# DIOSCURI

*Secrets of the Fey*

Book 2 of

The Infernal Artifacts Collection

The Infernal Artifacts Collection

Timeline Order:

Corpse Walker: The Night Parade (1940s)

Dioscuri: Secrets of the Fey (2002)

# DIOSCURI

*Secrets of the Fey*

RALYNN KIMIE

Steely Co. Publishing

For information contact: www.ralynnkimie.com

Paperback 5x8

Second Edition: 2023

# Contents

# IN LOVING MEMORY OF

*Twix,*
*my beautiful brown dachshund who gave me more than I could have ever hoped for. I don't possess the vocabulary or intelligence to express how much she meant to me and how much I have felt her absence since her passing.*

*I miss you every single day.*
*2007-2023*

# DEDICATION

*to these amazing individuals:*

*Norma Aranda*

*Kristy Carroll*

*Daina Elvenia*

*Jaclyn Fett*

*Tracey Hazel*

*Jennifer Stubbs*

*Thank you for all of your love and support.*

*What fates impose, that men must needs abide; It boots not to resist both wind and tide.*

-Shakespeare

# INTRODUCTION

## *The Iroquois Theater*

On a chilly winter afternoon in Chicago, smog overtook the city. The Iroquois Theater was ablaze. Teachers, families, and children had all gathered to watch Mr. Bluebeard, a musical comedy starring a Chicago native that would end in tragedy. Black smoke filled the fireproof theater, rising quickly. Audience members bolted from their seats to the exit doors locked by metal accordion gates. The frightened patrons clogged the aisles frantically searched for an escape. The upper levels held an animal-like stampede. A backdraft from an open door caused a ball of flame to explode, killing dozens instantly. The screams would haunt those who survived and the many outsiders who tried to assist.

One-third of the patrons perished the evening of December 30, 1903, branding Chicago as the unhappiest city on the face of the earth.

# CHAPTER ONE

## *1*

The world was on fire.

The smoke was suffocating. Poisonous air filled his lungs with every breath he struggled to take. His bright green eyes were red-rimmed and teary, trying to wash away the flames surrounding him. Sweat beaded on his forehead, his curly brown hair was drenched, and he pushed it out of his face in a hurry.

"Please! Help me!" she screamed. Terror and agony dripped from each of her words as her voice grew hoarse from the strain. He could hear her clearly above all other noises, above all other surrounding screams of terror as people rushed the gates, getting crushed against the iron bars from the force of each other. But hers—her fear was particularly haunting. His eyes searched the smoke and fire for her, but the fumes burned and clouded his sight. "Please!" she cried again.

Finally, he spotted her in the air as the smoke engulfed her. Tied up and tangled like a marionette, the ballerina on stage struggled with her harness before her large emerald eyes locked with his. Her hand reached out to him, and his to hers, just before the fire claimed her.

Something came out of his mouth, some words—or maybe it wasn't a word at all, but something that didn't quite sound human but was louder than the commotion that surrounded him. He dropped to the ground, pain in his chest, his hand clutched at his collar and neck. Piercing screams came from every direction, deafening him to the sounds of everything but his heartbeat that fluttered rapidly like a wild bird trapped in a cage.

The sound grew louder, his heart raging against the smoke, desperately seeking an exit.

The fluttering rose to a roar, descending upon him from above. Wings surrounded him. Loud flapping, and then sudden silence.

His body jolted.

Arlo awoke in his bed, drenched in sweat. It continued to bead on his forehead, his dark brown hair, soaked. He sat up quickly, heart still beating rapidly. Arlo's hand smoothed over his bare chest as he took a deep breath and blinked several times. He ruffled his wet curly locks and pushed them back and out of his face as he looked up at the ceiling. *It was just a dream*, he thought with a sigh. *Just another nightmare.*

Still, he sat in bed a moment longer, trying to remember the girl's face that he had seen so vividly only seconds earlier. The ballerina puppet in the air. She looked so familiar, but he couldn't piece it together. His brows furrowed as he raked through his thoughts and scattered memories. Who was she? She couldn't be a figment of his imagination—Arlo had the imagination of a flea, or so he was often told by his friends. But his nightmares of her were so vivid, so real, and yet he couldn't recall ever being in a fire or watching a play. In truth, he hated theater.

He turned his head, listening to unexpected sounds from elsewhere in the house. He could hear voices drifting up from downstairs. He frowned. His father rarely had company this early in the morning—in fact, his father never had company any time of the day. Ambrose was hardly a social Fey man. Most days, he rarely even spoke to Arlo.

Curiosity got the best of him, and Arlo immediately slid out of bed. He kept his ear facing each door he slipped through and continued on toward the noise, trying to make out the other voice, wondering who in the world it belonged to.

Arlo could hear Ambrose clearly. His father spoke in a brutish, grunting manner, but the other voice remained indistinguishable and unfamiliar. He grabbed a tunic hanging off of a nearby stool in the hallway as he headed down the stairs—not too loud, but loud enough that his father wouldn't accuse him of sneaking about. Ambrose hated that, or at least hated when Arlo startled him.

Arlo stopped in his tracks when he realized who was in their company. He blinked several times, and once more pushed his damp hair out of his face as he tried to make himself believe what he was seeing.

Ambrose sat with an older Fey man Arlo knew as Magnus Aster, who belonged to one of the wealthiest families in the Autumn Court. Ambrose didn't acknowledge Arlo's sudden appearance, but then again, he rarely did. Magnus, however, gave him a quick and immediate once over, his eyes raking Arlo up and down. He rose from his seat. Magnus was an elegant man, well-dressed with combed silvery blond and red hair, almost resembling that of a tamed fire behind his pointed ears. His eyes were a similar color. Arlo closed his eyes, thinking of the raging hellfire in his dreams. It was strange to see Magnus in their home. It wasn't that Ambrose and Arlo were poor, but they certainly didn't move in the same wealthy circle as the Aster family. It was unlikely Magnus would visit them unless it was important.

"I'd best be on my way," Magnus said, straightening his dark brown cloak, eyes still wandering over to glance at Arlo. "I'm glad we could come to an agreement." He looked back at Ambrose and nodded once.

"An agreement about what?" Arlo asked. He fumbled with his ears, realizing he had forgotten his pointed ear cuffs that hid his badly damaged ears. The tops of his ears had been brutally sliced off during a FeyForce mission when he was captured by the Winter Court. He hated the mutilation, and he hated it even more when others saw it. He silently swore at himself for accidentally drawing Magnus' attention to them as he scratched a subtle itch that felt like it was coming from the missing tip of his left ear.

Ambrose held his hand up and silenced Arlo immediately.

"Pleasure doing business with you, Magnus." Ambrose shot Arlo a glare as he moved toward the door to show their guest out.

Magnus looked at Arlo once more, a small smile peeking at the corner of his thin lips as his eyes again wandered up Arlo's body, landing on his twitching ears. He bowed slightly before excusing himself from their home without another word.

Ambrose closed the door while Arlo quickly approached the wooden table and peered into the burlap sack left upon it. It was filled to the top with tiny trinkets for trading.

Arlo frowned.

"He gave us money?" His hand dug through the sack, through all the little pieces. The Fey loved trinkets, and they functioned as currency in the Autumn Court. "For what?" he asked as he looked up at his father.

Ambrose shrugged nonchalantly as he sat back down in his chair. "For you."

"For me?" The crease of the frown etched between Arlo's brows deepened. "What do you mean *for me*?"

"He heard about what you did for the queen and believes you'd be a good suitor for his youngest daughter, Marigold—despite your obvious *imperfections*." He acknowledged Arlo's ears, which sent Arlo right back to fumbling with them. Ambrose's satisfaction quickly turned to disgust when he took a better look at his son. "Why are you wet?" he questioned, demand in his voice as he wrinkled his nose and waved his hand dismissively. "I can't believe you appeared before Magnus like that—you're drenched. And you smell."

"I—I had another nightmare." Arlo was almost embarrassed by the admittance, especially to his father. He rubbed the back of his neck and looked away, his hand falling from the sack of trinkets. "And I didn't know you had company—I can't believe you sold me."

His father scoffed, rolling his brown eyes as he gripped the armrests of his chair and got up again.

"I didn't *sell* you," Ambrose grumbled, "I just agreed that you would marry the girl. Don't be so dramatic." Arlo watched as Ambrose moved to a cabinet. He got a box out. Holding it with one hand, he opened the lid and got something out of a small jar. He walked over to Arlo and placed the item in his outstretched hand.

It was a small purple crystal.

"Try amethyst," he sighed, closing the box again. "Keep it in your room. It should help with the nightmares."

The two men couldn't have been any less alike. His father, Ambrose, was a large man, robust and rough around the edges. He was well over six feet tall with a sturdy build and had been through many fights in his lifetime. Ambrose was blunt, the sort of man who preferred to pretend life was an ongoing business deal rather than a series of relationships that ebbed and flowed like tides. In comparison, Arlo looked malnourished beside him, even if he wasn't. His thin, lean frame let his body move like a branch in the wind. He was stealthy and observant, aware of every sidelong look at his ears, noticing every change of tone in his father's voice. Ambrose often likened Arlo to that of a cat—though he didn't mean it as a compliment.

"Thanks," Arlo said quietly.

Just as he was about to head back to his room, his father spoke up.

"There's one more thing."

Arlo stopped in his tracks. He looked back at Ambrose, whose hand was now tightly gripped around the sack Mr. Aster had brought over.

Arlo raised a brow. "Which is?"

"She mustn't know."

"Who mustn't know what?" Arlo asked.

"About the arrangement," said Ambrose.

Arlo stepped down from the stairs. "I'm not sure I follow."

Ambrose rolled his eyes. "Magnus says his daughter has an obsession with marrying for love rather than status. She doesn't think marriage is transactional, despite what's customary in the Autumn Court. So, you have to make her fall *in love* with you. She can't know."

Arlo scoffed. He wasn't sure whether he was disgusted or amused.

"This will end well," he said sarcastically.

"Don't think you can do it?"

"Oh, I think I can do it—haven't you met me? I'm charming. Everyone loves me. Even the queen adores me."

"That's different," Ambrose said, still gripping tightly onto the bag as though someone was going to yank it from him. "You saved her life."

Saving the Autumn Queen's life was a blur Arlo had difficulty remembering. He remembered seeing her severely wounded and near death. He could hear echoes of the foul words spoken by the Court of the Imps who'd initiated the attack. He remembered the cries afterward that the Winter Court had been responsible and deserved retribution, but everything else was a blur. The healing, the loss of his senses—a fuzzy memory that fought, and failed, to find distinction among the rest. Though slowly gaining them back over time—that bit he definitely remembered.

The Fey he worked with all had their opinions of course. Some believed Arlo couldn't properly remember because he was wounded so badly by his abilities as he healed her, reasoning that was why he now struggled to use magic without the aid of his FeyForce suit. Some believed he may have just been hit on the head during the attack. Others just noted that Arlo never had the best memory to begin with.

They certainly weren't wrong. Everything was often hazy. Short-term memories were okay; long-term was nearly impossible for him to recall.

Arlo shrugged and acknowledged the sack.

"I don't think you would've taken that if you didn't think I could succeed." He smiled confidently, which made his jawline only appear even more defined. Arlo had a very pointed chin and laugh lines deep in his cheeks that became even more prominent when he smiled.

"Don't let me down."

"When have I ever?" Arlo asked, feigning slight offense as he put his hand over his heart. He smirked and turned back toward the stairs before heading back to his bedroom, the smile fading quickly.

Arlo wasn't exactly pleased with the arrangement. He had anticipated a few more years of enjoying the none-too-infrequent fling with whatever Fey woman struck his fancy, and his stomach felt an unusual weight as he faced the prospect of settling down with someone he'd never even met. But he also hated the idea of failure.

He wasn't a failure.

He placed the amethyst on the table next to his bed before groaning in frustration. He knocked over a chair and sank into his mattress, clenching his fists. His legs bent awkwardly, feet still flat against the ground. Raising his arms, he combed his fingers through his matted, slightly greasy hair that had begun to dry.

Something tapped his foot. When he looked down, he noticed a small rock. He furrowed his brows just as another knocked against the floor and rolled up against his foot. Then another. Arlo glanced toward his window as another came soaring in.

He got up from his bed and looked outside.

Outside on the ground below stood a young woman with pebbles still in her hand. She was winding up to throw another when she spotted him. She lowered her arm and smiled as she waved. Just as he was thinking about his flings…

"Arlo!" Her voice was pleasant, and it drifted up towards him like a line of music.

Brigit was beautiful. Her raven hair and captivating dark eyes created a striking contrast against her pale skin. While happy to see her, he was reminded of the deal his father had made with Magnus Aster. Arlo's expression faltered and went stone cold. He dropped the pebbles onto the ground, and she watched them fall, her happiness fading as fast.

"Go home," he told her. He had to end it. "And don't come back."

"But Arlo—"

He had already left his window by the time her eyes had made it back up to him. Arlo didn't particularly have feelings for Brigit, or any of them really. But it was the company—and fun—he would miss. He shook himself slightly, trying to accept and focus on his new future.

Marigold.

There were waves of emotions hitting him from every angle, many of which were unpleasant. Many of which were fuel to a fire he wasn't sure he could contain. Arlo glanced outside again, and Brigit was gone. He leaned back against the wall and sighed. It was only morning and today was turning into a much longer day than he had anticipated.

Arlo strolled back downstairs to heat water for his bath. He ignored Ambrose's voice as the water began to bubble. He didn't particularly care at the moment what his father had to say.

"Arlo!" Ambrose snapped. Arlo blinked several times before looking up at his father. "I don't want that girl coming back here, you hear me?"

"I told her not to," he answered softly.

"Good, or I'll stop her myself."

"She won't be a problem, you have my word."

"Sure," he said, less than convinced. His eyes were focused on the door that led to where Brigit had been throwing pebbles at Arlo's window.

"You best hope Mr. Aster didn't see her."

"Even if he did, I doubt he would've known she was coming to see me. Fey walk through our fields all the time."

Still, Ambrose scowled. "What time are you leaving?"

"Just after my bath," Arlo said.

"Has Bane said anything else about the Imps?"

Arlo shook his head. "I've told you everything I'm allowed to tell you."

Ambrose licked his lips and nodded. "I should be out there—I should be fighting against those nasty—"

"We've got it handled, father. You did your time in the FeyForce."

Ambrose nodded slowly as Arlo transferred the boiling water to the buckets to bring back to the bath to mix with the cool water from the pump. Bathing in the morning wasn't ideal, but since the nightmares started coming and refused to stop, Arlo wouldn't dare go to work sweaty and disheveled. Though he and his father weren't rich, poor and dirty wasn't how they carried themselves regardless of what their home life looked like. *Appearances are very important*, Ambrose frequently reminded Arlo, his eyes flicking up to the mutilated cartilage of his ears. Arlo would squirm, wondering why they needed to give off the illusion they were better off than they were. That they were just as classy and noble as any other respected family in Fae, even if they weren't.

Most respect came from Ambrose's ruthless nature as a former commander, which was also Arlo's current rank. They may not have had a lot when it came to material wealth, but they had skills, and that got them places. It was one of the few things that made Ambrose proud of his son.

All Arlo wanted was to be of use in the world—primarily, to be seen as useful in his father's eyes. What a sad sentiment that was.

He carried the buckets of water to the tub and dumped one in as he began pumping the water from the well, leaving the other bucket for a rinse when he finished. The mixture always came out near the perfect temperature for a morning wash. Arlo undressed and sank into the tub of water, soaking his body before completely submerging himself beneath the surface. He went over the nightmare once more while beneath the water. The flashbacks caused his chest to tighten, and his lungs felt like they were closing up. He gasped, inhaling a mouthful of water. He quickly got up and coughed. Ambrose burst through the door.

"Are you alright?" he asked. Arlo coughed, pounding a fist to his chest. He nodded and swept his wet black hair out of his face. There were moments when Arlo felt like his father cared. "Well, try to at least stay alive until after the wedding ceremony."

Then he was always quickly reminded that he didn't.

*Thanks, Dad.*

# CHAPTER TWO

*2*

The Autumn Court in Fae was always rich and full of a myriad of colors. It was permanently autumn year-round, and the reds, yellows, and oranges never failed to fill trees, the grounds, and the sky. They were the colors of the wind, always. Even in strong gusts, leaves were freed from branches, yet they never seemed fully absent from the trees, always rustling in the wind, no matter how many of them fell to the earth.

Arlo stood at the carved open window of the stone building, watching a gust of wind carry several leaves like music notes across the sky while he awaited for their meeting to start.

"Have you ever been to any other Courts?" he asked.

Salvatore came to stand beside him. Salvatore was a tall Fey who towered over him by nearly seven inches.

Salvatore tilted his head, his dark brown hair moved just as he did before he swept it out of his face with his hand.

"Once. The Spring Court. It's basically the opposite of this one. Rather than everything always dying or near death, everything is at the beginning stages of life. Birth and bloom. I'm curious about the Winter Court, though," he said, turning his head toward Arlo, knowing he had been captured by them once. He lowered his voice. "I hear the Winter Queen—"

"You heard the Winter Queen—*what*?"

The two young Fey turned around, interrupted by Salvatore's wife, Acacia, who also happened to be Marigold's older sister. Her gaze was focused on her husband, and she briefly narrowed her eyes. Acacia had straw-colored hair, long and usually pulled back tightly to show her long, pointed ears. Her hair was neat, not a strand out of place, but was always so tightly bound that it often gave her a permanent look of surprise mixed with a smidge of disgust.

Salvatore often argued that's just how she looked, even with her hair down.

It wasn't that she wasn't pretty—all three of the Aster girls were stunning. Acacia was just high-strung and not easy to get along with—and that was putting it nicely.

Salvatore simply stared back at her, and eventually, Acacia swept her gaze toward Arlo. A smirk crept across her lips.

"I've heard the news," she teased Arlo playfully, or as playfully as *Acacia* could manage. She was normally cruel in her demeanor, and everything she said came out with malice, and she teased him to get under his skin.

Arlo rolled his eyes. Exasperated, he sighed and looked back out the window.

"Heard what news?" Salvatore asked curiously, cocking a brow as his gaze shifted between the two of them. Acacia didn't take her large, piercing red eyes off of Arlo though, even if he wasn't looking at her himself.

"Arlo's going to ask my sister to marry him."

Salvatore raised his brows. "Zaria?"

"No—" she hissed and smacked the back of his head with her hand despite being over a foot shorter than him. "*Marigold*."

"You're *what*? Marigold? Really?" He made a face, his large nose crinkled in disgust. "Why? She's like—she's a child."

"She's an adult—" Arlo began, knowing Marigold wasn't much younger than he was.

"Barely," Salvatore cut him off. "Why in the world—"

Acacia crossed her arms. "Because it's time for my father's perfect little princess to get married."

Arlo pursed his lips together and turned around again. He leaned against the windowsill as he crossed his slender arms as well. "My father told me she can't know about it though. That your father arranged it, I mean."

Acacia rolled her eyes. "Like I said, princess. Her desire to marry for love is stupid and childish. No one in the Autumn Court marries for love. It's a contract. You marry for status." Her gaze swept over Salvatore. There was a coldness in her large eyes.

"You two don't love each other?" Arlo asked.

"We grew to," Salvatore said, nonchalantly. "It didn't happen overnight. And Acacia is a nightmare to live with—"

"Speak for yourself!" she sucked in air sharply through her gritted teeth. "You're the slob."

Salvatore rolled his eyes. "Does this not speak for itself?" he asked Arlo.

Arlo could only grin. While they constantly bickered in front of others, he had seen the two of them often whispering to one another, even stealing kisses when they thought no one was looking. He saw the way they looked at each other. He wondered what part was just for show.

More members of the FeyForce filed into the room, including Salvatore's younger brother, Sebastien.

Sebastien was even taller than Salvatore. The Sanguine brothers were a lot taller than Fey men typically were, both closer to seven feet tall with a strong jaw structure and thick brown hair. The two of them weren't very social. Salvatore only really spoke to his team and his wife, while Sebastien only really spoke to anyone was when he was flirting. He wasn't boisterous either. If he wasn't attracted to you, he was still quiet and withdrawn. If he was, then it was hard to get him to shut up.

"Arlo's gonna marry Marigold," Acacia said.

Sebastien shrugged as he grabbed one of the rolls from the table. It looked so small in his large hand. "So?" he asked, creasing his brows together. He was almost identical to Salvatore, just taller. They both resembled their father, Sebastien's features just a tad more feminine like his mother's.

"So? You're his age. Isn't it about time you get married too?"

He rolled his eyes. "I like being single." He smiled smugly, pleased with himself. "The men and women of Fae like it too."

Acacia curled her lip in disgust as Salvatore laughed.

"Oh, shut up," she growled at the younger Sanguine brother before hitting her husband in the chest for laughing. "Honestly, you should be proud my father chose you," Acacia said to Arlo. "A lot of men were willing to pay him large sums to marry her, but he wanted you."

"What's so special about Arlo?" Sebastien asked, stuffing the rest of the roll into his mouth. He wiped the corners of his lips with his thumb.

"He saved the Autumn Queen, remember?"

"How could I forget—" Sebastien said, staring at the table of food. There wasn't much, aside from the bread rolls and some cheese. "Wonder what things would be like if she died. Maybe we wouldn't be starving."

"We probably wouldn't be going to war with the Winter Court either." Sebastien raised his eyebrows at Salvatore's comment as he reached for another roll to toss into his mouth before he made another typical Sanguine comment.

"*They* attacked *us*—"

"In retaliation—"

"You guys really shouldn't be talking about her like that," another member of their team warned as she looked around. She was extremely shifty and paranoid. The Sanguine brothers just exchanged glances. "You know she has eyes and ears everywhere. We don't really know who all the members of her guard are."

"You mean her sex slaves?"

It was well known throughout the Autumn Court that the queen had slaves who doubled as spies for her throughout the realm of Fae. No one wanted to be called to meet with her—many never left once they were.

"Weren't you nearly made into one?" Sebastien asked Arlo, who ignored him as his gaze returned to the window.

While there were a number of things Arlo couldn't remember, unfortunately, that wasn't one of them. He could clearly remember her touch on his skin, the smell of her breath against his neck. He clenched his jaw and didn't look at Sebastien again.

Lord Ignatius Bane entered the room with Commander Kall-An. Immediately everyone went quiet, and all eyes found the two of them. Lord Bane raised his head, standing tall. His eyes moved from one person to another as they made their way around the room. Ignatius wasn't a very tall man, but he had a sharp jaw and a strong nose. He had large blue eyes and pointed ears sticking up past his dark brown hair. His eyes stopped on Acacia.

"Zaria has not returned from her mission on Terra," he announced to everyone, though his eyes stayed on her as if addressing her directly.

Acacia's lips parted slowly as her wide eyes flicked instinctively up at Salvatore, whose arm snaked around her waist. Zaria was her younger sister, the middle child. She clenched her jaw and lowered her gaze to find Bane's. "Where is she?" Acacia asked.

"Still on Terra," Commander Kall-An said. "She and Alden were doing an investigation regarding the sighting of Elves in Chicago. We received an S.O.S. from Terra, but when we showed up, we only found Alden—dead. His body was recovered, and we'll be honoring him at the river this evening." Kall-An's eyes moved to each of the members of his FeyForce. "As for Zaria," he said, fixing his gaze upon Acacia. "We'll leave tomorrow afternoon to find her and bring her home." He cleared his throat, preparing for the more expansive briefing. "We believe this is the work of the Imps. We already know they've been invading Terra and surrounding realms for the last few decades. They've become bolder. If they're behind Alden's death, we need to be ready for anything."

Everyone took seats at a round table that sat thirteen. Lord Ignatius Bane sat on the opposite end so that he could face the door, and Commander Kall-An sat to his right. Acacia sat to his left, her husband to her left, Sebastien next to him, and Arlo sat beside Sebastien. The other high-ranking officers of the FeyForce took their seats, filling the remaining seats.

The rest of the meeting lasted a few hours, and Arlo tuned in and out. He had trouble focusing after the events of that morning—the situation with his dad and Mr. Aster, then Zaria not returning from her mission. He passed his hand over his face, trying to wipe away his clamoring thoughts. Arlo looked over at Acacia and wondered what she was thinking as today seemed to revolve around her family. Her cold eyes remained fixed on Ignatius as he went over things with Kall-An. She didn't even notice Arlo staring at her. Perhaps she was just as tuned out as Arlo but better at hiding it. He tried to refocus.

"Terra's a lost cause," Commander Kall-An was saying. "Do not bother with the locals—we're going there to save Zaria and leave. The Imps have made their home there, and we don't want any of them following us back to Fae again." He rose, signaling the end of business. "Tomorrow, everyone meet here when the sun reaches the center of the sky. Now, you are all excused."

As several members began to file out of the room, Commander Kall-An held out his arm and stopped Arlo from leaving.

"You will not be going," he said without looking at him.

Arlo frowned as he looked up at him. "What? Why not? I'm your best asset, and you know it." He quickly added, "sir," as a respectful afterthought.

"I've been informed that Mr. Aster has another mission for you tomorrow. You know his wealth grants him power. It's not up to Bane." Kall-An consulted the sheaf of papers in his arms. "I have been instructed to pass along particular… assignment instructions for you for today. Mr. Aster has asked that you be ordered to go to the White Crest tonight for a more detailed briefing."

He sighed, or maybe it was a snort. He looked up at Arlo, "Don't be late."

Acacia looked over at her husband while Salvatore kept his chin tucked down. Arlo looked over at the two of them, then at Sebastien, who was busy flirting with another member of their squad.

"How could that be more important than rescuing one of our own?" Arlo asked, and Commander Kall-An just shot him a glare. "I should be there—you guys could use my help. Especially if someone gets hurt—"

"Are you trying to get on Lord Bane's bad side, Arlo?" he asked. Arlo averted his eyes and looked down. "Didn't think so," Commander Kall-An added.

"I'm not trying to step out of line," Arlo continued, and Commander Kall-An stopped in his tracks.

"Then don't," he said over his shoulder and left with Lord Ignatius Bane without another word.

Arlo looked at Acacia and Salvatore.

"What could be more important than rescuing your sister? Does your father even know Zaria is missing?"

Acacia stared at him with a deadpan expression. "You really have to ask? I'll give you one guess who comes before me and Zaria."

*Marigold.*

***

The White Crest was an upscale eatery near the Autumn Queen's castle beside the river that connected and divided the four Courts in Fae. Standing close enough to the river, you could see the edges of each Court and the way the different seasons affected the water. Fey only came down to the river for funerals. The other Courts were typically respectful of that.

White Crest was located in the trunk of a large white oak tree. The tree was full of colorful leaves, but many still loosened in the wind. Arlo stood beside the door wearing the finest cotton he could dig up from his closet. He was dressed in an assortment of browns and blacks, as he planned to head over to the river once his meeting with Mr. Aster was complete.

The chilly wind coming from the direction of the Winter Court tickled at his neck. Arlo readjusted his scarf and pulled his cloak closer to his body.

"Good evening, Arlo. You clean up nicely."

Arlo looked up to see Mr. Aster approaching from the left.

"Sir," was all Arlo managed to muster.

"Shall we go inside?" Mr. Aster asked, acknowledging the White Crest's door.

Arlo nodded, grabbed the stone embedded into the bark, and pulled the trunk door open with ease. Immediately, an assortment of smells filled his nose from different meads, toffee, and other sweet, sugary treats. His stomach growled.

"Hungry?" Mr. Aster asked, noticing the noise emitting from his stomach.

Arlo quickly ran his hand over his abdomen as if attempting to silence the noise. "It's been a long day," he said. "Haven't really had the time to eat."

"Lord Bane not feeding you all on the Force?"

Arlo recalled the minimal scraps of food on the table at headquarters.

"Sebastien was eating all of it," he said plainly.

Mr. Aster smiled. "I'm surprised at how skinny that boy is, given he never seems to stop eating." Mr. Aster grabbed Arlo's wrist and turned it over in his hand. "You could stand to gain some weight also."

"Being well-fed is a luxury," Arlo noted.

"A luxury indeed." The workers at the White Crest only had to catch sight of Mr. Aster and they moved to find him a table without a word. The two were being seated before Arlo could close the door. "Given you saved the Queen, you should be rich."

"I didn't do it for payment," he admitted.

"So then, why did you?"

"She needed help, I could help."

Mr. Aster narrowed his eyes and stared at Arlo for a moment. This made Arlo adjust and readjust in his seat, unaware of what to do while the elder Fey man stared at him.

"It must have been quite an experience, being in the Queen's presence like that. Must have been memorable for you," he commented. Arlo pondered the thought.

He remembered narrowingly dodging being a part of her guard, but that was the extent of it. Arlo shook his head. "Not really. There's a lot I don't remember." He shifted in his seat as the workers placed golden plates piled with extravagant food upon their table. "Sir—do you know about Zaria?"

"You're bringing up the wrong daughter—"

"I know, I'm just—"

"Of course I know, and I'm sure she's fine. All three of my daughters have their mother's spirit." Mr. Aster tilted his head to the side absently as he dug into the food before him. "You're worried about her?"

"Well, she's my friend," Arlo said. "She's stuck on Terra, and we were just told of Alden's death and—"

"She's fine, I'm sure. Zaria can take care of herself. I'm not worried," he repeated, tucking a lacy napkin under his chin. "Eat up, boy."

Truthfully, Mr. Aster didn't even need to speak; it was obvious he was unconcerned. There wasn't a tense thing about the man; he was relaxed and in his element. Nothing seemed to bother him, not even the bustle of the busy restaurant happening all around them, something Arlo was often distracted by as his eyes continued to wander back and forth between Mr. Aster and everyone else in the White Crest. While no table was directly beside them, Arlo's gaze seemed very shifty. He couldn't focus. He poked at the food in front of him, cursing himself for not even being able to enjoy the most expensive meal of his life.

His mind bounded far away from Mr. Aster and the reason he requested his presence. Marigold was a nice girl, and Arlo had known her for a while as Acacia's and Zaria's kid sister. But his mind was on Zaria and her mission in Terra—and Alden.

Alden's funeral.

"Arlo?"

"Huh?" Arlo looked at Mr. Aster, who was raising his thin red-orange eyebrows at him, a spoonful of what appeared to be caviar halfway between plate and lips.

"Did you hear me?"

"Sorry, I'm just—things with the FeyForce—"

"Well, good thing you're getting a break tomorrow," Mr. Aster said, putting his napkin on the table. "I know the FeyForce is going to Terra, but I would like you to take Marigold on a date."

"Tomorrow? How am I supposed to swing that if she doesn't know I'm even," he searched for the right word, "interested?"

"You will ask her when you see her." Dabbing his lips with his napkin, Mr. Aster placed the soiled cloth and a conspicuous pile of money on the table before rising.

"Will she be at the funeral?" Arlo asked, but Mr. Aster continued through the crowd of Fey, who all seemed to move out of his way as he walked, like a force field was pushing them away before they could bump into him.

Arlo sank back in his chair.

"Excuse me, you can't stay here." The same waiter who had quickly managed to get this table for Mr. Aster was now hurrying Arlo away from it. Arlo sighed and got up. No one cares if you're not rich. He quickly tossed his napkin on the table and left.

There were more Fey near the river now, just outside of the White Crest. The tone was somber, and Arlo slowly walked toward the Sanguine brothers once he spotted them sprouting out of the crowd like giant weeds. Arlo quickly fell in line with the rest of the FeyForce standing at the edge of the river while Alden's body floated down. He was placed upon a bed of vines and branches intricately woven together beneath a sheet of colorful autumn leaves.

An archer, standing on the balcony of the Autumn Queen's castle, aimed his arrow up and shot a flame into the night sky. It arched gracefully through the air, suspended in the darkness, falling eventually at Alden's feet, setting the intertwined vines ablaze.

Arlo clenched his jaw. The Autumn Queen herself stood on the balcony now, her fingers laced together in front of her. She stared at Alden's body floating down the lake before shifting her gaze to look at Arlo. Surrounding her were members of her guard, all masked and shirtless.

Soon, she turned away and went back inside.

Arlo looked back at Alden just as his body was overtaken by the flames. The fire crackled, and his body began to flake into fiery bits that resembled dry leaves and floated up toward the sky until there was nothing left on the river. Up above, a silhouette of Alden could be seen, bidding farewell to his Court.

Arlo clenched his jaw and turned away.

His eyes scanned the many faces that surrounded him. Briefly locking eyes with Brigit, Arlo quickly turned in another direction, hoping she wouldn't make her way over to him. He closed his eyes and stepped behind Sebastien who was tall enough to block him and several Fey behind him.

"If you're looking for Marigold, she isn't here. Not even sure if my dad told her."

Arlo glanced at Acacia, who leaned her temple against Salvatore's shoulder. He rubbed the back of his neck and looked back at the night sky as the sparkling pieces of Alden's silhouette began to disappear in the darkness. He peered around Sebastien again, and Brigit was gone.

"I can't believe you aren't coming tomorrow," Salvatore said quietly, looking down at Arlo before directing his gaze back to the river.

Arlo glanced over at him as his mind wandered over his options. "Just stall them, okay?" Arlo whispered to him in the softest voice he could manage as if Mr. Aster was listening in on him. "I'll be there."

# CHAPTER THREE

## 3

The nightmares returned that night, even with the amethyst under his pillow.

Arlo punched his pillow in frustration and sat up. Twisting his body, he planted his feet on the floor, the cold shooting through his feet, rousing his brain. He rested his elbows on his knees as he did his best to steady his breathing. His hand smoothed over his chest as he took a deep breath. Running his fingers through his hair, he glanced to the left at the night table beside his bed. Arlo grabbed his pointed ear cuffs, fixed them upon the top parts of his ears, and got up.

Most nights, he slept until the nightmare was over.

Until, he supposed, he perished in the fire.

Not this time.

That early morning, he awoke just after the ballerina girl locked eyes with him. The sun in Fae hadn't yet shown itself over the horizon, but Arlo never could get back to sleep after waking. He did his best, tossing and turning in his bed, trying to get comfortable enough to drift back to sleep, but his attempts were fruitless.

Arlo got out of bed and ran his fingers through his hair again. Rubbing what sleep was left out of his eyes, he got dressed.

He pulled on his cloak and slipped outside soundlessly.

The night was cool, colorful and crunchy leaves still loosening from trees floated to the ground. He made a conscious effort to step on a few as he walked, leaping from one part of the path to another.

The dark path led him down to a small waterfall about twenty feet high. Beside it was a large wooden, moss-covered door, wet from the splashes of the waterfall. With the back of his hand, he knocked three times, his knuckles rapping against the wood. Arlo then wiped the back of his dampened hand against his cloak. He took a step back when the knob twisted.

"Why are you *awake*?" Arlo asked when the door opened, surprised the door had opened at all.

His tall, slender friend leaned against the doorframe and crossed his arms.

"Why are *you*?" Salvatore asked, raising an eyebrow as his eyes gave Arlo a once over. Arlo only shrugged at his question. "And why are you here?"

"Nightmares," he mumbled.

"Ballerina girl?"

Arlo nodded, averting his gaze.

Salvatore stepped aside, allowing Arlo into his home.

It was very dark and cold inside the stone mountain. The rushing water from the waterfall could be heard loudly throughout the structure, and Arlo turned around. He had been in Salvatore's and Acacia's home often, and every time it struck him as quiet, unnerving, and unwelcoming. Cold and damp, Arlo pulled his cloak closer to his body.

"Has Acacia said much since Kall-An delivered the news yesterday?" Arlo asked, glancing up at Salvatore, who moved routinely around the kitchen to grab a few mugs.

Salvatore shook his head as he poured tea.

"You know she's never really gotten along all that well with her sisters, especially Zaria. Zaria's the black sheep, and Marigold's the favorite." He tilted his head to the side to acknowledge the stairwell. "Then there's Acacia, just... the oldest."

Arlo pursed his lips together and pushed his wavy brown hair out of his face. "Yeah, but I figured with Zaria actually *missing* and all, that might affect her a little more."

Salvatore shrugged.

"It's Acacia. Between you and me, I'd be more weirded out if it was openly affecting her. She deals with things in her own way. Most of the time, I don't understand it." He pushed one of the mugs toward Arlo before cupping his own in his oversized hands. "I just let her be. It's easier that way, you know? Just let her be Acacia. You ready for your date?"

Arlo tilted his head and raised his brows. "Well, I haven't asked her yet."

"You haven't asked her yet on the date you're supposed to have this afternoon?"

"It's still early—and I was intending to ask Acacia where I might find her." Arlo sighed. He turned his head to look outside a window, briefly forgetting their home had no windows. He returned his gaze to meet Salvatore's. "Honestly, it's been a while since I've actually asked someone on a date—a real date."

"You and me both. Mine and Acacia's first date was a bloody nightmare." Salvatore hit the back of Arlo's shoulder before giving it a squeeze. "It'll be alright. I mean, you have it easy. Marigold's had a crush on you for years. Acacia couldn't even stand to look at me, let alone be in the same room as me."

"And look at you now, a happy couple."

Salvatore chuckled. "A happy couple," he repeated quietly, barely audible for Arlo to hear. "It could definitely be worse."

"Yeah, she could be pregnant."

Salvatore closed his eyes and rubbed his temples. "That is not funny—please don't speak that evil into existence. Can you imagine a baby Acacia? No, thank you. I'd quit. Send me on a suicide mission."

Arlo laughed.

"I'm curious about the girl you keep having nightmares about," Salvatore said, keeping his hands wrapped around the clay mug. "You've been having them a lot."

"Almost nightly at this point," Arlo said.

"What does she look like?"

"Well," he considered. It wasn't that he didn't know what she looked like, it just felt strange saying it out loud. "She looks like me, actually. We have the same eyes, same facial features, but I don't remember her—and I don't have a sister." Arlo blinked several times. The last time, he kept his eyes closed for a moment longer as he visualized her face. "You would've thought it was me in a skirt."

Salvatore flinched and shook his head as if trying to shake the thought. "Great, now that image is in my brain."

Arlo chuckled, shaking his head disapprovingly at the comment.

"What's so funny so early in the morning?" Acacia asked, emerging from the darkness. Her blond hair was down, but still neat, especially for having just woken up. She pulled her robe close to her body as she took the mug from her husband and took a sip.

"Arlo's having nightmares about himself as a girl."

Arlo frowned at Salvatore's explanation. "I mean, it's not exactly like that—" Then again, it was better than any explanation he could muster. He didn't say anything else and, instead, looked over at Acacia who was also frowning and appeared somewhat confused by Salvatore's description of Arlo's dream. "Anyway," Arlo said. "I was wondering where I might find your sister this morning? I'd like to ask her out on a date."

Her expression turned into a mixture of both amusement and disgust.

"This early? She's still asleep."

"Do you two misunderstand me on purpose? I don't mean right now." He looked over at Salvatore. "And you know I'm not dreaming about myself."

Salvatore grinned, clearly amused with himself.

Acacia scowled.

"She normally goes to see Ms. Mabel for tea right after sunrise. She used to always get a cup with mom and kept the tradition going."

"That's cute," Salvatore said.

"She'll grow out of it," Acacia muttered. "We all did."

Arlo didn't linger in the Sanguine home for much longer. While Ms. Mabel's Teahouse was within walking distance of their home, it wasn't exactly nearby.

His hands were stuffed deep into his pockets as the sun rose. The cloudless sky brightened into a prismatic array of pinks, purples, and oranges. It was chilly that morning and puffs of his hot breath could be seen in the air as he breathed.

Ms. Mabel's Teahouse resembled a large Angel's Trumpet flower laying open face on the ground. It blended nicely with all of the autumn leaves scattered around it and had small wooden tables and chairs sitting both over and under the large petals for those who wanted to enjoy the sky and for those who wanted shade.

He paused outside the door and jingled the trinkets in his pocket as he went over what exactly he was going to say to the youngest Aster girl.

"Are you going to stand there like a golem or are you going to come inside?"

His train of thought was interrupted by none other than Ms. Mabel herself. Arlo caught a small glimpse of blonde hair quickly ducking behind Ms. Mabel's shoulder while Ms. Mabel raised an eyebrow at him.

"I was just admiring the—furniture." His hand moved to fumble with the edge of the chair. "Excellent craftsmanship. I'm sure these cost a fortune. Did Hansel make these?"

Ms. Mabel smiled as her attention focused on her gray wooden tables.

"That he did." Her attention then was brought back up to Arlo. "How did you know that?"

"I apprenticed for him a bit ago. Grumpy man."

She chuckled. "That he is."

"Maybe he has a thing for you. You do have a beautiful smile, Ms. Mabel." Arlo straightened his scarf as he approached her. There were small crows feet at the other corners of her eyes and laugh lines deep in her plump and rosy cheeks. A few graying hairs were tucked in her messy brown bun, and she simply rolled her yellow eyes at his remark.

"I'm much too old for you, Arlo."

"A Fey can dream," his voice was smooth as he stepped closer to her at the small fold between the petals that allowed entry into the teahouse. "But there is someone closer to my age I have a thing for," he said, fully knowing Marigold was standing behind her.

"Oh?"

"Do I detect jealousy?" he teased.

Ms. Mabel pursed her lips together. "Absolutely not." She quickly stepped aside before Marigold had the chance to move from her hiding spot.

A small smirk peeked at the corner of Arlo's mouth.

"Good morning," he said.

"Is it?" she asked flatly before straightening her skirt. She smoothed it out, focusing on an invisible wrinkle to avoid looking up and revealing her deep blush. Her blonde locks fell in front of her face as she looked down at her hands, smoothing out the material.

"Is it not?" he asked, stepping in through the petals of the teahouse.

"I guess that would depend," she said, finally looking up at him. She huffed, purposely blowing some of her blonde hair out of her face.

Arlo raised an eyebrow. It took all of his self-control to avoid looking her up and down. She looked perfect. Her light hair looked weightless, and her dress draped over her form perfectly, its color bringing out the particular emerald of her eyes. She appeared flustered.

"Would you like to have tea with me, Ms. Aster?"

"I—Well—I can't right now. I was just on my way out, actually." Her gaze wandered around the small teahouse. "I have to go to the garden, and—"

"Well, what about this afternoon? We could have lunch." Now that he was standing in front of her, the idea of getting to know her better seemed rather appealing.

She narrowed her eyes as she finally let her gaze fall upon him. "A little last minute, don't you think?"

"Are you saying no?" he asked.

"No."

"So is that a yes?"

"No."

"Please?" Arlo said, tilting his head. He almost blushed. "Do allow me the pleasure of your company."

She crossed her arms. "A week ago, you didn't even know I existed."

"I always knew you existed, Ms. Aster… and then Acacia told me that you've had a crush on me for quite some time." Her pale face reddened at his words. "Though I admit I already knew. I often noticed you staring at me," Arlo continued as Ms. Mabel handed him a hot cup of tea. "It was cute," he said before nodding toward Ms. Mabel as a 'thank you' for the tea.

Marigold clenched her jaw. "Yeah, that's what I want to be. Cute."

Arlo's stomach lurched slightly. He hadn't meant it that way. Maybe she did have more in common with Acacia than he'd anticipated. He leaned forward. "You're beautiful, Marigold." With his free hand, he brushed a few strands of wispy blonde hair out of her face and tucked them behind her ear. "Far more beautiful than the flower you were named after." He was surprised to find that he truly meant it.

He had approached today as a mission—a goal to be conquered. But he was finding it more complicated than that. He was beginning to worry that his own surprising feelings of awkward attraction would make him fall on his face. Flirting was apparently more difficult if you were interested in more than a one-night stand.

"Yes," she said immediately.

"Yes, what?"

"White Crest at noon," she said quickly and hurried off before he could say another word.

Arlo looked over at Ms. Mabel, slightly perplexed.

"You make her nervous," she said sympathetically before glancing at the entrance Marigold had scurried out of.

"Oh, is that what that was?" His ears felt slightly warm under their cuffs, unsure how successful this first interaction had been.

Arlo swallowed the tea in nearly one gulp before putting the cup on the nearest table. He dug his hand into his pocket.

Ms. Mabel lifted her hand and shook her head.

"It's on the house—for the entertainment."

He scoffed, though not in a cruel or annoyed way. He had actually enjoyed it too. Arlo looked back at the entrance and smiled to himself.

***

The next few hours seemed to pass by in a blur, and he found himself at White Crest, the same upscale eatery he had been the day before with Marigold's father. He sat across from her as she poked her fruit around her polished plate with her utensil.

"You know, after you told me Acacia said I had a crush on you, I was fuming, but I'm glad this turned out the way it did. It's nice to finally talk to you." She glanced up at him and smiled.

Arlo felt an unexpected warmth in his chest. "It's nice to finally talk to you, too." He meant it. He searched for a suitable conversation topic. "So, you're the third Aster sister. The only one who didn't choose the FeyForce."

Marigold blushed.

"No," he added quickly. "I think it's good that you've chosen your own life. It must be hard to forge your own path after watching both of your sisters choose the same vocation." He tapped the table. "What is it that you do every day? Besides assisting Ms. Mabel, obviously," he added with a smirk.

Marigold blushed still, though not in embarrassment. "I read." She grinned at Arlo. "I read a lot."

"What do you like to read about?"

Marigold's eyes wandered over the restaurant expansively. "Just about everything, honestly."

"Everything?"

"Pretty much. I like stories, and I like learning about trees and animals. And I like history and legends!" She leaned in closer. Arlo found himself instinctively leaning in closer too, as if receiving a secret. "Zaria once told me about the legendary Book of Fate, and I've been reading everything I can about it. Mostly old history books and even older myths, but it's fascinating. I've read everything I could get my hands on, and I still want to learn more. I'm thinking of trying to become a librarian of a sort for the Queen, but Acacia tells me that working for the Queen is comparable to slavery." She made a face, though her annoyance seemed directed primarily at Acacia rather than the Queen.

Arlo smiled back, though his lips remained closed. He was never really one to show teeth when he smiled. "She does care about you, you know."

Marigold looked back down at her fruit. "Acacia? She has a poor way of showing it."

Arlo chewed on the inside of his cheek, before shifting in his chair, knowing there was somewhere else he wanted to be.

"How's working with her? With both of them, actually?" Marigold asked, still not bothering to look up. They had eaten a light lunch, and only the final course of fruit remained though neither of them were hungry. She continued prodding the berry in front of her.

Arlo shrugged as he leaned back in his chair before stiffening a little and straightening his posture.

"Well, with Zaria missing in action after her mission on Terra and the team's—"

"WHAT?" Marigold cut him off. She stood up so quickly, her chair slid across the floor from the force. She drew a lot of attention from the other patrons. "Then what are you doing here? Why aren't you going to Terra?"

He looked up at her from his seat as he sat back in his chair. He wasn't quite sure how to answer. Surely he couldn't tell her the truth.

"We had a date."

Marigold's jaw dropped, the color nearly gone from her face. "But my sister is missing! That's a little more important than a date, Arlo. I'd rather you bring her back—rather than—rather than be here eating lunch with me—this—this is so dumb."

"It's not dumb to me." He hadn't intended to upset her, but, at the same time, the conversation was going in a hopeful direction if he was to join the Terra mission.

Marigold remained standing. Others in the eatery glanced over at them and whispered to one another.

"We can go on a date after you bring my sister back."

*There it was. Perfect.*

"Well, if you insist."

He stood up and wiped his face then his hands with a beige cloth napkin. Arlo's gaze wandered over the features of Marigold's heart-shaped face. She really was a very beautiful young woman, with brilliant gold-flecked green eyes and silky smooth blonde hair. The tips of her pointed ears poked between strands of her hair. He gently grazed the back of his fingers against her freckled and rosy cheek before pushing her hair behind her ear. Leaning in close, he whispered a 'thank you,' lips nearly touching her ear, and softly kissed her cheek. He meant it.

Marigold's heart fluttered like a newly emerging butterfly. Her fingertips lightly touched where his lips had been as she watched him run off. He glanced back at her once, and she smiled when their eyes met, even just for a moment.

Marigold wasn't as bad as Acacia tried to make her seem. If he had to marry someone, he wasn't exactly upset that it would be her.

***

"I see you've managed to escape," Acacia said with a grin plastered on her face as Arlo practically flew into the room.

"She's not that bad," he said, paying no real attention to the eldest Aster girl.

Commander Kall-An turned his head to notice the commotion and narrowed his eyes when he spotted someone he knew had other arrangements.

"I thought you had a date," he said, staring directly at Arlo.

Arlo shrugged as he put on his belt, not bothering to look at the commander.

"She wants me here," he said plainly, as he tightened his belt around his waist. "Said we can go on a date after I save her sister." He put his palm innocently against his heart. "And I'm not going to argue with Mr. Aster's daughter."

Acacia scowled. "Oh, beetle dung, Arlo. You argue with me all the time."

Arlo waved his hand dismissively.

"Obviously, I don't mean *you*."

Commander Kall-An directed his attention onto Acacia. "You made contact with your sister, yes? She'll be at the meeting point?"

Acacia nodded as she checked the time.

"We should go."

# CHAPTER FOUR

*4*

The Fey warriors were ambushed.

Their rapid appearance was supposed to be unexpected and catch the Imps by surprise, but luck was clearly not on their side. They'd opened their portal from Fae to Terra in a Chicago alleyway. As they passed through the brick wall, Imps jumped out from behind the industrial dumpster where they'd been hiding, ready for the first Fey to come out of the portal.

"How did they know we were coming?" Sebastien sliced through the body of an Imp with his sword. He huffed as the two pieces burst to dust before glaring at Acacia. "You told her to meet us here, didn't you? Where is she?" he demanded.

Sebastien was normally soft-spoken and withdrawn but rarely during battle. His stress forced itself through his voice, and he sounded furious.

Acacia just shook her head as she took a step back toward the wall and stabbed an Imp against the brick with her dagger. Her eyes searched for her husband. He was so tall it was usually easy to spot him, so where was he?

Her eyes found Arlo and followed him as he fell to his knees. The world wavered for a moment.

Salvatore lay on the ground in a widening pool of his own blood. His chest shuddered then fell still.

"Fall back!" Lord Bane shouted into his communications. "Fall back!" There was strain and urgency in his voice. While they had strength, the Imps outnumbered them significantly, and they were ruthless in their attack, coming at them from every angle. Even as Lord Bane shouted to his squad, he watched the Imps' attack patterns. It was quickly becoming apparent that the Imps' target was not the portal, or even most of the Fey.

They wanted Arlo.

While Salvatore's vision was blurring as he slipped in and out of consciousness, he noticed that many of the Imps seemed to hold back against the Fey, only attacking with disproportionate force when the FeyForce got between the Imps and Arlo. They were clearly after him specifically.

Salvatore's vision blurred as Arlo's powers manifested before all of them. Although some of Arlo's powers had been interrupted by his maiming, his suit was able to augment his weakened abilities. Interestingly, Arlo had retained powerful healing abilities that he could use at any time. It was an odd spectacle to watch as, if he focused hard enough, he was briefly able to render others powerless as he healed someone's wounds. It was an uncommon ability, even among the Fey, but despite his broken memories of his childhood, Arlo's healing skills always felt second nature to him. He wasn't entirely certain how his abilities worked, but it felt like he merely extended his own life—his own soul—into the broken parts of someone or something else. In those moments, although Arlo's body was weakened, he could feel a thrill of life as his life force nourished the wavering life of whoever had been harmed.

As Arlo neared Salvatore's prone form, it almost appeared as though something else had taken over his body in the process. His body glowed a faint smoky white-gray color, and his eyes turned white. He managed to keep several of the Imps at bay, so Lord Bane could reopen the portal, and the Fey could make their escape back to the woods of Fae from which they came.

Arlo quickly crawled across the cemented ground and tightly wrapped his hands around Salvatore's wrist. His glowing gaze crossed over the wound in Salvatore's chest. A burrowing Imp had fought hard to expose ribs and flesh that now dripped onto the dirty ground of the alley.

The blood of many Fey warriors, including Salvatore, mingled, painting the alleyway bright crimson. Arlo sent his own energy to his teammate. He felt part of himself transfer through his fingertips, sending that life towards the gaping gash in Salvatore's chest. As the energy flowed out of Arlo, his vision blurred. The alleyway blinked a few times, then vanished.

He cursed under his breath.

*Why did it have to be sight?*

He could heal others, but the process usually cost one of his five senses, and depending on the severity of the wounds, sometimes he lost all of them. Arlo would eventually regain it, but it would take some time and a lot of nourishment, unless he took the energy back, reversing the healing, or took it from something else.

"Of course it had to be sight," he mumbled again, now entirely blind to his surroundings. He was now in the middle of an ambush, blind, relying primarily on his hearing to assist him in the fight. He felt Salvatore's body being lifted roughly. He struggled to his feet, trying to follow the sounds of his FeyForce companions.

"Arlo! Quickly, follow my voice!" Acacia shouted.

He took one step forward before something smacked him in the back of the head, and he fell to the ground, his temple crashing into the cement.

All sound, all sensation vanished immediately as Arlo lost consciousness.

***

Acacia watched as the portal closed. Her large eyes were bulging out of their sockets even further than normal as she cradled Salvatore in her arms. The uprooted tree they had tumbled out of had flattened its roots and firmly sat back down on the earth of Fae. What was left of the FeyForce sat discombobulated and silent in the forest. They all looked questioningly at Lord Bane, waiting for him to speak, waiting for him to address the disaster they'd just faced.

Lord Bane shot Salvatore and Acacia a glare before getting up. He dusted the autumn leaves from his body and straightened his uniform. The cuff was stained with blood, but it didn't seem to be his own.

"We have reason to believe Zaria has switched alliances," Lord Bane said. While he spoke to the entire FeyForce, he kept his focus on Acacia, who had been responsible for communicating the meeting point with her sister. "Zaria was supposed to be there, and, instead, we were ambushed. We will not be returning to Terra for her again."

"We have to go back though," Salvatore said, holding his abdomen. While he was healed, the pain of having his ribcage torn open still lingered in his body. His palm ran over the front of his ripped uniform as Acacia helped steady him. Her own hands were coated in his drying blood. "Arlo is still—and he's blind because of me—we have to save him—"

"You almost died," Acacia said sternly, not taking her eyes off of her husband. "I saw you—I'm not losing you too."

"We should get back to headquarters," Lord Bane instructed. "We'll regroup there. Anyone who is injured should report to the hospital wing immediately."

Thirteen had gone out, and only six had returned unharmed.

Acacia didn't take her focus off of her husband, not even as they walked through the doors. While she noticed her little sister waiting for her, she paid no attention to her.

"I've been waiting ever since you left—" Marigold began, noticing the bloodied uniforms and the lack of members. Her eyes searched for Zaria, but she was not among the returning Fey. "I thought you guys were going after Zaria? Where is she? Is she at the hospital wing? What happened?" Marigold asked as she looked amongst the warriors who'd come back. She frowned as she counted the members of the FeyForce who entered the room. There weren't many. Her expression faltered. "Where's Arlo?"

The remaining members of the FeyForce collectively ignored her, including her sister and her brother-in-law.

"What is she doing here?" Lord Bane asked at the sight of Marigold. He ripped his belt off of his waist and threw it down on the table, frustrated by their performance in Terra. Frustrated by the ambush.

"Where's Zaria?" Marigold asked again as she turned away from Lord Bane. She knew she would get no answers from him directly, but hoped another member of the team would empathize with her and speak up. To her dismay, none did.

"Your sister is a traitor, and your boyfriend will die an honorable death on Terra. Now get out of here before I have you forcibly removed."

"A traitor?" Marigold furrowed her brows as she turned back around to face him. Her silky blonde hair bounced with her movement. She began backing away as she cupped her mouth with her hands and shook her head. "Zaria? No." She looked at Acacia, who averted her gaze. "You can't be serious—Zaria? She would never—"

"You don't know what your sister is capable of," Lord Bane sneered at the young Fey girl. "When have you last spoken to her?" he asked, taking forceful steps toward her. He grabbed her wrist and shoved her against the wall. "When have you cared about anything or anyone but yourself and the little fantasies going on in your head about love and romance?" He was inches away from her face as he scowled at her. Lord Bane grabbed her chin and forced her to look at him. Marigold's eyes were beginning to water. She shut them tightly and struggled against him.

"Lord Bane. You're scaring her."

Lord Bane looked over at Acacia, who immediately turned away after meeting his glare. He released Marigold from his grasp and stepped away from her. She quickly rubbed her wrist, skin reddening from the force of his grip. Her eyes were shiny and watery, and she looked down, embarrassed.

Lord Bane walked over to Acacia, tilting his head as he approached her.

"It's not like you to talk to me like that," he said. Grabbing her by her chin, he forced her to look at him too, the same way he had done with Marigold, only Acacia was taller and looked up at him willingly. He didn't have to use much force. Lord Bane then looked over at Salvatore, who was watching the two of them with his arms crossed. Lord Bane let go of Acacia's face and pushed her away from him. A part of him blamed her for Marigold's interference and Zaria's desertion. They were, after all, both of *her* sisters. "You need to learn to keep better control of your family, Acacia," he said. "They look up to you, do they not?"

Acacia didn't say anything. She just looked up at him, before looking away. She even avoided making eye contact with her husband.

"We need to make sure Zaria is cut off from all intelligence. We do not want the Imps infiltrating the Autumn Court the way they've done with Terra. We don't know what other demonic scum they may bring through with them. We have enough happening with the war of the Courts brewing."

Marigold hovered near the wall and watched from the sidelines as the FeyForce began devising a strategy to keep the Imps from entering Fae. She knew she wasn't supposed to be listening to their meeting, but she felt so intertwined. After all, both her sister and her crush were lost on Terra, and no one was willing to talk to her about it. She kept shaking her head, trying to shut out the voices of worry in her head, trying to listen to the plan.

Surely she'd misheard. She did her best to focus on the words of Lord Bane and Commander Kal-An. She was not well-versed in military tactics, but the more she heard, the more certain she became. Her eyes grew larger as full comprehension dawned. They weren't planning a rescue mission for Arlo but were rather accepting his fate on Terra as his death. She waited a little longer, hoping someone would bring it up, challenge the decision. Her eyes moved from Acacia, to Salvatore, to Sebastien, then back to her sister before turning to their commander.

"Is no one going to go after him?" Marigold looked at Commander Kall-An before turning back to face her sister. "Acacia?"

She ignored her and continued fumbling with the beads on her wrist that connected to the intercommunication mechanism of her suit.

"He knew the risks, Marigold," she said plainly, not bothering to look up at her little sister, whom she just knew was staring at her with her ridiculously large and sad eyes. "We all do. It's part of the job. It's more than likely his father will be proud—I'm sure Dad will be proud too that you liked a man capable of such sacrifice—"

"You can't be serious—Acacia!" she snapped, interrupting her sister. She then turned around to look up at Salvatore who turned away from her, looking down at his hands. "Salvatore! He's your best friend—"

"Why is she still here?" Lord Bane looked in annoyance at the ceiling as if he didn't even have the time to look Marigold in the face as he gave up on Zaria and declared Arlo *dead*.

Marigold hadn't even realized she had walked up to Lord Bane. She grasped his arm pleadingly. "You can't—"

"Silly girl," Lord Bane snapped, roughly brushing her aside. "You have no idea what you're talking about—so stay out of this."

"You don't know what's happening there," Salvatore added softly. "Sometimes a sacrifice has to be made for the greater good—for the safety of Fae. The Fey come first, Marigold. The Court comes first. I don't want to leave him there either but—" he glanced at his wife, "—I think rescuing him would be a suicide mission."

"Now leave." Lord Bane pointed towards the door.

Her large, watery eyes wandered over each of them. She backed up, shaking her head. She looked at her older sister, who didn't bother to make eye contact with her.

"She'll get over it," Acacia mumbled, watching as Marigold ran out of the room. "She doesn't really have a choice."

"What's your dad going to say? About the arrangement?"

Acacia shrugged.

"He'll have no problem making the money back he spent on Arlo. Many were offering huge sums for Marigold's hand. I'm sure he'll just settle for one of them. Besides, Ambrose isn't going to give that back without a fight—as much as I would really love to see that." Acacia's voice was light, unconcerned as if they hadn't just been fighting for their lives—as if their hands weren't still stained with blood.

"I second that," Salvatore said, his hand still pressed to the hidden wound beneath his coat. "Ambrose was one of the best commanding forces in Fae."

"While I'm not ready for my dad to die, I certainly wouldn't be rooting for him if the two of them did fight."

The pair didn't linger much longer at headquarters. There were too few of them to plan another attack, but Commander Kall-An mentioned allying with other FeyForce teams within the Autumn Court to fortify a defense system should the Imps manage to get through, but many were already busy with trying to set up defenses between their Court and Winter's. Salvatore checked in with Sebastien before leaving with Acacia to return home.

Their walk was a quiet one. Salvatore stole frequent glances at his wife, who kept her posture straight, shoulders back, and focus straight ahead. Her slender fingers, now scrubbed clean, were laced together in front of her. Acacia wasn't conventionally beautiful the way Zaria was, nor was she near-angelic in appearance the way Marigold was, but she was beautiful in her own way. She was still elegant, and while she could be cold at times, she was also calm and patient. Calculating.

As they approached the waterfall, Salvatore stopped.

It took Acacia a few seconds to realize he was no longer at her side. She turned around and, unlacing her fingers, pressed the tips together. Her large eyes rose to meet his, and she raised her eyebrows.

"You clearly have something to say, so you might as well spit it out."

"Does Zaria's betrayal really not bother you?"

Acacia chewed on the inside of her cheek. She stared at her husband for a second longer before turning away.

"I don't want to talk about her," she stated so simply and sharply that there was nearly a hiss at the end of her sentence. "We have more important matters at hand. Like the possibility of the Imps coming through. They got so close to the portal we opened."

"Are we really just going to let Arlo die on Terra?" he asked. The memory of Arlo, sprawled on the ground without sight, replayed guiltily in his mind. Survivor's guilt, perhaps. After all, Salvatore would have died on the pavement if Arlo hadn't sacrificed his own ability to escape to save him. Salvatore clenched his jaw and tightened his fist, trying to shake the helpless memory from his thoughts. "I understand what we would be risking, but—"

"What exactly do you propose we do, Salvatore?" she asked plainly, looking down at the splashing of the waterfall. "I just found out my sister is a traitor, and one of my best friends got kidnapped by those wretched beings." While she spoke of quite awful things, Acacia's voice was unnervingly calm. "Who knows what they're doing to him—who knows what will become of him by the end of it."

"All the more reason we need to do something."

"There's nothing we can do!" she hissed, slamming her fist down against the door she stood beside, finally betraying her emotion. Her thin, stringy blonde hair fell in front of her face like a curtain. "He's as good as dead. At least the Arlo we knew. Or did you forget?"

Salvatore averted his gaze and looked down at the dried blood on his hands. He started fumbling with the shredded pieces of his torn uniform. The blood in the fibers diluted and ran from splashes of water spraying him from the waterfall. He rubbed the skin across his abdomen.

"But he saved me," Salvatore said quietly, barely over the nose of the rushing water they stood beside.

"He made that choice."

They both fell silent, listening to the stream of the waterfall. Acacia finally began to open the door.

"What about Zaria?" Salvatore finally asked, staring into the water.

Acacia stopped. It was a question she didn't want asked, nor did she want to answer. Still, this was her husband, and while she respected him enough, she didn't bother to turn around.

"She's already dead to me," she said sternly and left Salvatore at the entryway alone.

Acacia went up to their room. As she walked up the stone stairway, she passed many pictures hanging on the wall, none of which she bothered to look at. Many of them were pictures from her and Salvatore's childhoods. Acacia clenched her hand into a fist and twisted her wrist as she walked past each image. The memory of Zaria began to burn from each one, leaving nothing but a charred black mark in her place.

By the time Salvatore had come to follow, Zaria was gone from every single picture. He looked up at the dark stairwell and inhaled deeply.

# CHAPTER FIVE

## 5

Everything was hazy, and Arlo couldn't tell a dream from a memory. Everything blurred together as he faded in and out of his consciousness.

***

"Can you believe it?" A young brunette woman squealed while holding several papers in her hand. Her feet were tapping quickly against the ground as she struggled to stay still. "I got it! I'm going to be in *Mr. Bluebeard*!" She was a very thin, tall woman, nearly the same height as Arlo. Her hair was just a shade lighter than his and fell in curls around her heart-shaped face.

"*In* Mr. Bluebeard? Why would you be *in* him?" Arlo cocked a brow and tilted his head, a subtle smirk tugged at the corner of his lips as he ran his fingers through his own curls. "Poor choice of words, Freya."

"You goop!" Freya frowned.

"Be happy for your sister," another woman nudged him before turning to Freya. "I'm so happy for you."

"Thanks, Halina." Freya smiled with a sigh, sounding almost exasperated. "I didn't think I was going to be anywhere near good enough."

"Of course you're good enough," Halina said. Her voice was very smooth and reassuring. "You're an amazing ballerina."

Arlo furrowed his brows as his gaze shifted between the two women. Halina slid her arm around the crook of his elbow and rested her head against his shoulder. She was much shorter than the two of them, hair almost black as night, with large pale blue eyes. She hugged his arm briefly before sliding her hand down to lace her fingers with his.

"So when will we get to see you in *Mr. Bluebeard*?" Arlo asked and Freya raised an eyebrow at him.

"Oh, I hate how you say it." Arlo grinned as she continued, "I'll get you two tickets, I promise. It's supposed to be in the new Iroquois Theater! I can't wait to see it. I bet it's beautiful."

"It's not even open yet."

Freya hit Arlo's arm with her papers.

"It's supposed to open soon—November twenty-something."

"Mama would be proud of you," Arlo said, finally giving her a genuine smile. His free hand reached for Freya's wrist as he pulled her into a hug. He whispered something to her in Polish. Freya wrapped her arms around Arlo's body and hugged him tightly.

She whispered something back as she let go. His hand found her wrist again before sliding against her palm. He squeezed her slender hand. Their gazes met, and she nodded.

Arlo smiled.

Halina, still holding onto Arlo's other hand, stared up at the two of them.

"You two with your silent twin language." She then focused on Arlo, her head tilting slightly as she tucked her thick black hair behind her pointed ear. "I rarely ever hear you speak Polish."

"It's something our mom used to tell us all the time," he said. "To believe in ourselves—"

"And that the possibilities are endless," Freya finished.

Arlo heard himself chuckle. "I was never going to amount to anything though, but Freya—*Freya*—"

His own voice echoed in his head as the two women dissolved into a blurry mist. Indistinguishable voices replaced the warm, reassuring words of Freya. Busy noises swirled around him like flurries of snow or fallen leaves in the wind before passing on, returning him again to shadowy memories that were locked deep down in the depths of his mind.

***

Arlo now stood in the finished Iroquois Theater with Halina, whose loose, flowing black hair had been twisted into two thin braids pinned into a crown that ran around her head, ornamented with small white flowers. The Iroquois Theater was a temple of beauty, as claimed, with marble staircases, soaring ceilings, and extravagant amounts of polished mahogany trim. It was clear that no other theater could match its claimed architectural perfection. He looked up, admiring the high ceilings.

"Where are we sitting?" Halina asked eagerly. Her large crystal blue eyes observed the other guests before her gaze landed on Arlo. She looked up at him, a small smile peeking at the corner of her thick lips, and she tenderly brushed some of his brown hair out of his face.

The gallery was accessed through a series of narrow staircases and landings, while the balcony would be up the sweeping marble staircase in the foyer.

"Orchestra," he answered, his fingers moving down the length of her forearm. "Up close and personal to the action. So we can see her."

Halina looked to her right and furrowed her brows, noticing iron gates pushed up against the wall. She turned to Arlo.

"Why are there gates?" she asked curiously, somewhat cautiously.

"To stop people from trying to get seats they didn't pay for, I'd assume."

"So they're locking us in?" she asked, holding tightly to her large Moroccan leather handbag. It was handsomely curved with gold plated mounting and chain, beautifully finished and lined in dainty colors of moire.

"Locking them out," he corrected. "We're supposed to be there, they aren't."

*Maybe it's in her bag.*

Arlo turned around once, noticing a familiar yet unfamiliar voice. Halina's hand was yanked from Arlo's as he spun around, but he didn't notice. He was too entranced by the voice. He didn't know where it was coming from and couldn't see anyone looking at them. All of the other guests were concerned with themselves and themselves only. Was it coming from inside his head?

*I know they had it.*

There was the voice again. Arlo looked over at Halina, then down at her bag.

"What's in your bag?" he asked her before looking around again.

Halina narrowed her eyes, holding it closer to her body.

"What do you mean?" she asked, somewhat defensively.

He shook his head.

"I—I—don't know," he muttered, rubbing his temple.

"Are you alright?"

"Yes, of course." Arlo snaked his arm around her waist and tugged her close enough to him so that he could gently kiss her forehead. A small smile appeared on her lips, feeling his skin against hers. She inhaled deeply, nestling into the safety of his embrace.

Once they found their seats, it was only a matter of time before the theater darkened, the patrons quieted, and *Mr. Bluebeard* began.

As the curtains rose, the scene melted into a cacophony of images and sound. Moments from dreams—or maybe it was the past—whipped around Arlo, assaulting his senses with the constant upheaval of light, smells, and volume.

***

Arlo blinked several times and rubbed his temples. He was no longer in the theater. He looked around at the black void surrounding him. A few yards away, he could see a figure hunched on the ground, shaking slightly. His feet took him forward, as if retracing steps from long ago.

It was Halina. Her large blue eyes were red-rimmed and watery. Arlo instinctively knelt and began to wrap his arm around her. But paused and allowed his arm to hover over her back and shoulder for a bit while her body shook from her unstable breathing.

"Halina?" he said tenderly, finally allowing his hand to gently touch her shoulder. "Are you alright, beautiful?" Halina averted her eyes. She blinked several times, her wet lashes causing several tears to dampen her cheeks. Arlo brushed his fingertips against her reddened face and softly wiped away her tears. "Talk to me," he whispered. The words came unbidden to his lips, and he listened as if he was merely watching the scene unfold between himself and Halina.

She chewed on her bottom lip as he touched the side of her jawline with the back of his fingers and turned her head to face him. Slowly, her brilliantly blue eyes met his green ones. Halina closed her eyes and inhaled deeply. Her lips parted as she exhaled.

"He said no," she said between staggered breaths. "My father. He said no."

"There has to be something—"

Halina leaned her temple against his as she closed her eyes, her black hair falling to hang in front of her face. "Destiny won't allow it."

"I don't believe in that," Arlo said, brushing her hair out of her face and tucking it behind her ear. "I don't care what some dead mythical being has to say about anything."

He heard his own voice chuckle quietly and murmur something indistinguishable as the scene faded into darkness.

***

Arlo's eyes fluttered again before he finally managed to drag his eyelids open.

*Nothing.*

*Maybe this was* finally *reality.*

He took a deep breath as images of Salvatore's inert body swam back into his mind. Of course. He was still blind from using his abilities to heal Salvatore from the ambush. Focusing on his other senses, a foul smell tickled his nose, and he lay strapped flat on a cold, steel table. He could feel the pressure of something—or someone—sitting on his chest, and when he struggled to move, they strengthened their hold on both his wrists and ankles. He inhaled sharply again—they were Imps. They were surprisingly strong for being so small in stature. The one sitting upon his chest kept its claws latched onto the sides of Arlo's head, digging further into his temples as he batted his wings in a fury, trying to stay low. Arlo could feel blood running down the sides of his head as the Imp continued to claw into his skull.

"Keep him under, Kaglu!" Szor hissed in demand, but Arlo could tell Kaglu's arms were shaking. Still, he did his best to keep his hold on Arlo's skull.

"Something's pushing me out of his mind."

"Szor!"

"What?" Szor hissed at Groljib, who was elbowing him harshly into his side. Groljib pointed a long, boney finger at Arlo, whose body had a faint white glow emitting around it. "What's he doing?"

"I don't think it's *him*."

"Freya?" the two of them said in unison as they glanced at each other.

"I'm losing—" Kaglu started to say.

"Don't let him go. He can't escape this time. Stand your ground!"

The weight on Arlo's chest was suddenly thrown back as if his own body had kicked it off with unimaginable force.

The Imps quickly backed up as they watched Arlo curiously, their black beady eyes were wide and didn't stray from him. A pale, silvery apparition encompassed his physical form as he got up. Arlo's body opened his eyes, and they were pure white. His pupils and irises had vanished.

"How dare you," a voice said. It came from Arlo's mouth, but it wasn't his.

The entire room filled with a blinding white light.

***

Arlo awoke abruptly on the sidewalk, the sun beating harshly on his face. He blinked a few times as his vision slowly began to return. Sweat beaded down his forehead, dampening his hair as he slowly sat up, massaging his temples. What had just happened? Instinctively, he rose to a defensive stance as quickly as he could, looking around for Imps, but there were only human pedestrians passing by, eyeing him curiously as they stepped around him and muttering things to each other about the strange boy dressed in bizarre clothes.

*Was it all a dream?* Arlo looked around for the alleyway where the team had been ambushed. He couldn't see it anywhere. *Where am I?*

He shook his head, ruffling his dark brown hair as he slowly got to his feet. He rubbed the back of his left ear cuff, and the silver of the end slowly slid into his ear. Arlo tapped it a few times before readjusting the bead comm on his wrist, but nothing happened.

He had awoken tucked behind a dumpster near the entrance to an alley, but it was obviously not the same one in which the FeyForce had been ambushed. The sun had warmed the trash bags around him, and he wrinkled his nose at the putrid smell. Before leaving, he looked around, trying to find any clue as to how he may have gotten there. His eyes landed on an old cellphone with a cracked and flaking screen. It wasn't a clue, but it was interesting, and Arlo picked it up. He knew enough about Terra to know this was a Terran communication device. He tucked it absently into his pocket—an interesting souvenir of what he hoped would be a soon-concluded trip.

He started walking down the street, continuing to tap at the silver that took up the space in his ear. Still, he heard nothing. He turned the corner and stopped in his tracks just in front of a movie theater. For a minute, he stared at the *Star Wars: Episode II—Attack of the Clones* poster, and his eyes fixed on the solid beam of light held by one of the motionless characters.

"I bet that'd be handy against the Imps," he muttered to himself, staring at the weapon featured on the movie poster. He looked at the poster beside it, *Spider-Man* and frowned at the creature dressed in red and black webbing scaling the side of the building. He glanced at the surrounding buildings to see if anything was climbing them. "For the love of gourd," he grumbled to himself. Arlo turned away from the movie theater and pushed his hair back and out of his face.

He took another step back, but when he tried to step again, he realized his shoe was stuck. Lifting his foot, a sticky pink gunk stretched between the cement and his shoe.

"Looks like you stepped on gum," a pedestrian noted wryly as he walked past Arlo, who continued to try to free his boot from the substance. "Shitty deals, man."

Terra. Rubbish blew across the sidewalks with the wind. Gum was stuck to the bottom of his foot. He sighed in annoyance.

He found it, for the most part, dirty and unimpressive. *Why would anyone want to live here?*

"*Hellooooo*!" he said in a frustrated, singsong voice into the comm, dragging out the end of the word as if it had three distinct syllables. Still, there was no answer on the other end. It remained silent.

Arlo scraped the bottom of his boot over the concrete to remove the remains of the globy gum before he continued down the streets of Chicago. Many pedestrians glanced his way, some of them muttering to one another as they looked him up and down, but Arlo paid no attention to it. If anyone was dressed strangely, it was them, not him, in their cotton clothing, collarless attire with weird symbols on their chests. Shuffling on his feet, he continued walking, still tapping on his communication devices.

"Is anyone there?" he said, still tapping ferociously.

"Arlo?" a voice finally emitted from the silver bud in his ear. "Are you alright? Arlo? Hello? Hello?"

"Salvatore!" Arlo said, exasperated but thrilled. A broad smile stretched across his face. "The Imps—they captured me—I'm still on Terra—I'm not sure how I escaped—"

"Arlo! I can't hear you—"

The line went dead. He tapped the comm in his ear again before groaning.

"Maple sap," he grumbled.

***

Salvatore quickly got to his feet as he continued tapping on the comm in his own ear. He ascended the stairs, where he found a sleeping Acacia, snuggled in their bed. Salvatore slid in beside her and gently touched her shoulder.

"Acacia," he whispered, brushing blonde hair out of her face.

"What?" she grumbled, not bothering to open her eyes.

"I talked to him."

There was no answer.

"Acacia," he repeated himself.

"To who?" she asked finally.

"Arlo," he said.

The mention of his name, at last, caused her to turn over in bed. For a moment, she lay flat on her back as she blinked her eyes several times, staring up at the ceiling. She inhaled deeply, and glanced at her husband.

"And?" she asked.

"Well, he still knows who we are," he continued. "I lost communication before I could find out anything else."

Salvatore sank into the bed beside her while she returned her gaze to the ceiling. "Did you notice during the attack, the Imps didn't really care about us. They targeted Arlo, and only us when we got in the way."

"They almost killed you," she recalled dryly.

"I got in the way."

She didn't answer.

"I think we need to go back to Terra," he said. He sighed, weighing his words carefully, almost afraid to voice his next thought. "I think—this must be about the Book of Fate," he said at last. "If anyone else there is closer to finding it than we are, then Arlo—"

Acacia looked over at her husband as his voice trailed away. They both knew what he'd been about to say. She narrowed her eyes, staring into his dark ones. She heaved a breath, her chest rising with each intentional inhale and falling with every nervous exhale.

"The book was lost, remember? It was destroyed in the fire," she said. "Arlo was all that was left. The Elves destroyed it when they set fire to the theater. It's gone now. End of story."

"Do you really believe that?" Salvatore turned to face Acacia, propping himself on his elbow to really look her in the eyes. "If that's true, then why does the Autumn Queen keep sending us to Terra?"

"Because of the Imps, remember? Those hideous creatures we just—"

"Again, you really believe that?" He tried to keep his voice calm, measured. "You saw them—the Imps didn't even care about entering Fae. They don't care about us at all, Acacia. None of it makes any sense. This is about the book. It has to be. It has to still be on Terra. Why else would they attack Arlo like that?"

Acacia chewed on her bottom lip, frustrated with Salvatore's probing.

"Sometimes you make me feel like I married the wrong Sanguine," she grumbled. "Sebastien wouldn't probe like this. Sebastien would just shut up and let me sleep."

Her eyes glinted slightly in the moonlight as she also pushed herself up. Acacia forcefully shoved Salvatore onto his back and climbed on top of him. She straightened her arms, and her palms were flatly pressed up against his shoulders as she looked down at him.

"We both know you'd have no fun with him," Salvatore noted, as Acacia sat back and ran her long, slender fingers down his biceps.

"Perhaps, but he doesn't talk nearly as much as you do."

"You're trying to distract me."

"Is it working?"

"I'm just trying to do what's best for Fae."

"Right now, you should be doing what's best for me—your *wife*." She returned her hands to his bare shoulders and pressed her nails into his skin before dragging them back down his arms. She wasn't rough enough to draw blood, just enough to leave a light mark, just visible in the dim room.

"Acacia," Salvatore said softly, looking up at her eyes.

Acacia raised her eyebrows.

"*Salvatore*," she said, almost in a mocking manner. "You woke me up for this," she continued. "You'll be putting me back to sleep."

He sighed.

"Fine," she yielded, but with resentment in her eyes. Acacia crawled off of him and got out of bed. She didn't like how Salvatore was suddenly questioning everything. Why couldn't he just accept what happened and move forward? There were bigger things to worry about than Arlo. "We'll talk to Lord Bane and Commander Kall-An about your concerns in the morning," she said, not glancing back at him. "I'm going to make myself some tea."

Salvatore grabbed her wrist before she had the chance to stray too far from the bed. "You don't need tea," he said, pulling her back down onto him.

# CHAPTER SIX

*6*

Out on the streets of Chicago, two agents caught sight of Arlo's uniqueness.

"Is there a renaissance fair in town?" Agent Eiríksdóttir asked Agent Harpy, who frowned at the sight of the young man dressed in a leather vest and cloak. "Maybe a Harry Potter convention? That new movie comes out in November, right?" she added with a small laugh, amused with her references. Agent Harpy, however, continued to frown.

The two agents sat on a bench near a bus stop. They sat slightly apart so that no passersby would assume the two knew each other. Agent Harpy observed Arlo over the top edge of her newspaper while Agent Eiríksdóttir fiddled alternatively with a crisp guidebook and a camera slung around her neck. She now peered through the lens at Arlo, snapping a few quick photos. The man was out of place in Chicago, and that was saying a lot given the eclectic array of ordinary pedestrians who were also glancing questioningly at Arlo and turning to each other to roll their eyes and shrug.

Both agents knew there was no fair in town.

"Do you think he could be a demon?" Agent Harpy asked, still frowning at him. She didn't take her eyes off of him, but he wasn't like anything they'd come across before. They were used to seeing unusual things regarding demons, but most demons tried to blend in, and they did a pretty good job at it.

This man wasn't trying at all.

"Look at him!" Agent Eiríksdóttir shrugged. "There's no way he's a demon. He looks lost." Agent Eiríksdóttir was still fairly new to the division, and new to being Harpy's partner, but she came from a well-respected group known as the Republic of Letters. Their knowledge and understanding of the paranormal was superior to newer S.M.O.K.E. & M.I.R.R.O.R.S. as they had been around for over a hundred years and had multiple international offices. In comparison, S.M.O.K.E. & M.I.R.R.O.R.S. was only a few decades old and was solely based and operated in the United States. Still, while the members of the Republic were booksmart, and known as Intellectuals, they tended to lack field experience, and even now, it was clear that Agent Eiríksdóttir expected demons to appear in their original, demonic forms.

"Demons can look like anything," Agent Harpy reminded her, trying not to be annoyed with Agent Eiríksdóttir's naiveté.

Eiríksdóttir cocked her head to the side, still staring at him in observation. She did her best to explain her reasoning. "I mean, sure, he's certainly not from around here, but I feel like most demons would at least try to blend in better than this. He's sticking out like a sore thumb. I doubt that's intentional."

"Excuse me," Agent Harpy said, completely ignoring Agent Eiríksdóttir as the strange man got closer and within earshot. She rose from her seat on the bench, tossing the newspaper into an overflowing trash can. Agent Harpy had one hand on her gun as she approached the young man. "I'm going to have to ask you for some identification."

"And who are you?" he asked, cocking a brow. He brushed his wavy hair back with his fingers and awaited an answer.

"Agent Harpy," she said before tilting her head toward the woman beside her. "And this is Agent Eiríksdóttir."

He nodded at the black woman who waved at him. "Daughter of Erik," he acknowledged before turning to the tall Asian woman in front of him. Agent Eiríksdóttir frowned slightly, caught off guard by his comprehension of her surname. "With a name like that, I expected bird wings and claws." He mimicked a clawing motion with his hands as he glanced over at her.

Agent Eiríksdóttir's eyebrows rose as an involuntary short of laughter flew out of her nose. Agent Harpy remained unamused.

"Not funny?" he asked before pausing. He raised his eyebrows in acceptance of defeat nearly five seconds later. "I thought it was funny—she thinks I'm funny—alright." He ruffled his hair and smoothed it back before placing his hand flat against his chest. "Arlo," he said.

"Just Arlo?" Agent Harpy asked.

He tilted his head to the side. "One should know better than to give more than one name. Names are valuable. They can be used against you. Everyone knows that."

The two agents exchanged glances. "We're with S.M.O.K.E. & M.I.R.R.O.R.S," Agent Harpy said, still pressing for his identification as she motioned for him to step off of the sidewalk and toward the alleyway to be out of sight of the pedestrians.

"Is that supposed to mean something to me?" Arlo asked. While hesitant, he took a step forward to her for a moment.

She frowned, unsure of what to say. He wasn't posing a threat to anyone, but Agent Harpy couldn't deny her curiosity. "It's the Sector of Managing Obscure Knowledge and Eccentricities & Maneuvering Irregular Rehabilitations, Removals, Obliterations, and Regulations Subdivision."

Arlo raised his eyebrows at the ridiculously long name.

"I can see why you go by S.M.O.K.E. & M.I.R.R.O.R.S.," he noted. "But if you'll excuse me," he said as he took the same step backward and away from the two women. "I'm a little busy right now. Have a good day."

"Going to a convention?" Agent Eiríksdóttir asked, unable to help herself. Her fluffy, cloud-like mane of black hair created a halo around her face. Her smile and her eyes brightened as she eagerly awaited an answer. Her energy was vibrant, especially standing beside Agent Harpy, a mixed Chinese woman whose long, straight black hair was pulled neatly back into a low ponytail, away from her pale, freckled stern-looking face. Her eyes kept the same unamused stare.

Arlo crinkled his brows together, confused by her question. He stopped and turned back to them. "A convention?" he asked. "What for?"

"I don't know—Harry Potter? Lord of the Rings? Maybe Star Wars? Star Wars comes out this summer, right?" she asked Agent Harpy, who just frowned at her still. Agent Eiríksdóttir didn't know why she bothered with

Agent Harpy as she turned back to Arlo. "You just look like you stepped out of a fantasy world."

"Are you mocking me?" he asked, stepping forward again into the alley.

Agent Eiríksdóttir's expression changed immediately, seeming taken aback by his words. "No, of course not," she said, glancing at Agent Harpy who just rolled her eyes. "I want to know where you came from, or where you're going—because, well, hell, I'd like to go too."

"Oh, would you stop already?" Agent Harpy snapped at her partner as Arlo combed his tousled dark brown hair back with his fingers.

"What are those things on your ears?" Agent Eiríksdóttir asked curiously, catching sight of the silver pointed cuffs he wore.

Quickly, Arlo ruffled his hair to cover them.

"Nothing," he mumbled. Even on Terra, people still drew attention to his ears.

Puffs of black smoke began appearing in the air all around the alley, shielding their exit.

The two agents immediately drew their guns.

"Those won't work on them," Arlo said dismissively as he cracked his knuckles. He reached toward his belt and unhooked what appeared to be a small keychain of a Burgundian Rondel dagger. Swinging the chain from the loop around his finger, the small replica landed full-sized as he caught it in his hand. The dagger was a heavy, hollow-ground, double-edged style with a reinforced point. The hilt was silver and gold plated as a two-tone effect with Fey inscriptions around both rondel.

"We have black tourmaline bullets—" Agent Eiríksdóttir started.

"Who's 'them'?" Agent Harpy interjected, cutting her off. But Arlo had his eyes on the puffs of black smoke that were constantly disappearing and reappearing.

Imps began to emerge as the smoke puffs got larger. They clawed out of the smoke as though they were little doorways in the universe. The two agents fired at several of them, but just as Arlo had warned, the bullets went right through them, causing absolutely no harm.

The bullets only angered the Imps. They shifted their energy away from Arlo and launched themselves at the two defenseless humans.

Arlo moved so quickly it looked like a blur. He stood between the Imps and the two agents.

"Leave them out of this."

One of the Imps curled his thin lip at Arlo, looking exactly like a small, hideous gargoyle. "We don't want them, we just want you."

"No harm will come to anyone if you come quietly—"

Arlo threw his dagger up in the air and caught it in his other hand.

"I doubt it," he said. He raised his arm as he bent his knees into a standard fighting stance that he'd learned in his first few days on the FeyForce. He charged.

Harpy and Eiríksdóttir stood on the sidelines as Arlo took on five Imps at once. His movements were fluid and quick, there were moments where he was nothing but a blur. As soon as he stabbed one of the Imps with his dagger, its eyes were sucked into its skull, leaving behind empty hollowed sockets as its body drained of all fluid. The Imp dried up instantly and broke into a cloud of dust upon impact with the ground. Arlo opened his hand, and the dagger quickly returned to it.

Hearing a groan behind him, Arlo spun around to face the agents.

An Imp had climbed out of a portal just behind Agent Harpy and was now doing its best to wrap itself around her, clawing her face as it used its other hand to pierce into her abdomen.

Arlo took this in in less than a second. In one fluid motion, he used the momentum from his turn to throw his blade at the Imp's head.

The same thing happened. The eyes were pulled into the skull, its body drained of all life.

Agent Harpy nearly fell to the ground, steadied by Agent Eiríksdóttir as the two of them coughed from the cloud of ash lifting in the air from the pile where the Imp once stood.

As the last Imp disintegrated in front of Arlo, he began to speak. "Imps exist between realms. Tourmaline bullets are good with most demons from the Underworld, or Purgatory even, but not ones that exist on the outside of what you and I know, the Inbetween."

"What are you?" Harpy asked him as Arlo spun his dagger back into a small replica. He knelt down to examine her wound as he hooked it back upon his belt.

"I'm Fey," he said. Tilting his head. He quickly and gently dragged his finger over her wounds and they began to stitch themselves. "What are you?" he asked quietly, before getting up. Arlo disappeared out of sight before she could even consider her answer.

*Human*, she thought. *Only human.*

***

"Director Quartermaine, I think you need to come out onto the field," Agent Harpy said, her hand pressing firmly up against her ribcage and the echoes of pain she felt. "It was like nothing I've ever seen. He called them Imps. He called himself Fey. He said the Imps are from an Inbetween—" She furrowed her brows as Director Quartermaine turned around to face her. The two agents had arrived back at their headquarters in Chicago only moments ago. They were in the sickbay, but given the information they'd gathered—both time-sensitive and top secret—the nurses had been asked to wait outside while the agents gave the Director their initial report.

Director Quartermaine observed Agent Harpy's wounds from where he stood before finally moving to approach her as she heaved herself onto the table. They were still in the process of healing from when Arlo touched her.

Agent Harpy cleared her throat before continuing. "I think he's a friendly—he helped protect us from the Imps. He started to heal me, I think. It was the damnedest thing. Black tourmaline doesn't work on them, by the way." She dropped her gun on the counter as she removed her weapons belt.

Director Quartermaine silently mulled over the words as Agent Harpy spoke. He was so silent, she wasn't sure he'd even heard her.

"Director?" she said.

"Do you believe him?" he asked, with his hand, he turned her head to face the other way as he took a closer look at her reddened and swollen cheek. "About being

Fey?" He turned to grab a bottle of disinfectant and bandages out of a cupboard.

"I don't know—I mean, those were definitely Imps—definitely not any creatures from *earth*." She scowled a little. "You should have warned us about what we were dealing with."

"I did," he answered flatly. "You just didn't believe me."

He continued to examine the wounds on Agent Harpy's cheek, collarbone, and arm. Director Quartermaine looked down and gently picked up her slender hand. Her index finger was broken. He turned her hand over within his own to look at her palm and ran his fingers along the cut. Director Quartermaine's eyes turned black, and smoky nether energy grazed along the cut. He looked up at her, and Agent Harpy could clearly see her reflection in his darkened eyes. She couldn't take her brown eyes off of his.

"We deal with *demons*, Director. Not Imps, and certainly not Fey."

"Imps are a kind of demon," he answered softly. He could sense it. The same energy from all those years ago. It had been so long. He daubed ointment on the cut, and Harpy winced. "Find Arlo," he commanded with urgency, letting go of her hand. "It is the most important—we must find him before—" He stopped himself and focused on the cut on her hand again.

"Who is he?" Agent Harpy asked.

"He's what we've been waiting for."

"We don't even know where to begin to look, Director Quartermaine."

"Try the Oriental Theater," he said nonchalantly. "Where he was supposed to die."

Director Quartermaine spun around, walking out of the room.

The two agents looked at each other, bewildered, but the nurse didn't enter. They waited only a moment before the Director returned, carrying a thick file. It was old and tattered, worn from use over the years. Slowly, he walked back to Agent Harpy, her fingers softly pressing against her cheek.

Director Quartermaine dropped the file onto the table.

"Arlo Jäger, twenty-two years old—twin sister of Freya Jäger. Came to the United States in 1902 with another woman named Halina. They died in the Iroquois Theater fire of 1903—where the Oriental Theater now stands. Although the bodies of both women were recovered and identified, Halina's body went missing after the fire. Interestingly, out of everyone in the theater that night, Arlo's body was the only one that was never recovered." He had recited it perfectly from memory. Director

Quartermaine only flipped open the file to the very beginning, where it depicted a picture of a young man. "Is this not the same man you saw?"

Agent Harpy stared at the photograph. Her face paled. She furrowed her brows in confusion before shaking her head.

"I mean, he looks like him but—no offense, Director, but that would make him over a hundred years old. The man I saw doesn't look a day over twenty-two."

"You age differently in other realms, Harpy. Time doesn't all work the same. After all, what did he tell you he was?"

*Fey.*

Her eyelids fluttered, as if attempting to blink away the thought. "Hang on," she said, "did you say Halina's body went missing?"

"The Elves collected it," he said. His tone was nonchalant, as if it were a normal thing to be said. The Elves. "She was the Elven princess. I always just assumed the Elven King wanted his daughter at home."

"It bothers me how normal this is for you."

Director Quartermaine only shrugged. "It wasn't always. I questioned the existence of Elves when I was younger and first assigned to Chicago, despite what happened to me as a child." He looked back at Harpy. "One thing is certain, we are not alone in this world,

Harpy. We never have been. Demons, Elves, Imps, Fey... We're only just scratching the surface."

That gave her chills. Agent Harpy readjusted her sleeves to hide her goosebumps, or, at least, doing her best without putting pressure on her broken finger. She looked over at Agent Eiríksdóttir, who had been oddly quiet since they returned to the office.

"What are you thinking, Ruthie? You're the Intellectual."

The agent looked up, her fluffy black hair bounced a little with the action.

"It's just a lot to take in," she said quietly. "I mean, these are all things I've studied, but I never in my wildest dreams thought I'd ever have the chance to witness anything like it." She smiled in disbelief. It was a large smile that took up half of her face. "Demons were one thing, but Elves? Fey? Imps? There's still a lot we don't know about those guys. My grandfather would have loved this."

Agent Harpy exchanged glances with Director Quartermaine, who only shook his head. "Find him, Harpy," he instructed.

"Yes, sir."

Director Quartermaine nodded to the nurse outside as he left the sickbay, and she walked through the door. He walked thoughtfully back to his office. He closed the door behind him before sinking into the leather chair behind his wide desk. Director Quartermaine had left the file with the agents, but he had memorized the whole thing years ago and photos and documents now swam before his eyes. His eyes fell to the photo on his desk of him with Dorothea Sharp and Dr. Ingram-Zander Stolly when he had first joined S.M.O.K.E. & M.I.R.R.O.R.S as a young man. He could recall it as clearly as the day it happened, when he was given the assignment forty years before, when he'd stood at the Pearl Harbor Memorial for the remembrance of his older brother. Chills crawled over his skin, remembering the look Dorothea Sharp had given him when he had made a joke about Santa's elves. A small smile peeked at the corner of his lips.

For forty long years, there was nothing but demons running amok. Nothing to do with the Book of Fate, his assignment.

Nothing, until now.

Everything prior had been mostly dead ends, but this was a lead they could finally chase. He leaned over his desk and picked up the phone.

It rang only once.

"Hello?"

"Mrs. Sharp," Director Quartermaine started, "I never did ask you why you never took your husband's surname."

Though he couldn't see her, Director Quartermaine knew she smiled on the other end.

"Finley Quartermaine," she said softly. "To what do I owe the pleasure?"

"Do you remember ten years ago—back in 1992—when you told me the Book of Fate would likely need a key?"

"Has it really been ten years?" her voice was still as tender and gentle as he always remembered it to be.

"Well, it's been forty since you gave me my assignment. How old does that make you now?" Director Quartermaine smiled as he asked.

Mrs. Sharp shushed him. "We don't talk about my age, young man." He grinned at her words. He was hardly young anymore. He tilted his head, awaiting her words, but there was a long, drawn out pause. "Yes, I do remember," Mrs. Sharp said finally. "Why?"

"I think we finally have a lead."

"What about the girl?"

"She's safe."

"Good." Mrs. Sharp sounded exasperated. "Because they will come for her."

"They'll try, but we'll protect her," Director Quartermaine reassured. "We'll have a lot more help once we get through to Arlo."

"That poor boy," she said empathetically. "There is so much he doesn't know."

"How are you doing?" Director Quartermaine finally asked.

Mrs. Sharp was quiet on the other end, but he could still hear the faint sounds of her breathing. "I'm fine, Finley."

He smiled. "You know, you're the only one who still calls me Finley."

"Old habits die hard, Director."

"I never said I didn't like it."

She chuckled softly on the other end while Director Quartermaine poked a stack of files on his desk. "How's your son doing? I heard you're a grandmother."

"Oh! Goodness. A *grandmother*—please don't." He laughed at her reaction and etched his thumb nail into the armrest of his chair. "I did want to apologize," she then said.

Director Quartermaine tilted his head, caught off guard by her comment. "For what?"

"Taking your brother away from you."

"Mrs. Sharp—" he started, but she had already hung up.

Director Quartermaine glanced out of his window as he sat back in his seat and hung up his own phone. Dr. Stolly had given him that old black rotary dial phone when Director Quartermaine was packing his things and headed to Chicago. He glanced at the picture again, of him with Dr. Stolly and Mrs. Sharp. Readjusting in his chair, he pulled open the top drawer of his desk and shifted through the many newspaper clippings he had held onto until he found the one about Mrs. Sharp's son and his wife—and their stillborn.

The Director's eyes rose to the seat that sat facing him on the other side of the desk. "Yes, it is strange," he murmured, as if responding to an invisible visitor. His fingers tapped the desk and his eyes wandered out the window. "Something isn't right."

# CHAPTER SEVEN

7

Finn Quartermaine still had nightmares about World War II.

He sat in his office, staring up at the wall of recognition he had received during his service in the Army. While he had been in wars of his own, it was World War II that'd left a scar that wouldn't heal. Director Quartermaine put his head in his hands and closed his eyes. He hadn't even fought in that war, not really, anyway. Not directly.

He was only eight years old.

It was July 16, 1944.

He remembered being at home, safe, playing outside with their family's Siberian Husky when the men came in their starched uniforms with brass buttons.

Young Finley had sandy blond hair with bright hazel eyes. He remembered seeing Sergeant Charles Kamuela in the driver's seat of a car with a man beside him Finley didn't recognize. Sergeant Kamuela was good friends with Finley's older brother, Hayden, and Finley was quite fond of the extremely friendly Hawaiian man, who always had a smile plastered on his face and sent him nice telegrams.

Finley smiled at Sergeant Kamuela and waved at him, only the Sergeant didn't smile back. Slowly, Finley curled his hand into a small fist and dropped it back down at his side, still not taking his eyes off of the stone-faced Marine.

The Husky paused at Finley's feet, eyeing the two men curiously.

Sergeant Kamuela tilted his head toward the dog, and the Husky whined, backing up behind the boy as the other man got out of the car. The man gave Finley a look, narrowing his eyes. Finley backed up farther, before darting into the house through the above-ground basement while the two men walked around the side to the front entrance.

Finley stood at the bottom of the stairway, just on the other side of the door as he listened to the commotion upstairs. He could hear his father ask who the man was while his parents warmly greeted the Sergeant, but after their initial meeting at the doorway, everything dropped to an inaudible murmur.

Everything went silent.

Finley backed away from the door and climbed into the bed, arms wrapped tightly around the Husky as he waited for what felt like an eternity.

He looked up at the ceiling as the floorboards above began to creak. Quickly, he got up from the bed and ran toward the door to lock it as someone descended the stairs. The above-ground basement had been remodeled into a bedroom for his brother after his injuries from the war left him unable to use the stairs necessary to reach the main level of the house from outside. Finley hid under the blankets.

They were coming for him.

He was just a child.

Director Quartermaine massaged his temples for a minute. He then ruffled his light sandy hair, now salted with whites and grays as he sat back in his seat before looking out the window. As his gaze once again fell to the picture on his desk, he heard the sound of the water and smelled the sharp metallic odor of construction. He could feel Mrs. Sharp's hand shaking his after she'd asked him to oversee a new S.M.O.K.E. & M.I.R.R.O.R.S. location in Chicago. He gripped the armrests of his chair before picking up the photo. *Pearl Harbor.* The memorial opened forty years ago, back in the sixties, and it still felt like yesterday.

He glanced at the rotary phone beside his hand before propping the picture back up. Director Quartermaine picked up the phone and started dialing.

No answer.

He tried again, and still, no answer.

Director Quartermaine hung up the phone for a moment, before picking it up again, unable to shake his sense of unease. He dialed a different number this time.

"How may I be of assistance, Director?" a voice on the other end asked.

"I'm going to need a flight to Honolulu—" Director Quartermaine started, his finger twirling mindlessly in the cord of the phone.

"For when?" the voice asked.

"For as soon as you can get me there."

"Yes, sir."

***

Less than twelve hours later, he was in Hawai'i.

Director Quartermaine knocked on the door. It took a few minutes, but an elderly woman finally answered it. Short in stature, she looked up at him through her reading glasses. "Finley—you came all this way." While she sounded exasperated, she hardly looked surprised to see him.

"Mrs. Dorothea Sharp," he said, crossing his arms. "You hung up on me, evaded my calls, and never even bothered to answer my original question."

She tilted her head and narrowed her already small eyes.

"My husband wanted space from his family name, so he took mine when we got married. He just wanted to be a simple businessman without the added pressures, and he was happy to take over for my father when the time came." She opened the door farther and stepped to the side to allow him entry. "But I know you didn't come just to ask about my last name," she said.

"Entering the *Sharp* family isn't what I would call simple," the Director said and tilted his head.

"Maybe," she said, "but it's a lot different than automotive innovations." Mrs. Sharp took off her reading glasses and tucked them into her breast pocket. "Now why are you here, Finley? Really?"

"Like I said, you hung up on me after apologizing and then wouldn't return my phone calls," he said as he entered her home. The Sharps were one of the richest families in America and had been for nearly eighty years now. Her home was extravagant, and he expected no less. Though he had known her for decades, Director Quartermaine wasn't a frequent visitor to her home, or Hawai'i, for many reasons. "What did you mean?" he asked finally, his gaze landing back on her as she shut the door behind him. He glanced down at her bandaged hand. His brows furrowed. "But first, what happened to you?"

"Arthritis," she answered softly, touching her wrist. She glanced up at him. "You were just a child when I met you."

He nodded, as he looked at her gallery of photos across the wall near the staircase. "I remember," he said quietly as she came up to walk beside him.

"It's been so long." She looked up at the pictures too. There was one of her with Dr. Stolly and of the famed Corpse Walker, Hayden Dáithí. It appeared to be a candid photo. Director Quartermaine didn't recognize anyone else in it—only his brother.

"I know there's—or at least was—a part of you that blamed me for what happened to your brother—when I gave up *Howard's* identity—"

Director Quartermaine chewed on the inside of his cheek and turned to look at her.

"I was a kid," he said finally. "I was angry, I lost my brother. More than once. I had to be angry with someone. Obviously I couldn't be angry at him." Director Quartermaine grunted. "But upon reflection, I should have known that it wasn't going to last." Director

Quartermaine shrugged, his gaze dropped down to the pictures on the table. "I should have known when he couldn't stay home. When he *had* to work. When he *had* to do something. When he became *Howard*. I'm sure he would've figured something out eventually, re-enlisting, I mean. Regardless of the part you had in it. *Once a Marine, always a Marine*," he muttered, mostly to himself. Director Quartermaine would be lying if he didn't feel some resentment toward Hayden, but mostly because he didn't get to experience what it was like to have an older brother. Even for the brief moment he had been home, Hayden wasn't the same. Stuck in a wheelchair, he had been a shell of his former self.

Director Quartermaine's eyes landed on a young girl sitting on Mrs. Sharp's lap in one of the photos. He picked up the picture frame to get a better look. As soon as his fingers touched the metal, his eyes turned black, and a surge of pain went up his arm. Director Quartermaine tensed and nearly dropped the frame. Mrs. Sharp came up beside him. There were only a few instances where he felt pain like that, and he was surprised to feel it in Mrs. Sharp's home.

"Are you alright, Finley?"

He blinked several times, his eyes returning to their normal hazel color.

"I thought your daughter-in-law miscarried," he said finally, still staring at the photo once his vision had cleared. He didn't mean for it to come out as blunt as he said it, but there were times words just came out like vomit. He couldn't control it. "I remember seeing it in the news a few years ago."

Mrs. Sharp clenched her jaw. "That was a little inconsiderate—"

He looked over at her, and his eyes darkened again.

Mrs. Sharp averted her gaze. She knew Director Quartermaine wasn't normal, he hadn't been normal the entire time she had known him. Not ever since she had rescued him from Guam. She forced herself to look down at the photo in his hand but still kept her gaze away from meeting his for a moment longer.

"She did," Mrs. Sharp answered finally. "My daughter-in-law miscarried. My granddaughter… is adopted." She tilted her head challengingly as she raised her eyebrows at the Director. "Did you not see *that* in the news as well?" she snapped. Even though she was now an old, frail woman, Mrs. Sharp still didn't threaten easily.

"I must have missed *that* one," Director Quartermaine said, though he doubted it. He took one last look at the photo and placed it back on the table while thinking about the news poking around in Mrs. Sharp's life. He supposed she was used to it. He certainly was. The press wouldn't leave his family alone for some time after the war ended. Mrs. Sharp didn't say anything, but her body language did as she turned away from him immediately. "Why won't you tell me the truth you're clearly hiding?" Director Quartermaine asked. She still didn't say anything. Mrs. Sharp seemed to be more tight-lipped that day than usual. He found it curious, and given the detection of nether energy, he wasn't curious in a good way. "You know what I'm capable of, Mrs. Sharp." Director Quartermaine glanced down at the photo again, at the young girl with frizzy, dark brown hair. He forced his voice to soften. "She looks a lot like you." He sighed and rubbed his eyes in weary frustration. "You've always been such a secretive woman. What did you do, Mrs. Sharp? She's not really adopted, *is* she?"

Mrs. Sharp's attention was now focused on the picture too.

"What are you accusing me of, *Director*?" She said it almost like an insult.

Director Quartermaine raised a brow. She rarely ever called him that except for the moments she wanted to distance herself from him and their history together. He supposed in that moment, she had the right to, but he didn't know how else to obtain the answers he wanted, that she wasn't going to give up so easily.

"Are you guilty of something, *Mrs. Sharp*?" he asked boldly and simply. The skin between his eyebrows creased out of concern while he waited for an answer. Deep down, he knew he wasn't going to get one. Not willingly. Not from her.

Mrs. Sharp clicked her tongue. "I just want her to have a normal life, Finley." There it was, some admittance, though she wouldn't say what it was. But there was something. He was right. She crossed her slender arms. "Please stop pressing. She's only seven."

"I was only eight."

Mrs. Sharp's bottom lip quivered.

He sighed, knowing he should let it go. Director Quartermaine was never too great with people, and age only made that worse.

"I'm just curious," he said, backing off of the subject. He even lifted his hands in surrender. "But she is part of one of the most influential families in America. How normal could her life really be?" he asked in a weak attempt at lightening up the mood. "After all, the great Mrs. Dorothea Sharp is her grandmother." But Mrs. Sharp didn't say anything. "Has she met Echo—"

"No," Mrs. Sharp said, quickly cutting him off before he had the opportunity to finish his sentence. "I hope she doesn't have to for a long time."

"Well, you have a beautiful family, Mrs. Sharp."

"Thank you, Finn."

Director Quartermaine could tell that she was still on edge with him, and she wasn't going to disclose any further information. He backed up and said his goodbyes before exiting her home. Once outside, he descended the porch steps and took a look around her property. Mrs. Sharp lived deep in Manoa Valley, her home was surrounded by tall trees and a large gold-plated gate. He stood beneath an archway held up by two large white pillars. His eyes moved back and forth, searching for the security cameras she most likely had.

Finn turned around to see her looking at him from her window.

He bowed his head slightly, and she tilted hers a little forward in return.

Mrs. Sharp remained at her window, watching as Director Quartermaine got in his car. The front gate opened for him, and he drove away down the long driveway. Only when the gate had securely clanged shut did she step away from the window. She returned to the pictures Director Quartermaine had stood before and carefully eyed each one, her gaze landing on the one he couldn't separate himself from. It was a picture of her with her little granddaughter. The resemblance was undeniable, but she shook her head, reminding herself that the only thing she was guilty of was having love for her family.

Mrs. Sharp began massaging her bandaged wrist with her fingers as she walked through the hallway toward the bathroom. Her fingertips fumbled with the edge of the bandage as she slowly began to unravel it. She entered the bathroom and quickly shut the door behind her. Mrs. Sharp pressed her back against the wooden door as she continued to unwrap the bandage. Her wrist was black and spidery with deterioration.

It was decaying.

The putrid smell hit her nose immediately. She tossed the bandage into the trashcan and quickly grabbed a bottle of ointment from her medicine cabinet above the sink.

Standing in the clean, bright bathroom, Mrs. Sharp gently massaged the ointment into what was left of her wrist. The damage went down to her bones, and she cursed under her breath as her fingers slipped, accidentally gouging into the soft, stinking flesh. The disintegration of her tissues created an unusual pattern over her hand and down her forearm, almost as though a fishing line had wrapped around her hand. Slowly, she began bandaging it back up with a new roll of gauze she'd gotten from her cabinet.

She glanced up at the mirror and nearly leaped out of her skin.

For a flash, a cloaked old man stared back at her where her reflection should have been, whose skin loosely hung off his body. His eyes were dark and sunken in, and his mouth sewn shut. Mrs. Sharp forced herself to look again, but upon second glance, he was already gone. The bandage had a floral lavender scent that only barely masked the smell of her decaying wrist and hand.

"Please don't do that," she muttered to herself, looking up at the mirror again, but only her reflection stared back at her. "You may send me to an early grave."

It wasn't that Mrs. Sharp had been overcome with fear. She was not afraid of the figure that had appeared in her mirror. She simply did not like surprises. She didn't like to be startled. She didn't like unexpected visitors. Little did she know, one of those unexpected visitors was standing outside her bathroom door.

Director Quartermaine had returned in a ghostly form. His feet made no sound as he walked, and he left no footprints. He could go through walls, and he could listen where he shouldn't be. He had watched, standing invisibly at Mrs. Sharp's side as she had unwrapped her wrist. He had seen the strange figure in her mirror. Director Quartermaine stared at Mrs. Sharp while she stood there, unknowing that she wasn't alone.

Although he partially blamed Mrs. Sharp for the experiences of his childhood, Director Quartermaine had never revealed the full extent of the abilities he'd gained as a result of his interaction with the Infernal Artifact known as Death's Scythe. Now, the gears in his brain were turning as he tried to make the connections between what he saw and what he knew. Her visitor must have been Death, and from there, it made sense. Director Quartermaine moved backward and left her home again. Once he was on the other side of her gold-plated gate and safely seated in his car, he returned to solidity. He put his hands on the wheel as he went over what he saw in his head.

Mrs. Sharp's wrist was *rotting*. It was decaying, and yet she still seemed normal, for the most part. He furrowed his eyebrows, wondering why she didn't want to tell him. Director Quartermaine looked in his rearview mirror at Mrs. Sharp's gate behind his car. He was tucked into a small side road, but her home was still in view. Director Quartermaine ran his fingers through his hair as he sat back in his seat, frustrated. He had more questions now than when he had left her home the first time. He felt caught between his desire to trust his first mentor and his instinct and duty as director. What exactly was her granddaughter? Perhaps he should respect her wishes and give her the space she desired. Maybe she would tell him in time. His hands gripped the steering wheel a bit tighter while he sucked in air sharply through his nose.

He clenched his jaw; his hands gripped the wheel so tight that his knuckles began turning white. Still, he didn't bother to start the car as he went over different scenarios in his head of what might've happened to her wrist. He knew he felt overwhelming levels of nether energy in her home, but was it coming from Mrs. Sharp? Or could it be her granddaughter? The surge he felt when he picked up the photo. It was so familiar, but it had been decades. Could her granddaughter be—

His waistband then buzzed, tearing him from his thoughts. Director Quartermaine shifted in his seat to look down at the pager on his belt. Destiny had made the decision for him, and his duties as a director won the internal battle this time.

It was Agent Harpy.

## CHAPTER EIGHT

*8*

Agent Harpy remained on her mission for Director Quartermaine to track down the strange boy of Fae wandering about the streets of Chicago. She had with her a small book of *Faerie Tales* that Agent Eiríksdóttir had given her. She briefly flipped through the pages after her drive but now sat in a cafe flipping through them again. The book was small but worn. It had either been well-loved or passed through many hands for its knowledge. Within the pages were many stories of Fae itself as a realm and of the Fey people who belonged to it. The Spring and Summer Courts were thought to be benevolent, while the Autumn and Winter Courts were not.

She sat back in her seat, staring at the tattered artwork of the Autumn Queen, whose red hair fell in ringlets against her shoulders that looked like a mane of fire, perfectly framing her face, with large, shimmering golden wings behind her body. The queen looked like a beautiful woman, from what Agent Harpy could see. She wondered how much truth was in the pages—how much Arlo could confirm.

Agent Harpy tucked the book into the inner pocket of her jacket and walked down the street. She stood outside the Oriental Theater, which had been repaired and restored since the fire nearly a hundred years ago. Her long black hair was now tightly bound by a rubber band, and she paced the sidewalk while looking up at the signs on the theater. Many pedestrians walked past her, but none were the one she was looking for. Arlo would stand out like a sore thumb. Everyone currently on the street clearly belonged there.

They belonged in the mortal world.

She sighed, wondering if it was a dead end. She hadn't seen Arlo or another Imp since the altercation in the alley, and she wasn't even entirely sure what she was looking for. She was seconds away from heading back to her car when she finally spotted him strolling down the street, his eyes focused on his surroundings. He was very observant, and it didn't take him long to spot her.

"I mean you no harm," she said, raising her hands when he stopped in his tracks. Arlo narrowed his eyes.

"I'm pretty sure you couldn't harm me if you tried."

"I actually know a lot about Fey," she said. "Maybe not as much as my partner, but enough." She took out the iron bar she had with her. "And if you're Fey, then I know this will leave a mark."

Arlo tilted his head forward, staring at the bar in her hand. She was more prepared now than she had been during their initial meeting. He too put his hands up as a sign of truce. "I'm not your enemy," he said softly yet clearly.

"Nor am I yours," she retorted.

"I simply want to get back home—if you do not wish harm on me," his head remained tilted toward her as he placed one hand over his chest, "then I mean you no harm as well."

"Why did you come here in the first place?" Agent Harpy asked. She tucked her iron weapon back into her jacket. "What business do you have here?"

Arlo straightened his posture. He then scratched his chin before looking around.

"I don't really want to talk about this *here*," he said.

"But you don't trust me to come along with me," Harpy concluded. Arlo shrugged, making no suggestions. "Do you drink coffee?"

"I prefer tea."

Harpy tucked her hands into her pockets and turned around. "Come, we'll have a drink." She turned back around on her soles and began walking backward. "I would love to hear this story."

Arlo scanned the facade of the grand Oriental Theater beside them before looking back at Agent Harpy. Reluctantly, he followed, still on edge, occasionally glancing over his shoulder just in case something was lurking behind him or tit was some sort of a trap.

He kept his distance from the agent—and observed her from afar as they walked to a small coffee and tea shop named Tashtegos on the street corner. He watched as Agent Harpy ordered an iced latte with nonfat milk for herself and a hot black tea for him. He trailed her to a table near the back, away from the rest of the customers.

"Are you going to sit, or are you just going to stand there and hover over me?" Agent Harpy asked, acknowledging that Arlo hadn't bothered to sit with her at the table. Instead, he stood there awkwardly. At first, he appeared to not know what to do with his arms. First, his hands were on his hips, then he crossed his arms over his chest at her criticism.

"How do I know this isn't some kind of a trap?" he asked. Arlo looked at the tea, then swiped his brown hair out of his face.

Harpy sighed. She fished the iron rod from her jacket and dropped it on the windowsill beside her, pushing it further toward his end. "You can keep it by you, if it'll ease the tension. I just want to know why you came here. To *Terra*."

Not only did her reference to this realm as Terra interest him, but he had to admit that seeing the iron rod beside him didn't actually make him feel better. Probably because it meant she knew more about him than he knew of her, and that caused an uneasy feeling in the pit of his stomach. However, eventually, he caved and took a seat across from her. His hands cupped the small paper cup that contained the hot liquid, and he took off the lid to inhale its familiar aroma.

"We didn't come here with the intention of causing any problems," he said finally. "That was the Imps, not us. We came to rescue one of our own."

"So, a rescue mission, alright." Agent Harpy nodded, stirring her latte with her straw. At least she was getting somewhere now. "So what were you rescuing them from?" she inquired.

Arlo shrugged. "I don't know."

Agent Harpy sighed. "I can't be of any help unless you talk to me."

"No, I really don't know. Missions are classified. We're given no knowledge of anyone else's mission but our own. It keeps everyone safe in case someone is caught and—"

"No one can capture you and torture you for information?"

Arlo was slightly caught off guard by her words, even though he'd been about to say something similar. "Well, yeah. Something like that."

"So, Fey, huh?" Agent Harpy began to reach in her jacket, which made Arlo tense. "Whoa, easy there," she said, pulling out the book her partner had given her. "I just wanted to show this to you." She placed the worn book on the table and slid it over to his side. Arlo stared at her for a moment, eyeing her curiously, before readjusting himself in his seat to get a better look at the cover she placed on the table.

"*Faerie Tales*?" he asked, looking up at her.

"Eiríksdóttir gave it to me." He continued to stare at her blankly. "The one who asked if you came out of Middle Earth." Still, he said nothing. She was likely speaking gibberish to him. "Oh, forget it. Look, there's information about four Fey Courts, and I was just wondering how much of it is true."

From where she sat, Agent Harpy reached over to flip open the book. Arlo quickly sat back on the defense, just in case. While Agent Harpy noticed his reaction, she didn't say anything.

He looked down at the book when she flipped it open to a page of the Autumn Court. "These are the colors you wear, correct? Is this your queen?"

Arlo shifted forward in his seat to get a better look. His eyes narrowed, and he tilted his head. He reached forward to quickly flip through the pages. "How did you recover this information?" he asked. "Who are you? Do you have spies in Fae?" He looked up at her, his expression tightening.

"It's a fable," she said.

"Beetle dung!" he snapped as he quickly shot up from his seat. He jammed his index finger into the book, pointing at the picture of the Autumn queen. "This is exactly what she looks like. Are you the ones who attacked her? Are you allies of the Winter Court?"

Harpy frowned and quickly shook her head. "I assure you, we've never been to Fae." Agent Harpy was not exactly what one would call a people person. She pressed her lips together and inhaled deeply, wondering how exactly to calm him as other customers in Tashtegos were beginning to look their way. He was drawing too much attention. "We are not your enemy, Arlo. Whoever you're at war with, whoever is allied with the Winter Court, it isn't us."

Arlo took a deep breath and quickly muttered an apology for his outburst.

"It's been a long few days," he admitted softly.

"I can't even begin to imagine," she said, glancing down at the book laying flat open on the table. Part of her wondered where he had been staying the last few days. Had he been on the streets the entire time? Squatting in a nearby building? She hoped for the latter, at the very least. Part of her wanted to ask but decided against it. It wasn't as though she could change anything about that anyway.

"I admit," Agent Harpy said, tilting her head as she stared at Arlo across from her. "When we consider our enemies as an organization, it never really occurred to me they could be coming from another realm."

"But you have demons here," Arlo said plainly.

"Sure, but that's because of what happened during World War II. A Japanese demon went to great lengths to open the portal that led them here. Gods and Goddesses, while I'm told they exist, don't interfere with humanity as far as I'm concerned. But the Fey… You just—" she sat back in her chair, dropping her arm into her lap. "Come and go as you please?"

"Clearly not, or I wouldn't still be here."

Harpy nodded her head as she yielded. "Touché." She smoothed out the material of her pants against her thigh and wrinkled her nose. "Are you hungry?" Agent Harpy asked finally. "I imagine you must be."

Arlo was slow to nod, but even he couldn't deny the growls of his stomach. Accepting food from strangers wasn't the smartest idea, but he was *starving*. "Yeah," he admitted finally and slightly against his will, "but I don't have a currency they'll accept."

Agent Harpy just shook her head. She gently touched the tabletop with her fingertips as she got up. "Don't worry," she said. "I'll take care of it."

Agent Harpy returned to the ordering counter to get the two of them something to eat. She ordered a toasted salmon bagel for herself and a Margherita bruschetta for Arlo. While she waited for them to prepare the items, she slipped into the nearby bathroom and dug her Motorola cell phone out of her pocket. Dialing several buttons on her phone, she quickly sent a message to Director Quartermaine's pager before returning to the counter to fetch their food.

Arlo was still sitting at the table, flipping through the *Faerie Tales* book she had left with him. He looked almost like a child, eager to learn as he turned every page, engulfed in its text. Agent Harpy pursed her lips together, not wanting to disturb him. It was hard to believe he was over a hundred years old. Director Quartermaine looked closer to a hundred than Arlo did. Agent Harpy smirked a little at the thought, knowing the Director wouldn't appreciate it.

Finally, she made her way back over and set the two ceramic plates down.

Arlo's stomach growled even louder once he caught wind of the food.

He ran his hand over his stomach, attempting to calm it.

"I guess you really are starving, huh?" Agent Harpy said, a small smirk peeked at the corner of her mouth.

"I think that's the first time I've seen you almost smile."

Agent Harpy shrugged. "I suppose there isn't a lot of smiling in my line of work." She pushed the Margherita bruschetta toward him.

"Daughter of Erik seems to enjoy it."

"Daughter of Erik enjoys everything," she said, copying him. For a brief moment, his dissection of Eiríksdóttir's surname made her wonder if her father's name actually was Erik. A large part of her doubted it though, but its origin was fascinating nonetheless. She quickly shook the thought. "That woman always has a smile on her face."

"Sounds like a nice way to live."

*Or foolish.* Agent Harpy tilted her head at the thought, but she didn't express that out loud. Eiríksdóttir was her partner. "I suppose so," she agreed instead.

Arlo waited till Agent Harpy began eating before he started to dig in himself. While he did his best to remain composed, he was starving, and the bruschetta certainly hit the spot. He finished it within a matter of seconds. Agent Harpy had barely made a dent in her bagel.

"So—*Harpy*?" he asked, wiping his face with a napkin.

"It's a family name."

"What's your first name?"

Agent Harpy looked down at the book before him.

"I did read that, you know. This sounds like a trap." Arlo smiled at her words. He then chuckled to himself as he sat back in his chair. His hands moved to cup the tea again. "One should know better than to give out more than one name." Agent Harpy nearly smirked as she repeated what he had said to them earlier as she wrapped her hands around her bagel. Arlo's smile broadened, spreading far across the width of his face. "Names are valuable, you know," she continued, tilting her head toward him as she raised the bagel to her mouth. "They can be used against you."

"Alright, alright," he yielded, a smile still plastered on his face, his laugh lines showing deep in his cheeks. "Point taken."

After she took a bite of her bagel, chewed the bit, and swallowed, she tapped the top with her fingers. "When I think I can trust you, I'll tell you my name."

Arlo nodded. "That's fair."

"So tell me more about you—about Fae. I'm curious. *F-A-E* is the place and *F-E-Y* is what you are?" She spelled out both to point out the differences.

"Sort of like how you're Terran and you live on Terra."

"But *Fae* and *Fey* sound the same."

Arlo shrugged. "I didn't make it up, but there is a very slight distinction, I suppose undetectable to Terran ears." He then looked at her bagel before looking at his own empty plate. He pushed his empty plate toward her and sat back in his chair again. "Get me two more of these things, and I'll tell you whatever you want to know."

Agent Harpy nodded. She could hardly put a price on the knowledge she was about to obtain from him, even if each bruschetta was almost seven dollars. She dropped her bagel back down on her plate and got up. Empty plate at hand, she returned to the counter to order two more of the bruschetta for him.

Arlo took a moment to look at the book again. It was still flipped open to the page of the Autumn Queen. He pressed his lips together just before inhaling deeply through his nose, wondering how his friends in Fae were faring. He considered Salvatore's wounds and wondered if he had managed to completely heal him before they all disappeared back through the portal. Arlo awkwardly fumbled with the cuff on his ear again. He tapped the comm and messed with the beads around his wrist.

"Hello?" he said softly, but there was no answer. He couldn't help but wonder if they were going to come back for him, or if they were simply going to cut their losses. He closed the *Faerie Tales* book and looked at Agent Harpy standing in line at the counter. Arlo chewed on his bottom lip and glanced down at the bagel she left on the table. He knew he should wait for her return, but he felt like sitting there was useless. What exactly did she need to know about the Fey? Or of Fae itself? The more he thought about it, the antsier he felt.

He began to tap his foot against the ground in anticipation, waiting for her to come back. He glanced outside absently. His eye was suddenly seized by what seemed to be a flicker. Arlo narrowed his eyes and got up from his seat, unsure if his eyes were playing tricks on him.

He looked back in Agent Harpy's direction, but she was fiddling with a small electronic device in her hands. Arlo looked back out the window, then at the door. Grabbing the book, he tucked it into his vest, picked up his black tea, and left without another word. Hopefully, Agent Harpy would understand.

When Arlo turned away from Tashtegos, he froze.

*She* was right there. In front of the theater, strands of her brown hair flowing in the wind while the rest was pulled back in a high bun. She was just across the street from him. So close, but so far at the same time. Her pointed jaw, large eyes.

The ballerina from his nightmares.

*Freya.*

# CHAPTER NINE

9

Salvatore Sanguine bowed his head before the woman before them. She was clearly older than the average FeyForce officer and had fiery red hair, a honey glow to her skin, and shimmering golden wings. Her lips were blood red, and her eyes glowed a sharp yellow color that could rival the sun. Her red hair fell in ringlets at her shoulders, and a crown twisted out of dark brown branches and amber leaves sat upon her head. She sat back in her chair of woven wood as her eyes swooped from Salvatore to Commander Kall-An, and then to Lord Bane. The three were standing before her, heads still angled slightly toward the earth after their bow. Acacia stood just behind Salvatore, keeping to his shadow as she looked up at the Autumn Queen through the darkness. Acacia hoped she would pay no direct attention to her and kept her gaze lowered to avoid drawing her severe gaze toward her reactions to the humiliating report.

"Where *is* he?" the Queen asked. Her voice sounded calm, but there was urgency and demand hidden beneath it. She gripped the armrests of her throne tightly, her long, slender fingernails digging into their undersides. Her large breasts nearly poured out of the top of her dress, but everyone was used to the way the Queen dressed. She was actually covered up then more than she normally was. Her usual regal attire consisted of a dazzling bra that appeared a bit too small for her, and a long, ankle-length skirt with a large, high slit that revealed a swath of skin from her foot to above her hip. The Autumn Queen was a voluptuous beauty, and she was very proud of her appearance. She had nothing to hide and didn't leave much to the imagination. She pulled a sheer brown robe over her shoulders as she sat back on her throne, awaiting an answer she would be pleased with. Unfortunately, she was not about to get one.

"My Queen, when we went to Terra to retrieve Zaria, we were ambushed," Lord Bane explained. Despite the tension of the assembly, his voice was strong and smooth as the creamiest butter, sounding almost like a parent offering confident solace to a volatile child. He was one of the few who could speak freely in her presence. Somehow, everyone was fond of Lord Bane. He could be charming but firm and rarely raised his voice in anger or frustration. Even Acacia found herself leaning into his presence—and she was a married woman. "Salvatore barely made it back alive. If it hadn't been for Arlo—"

"Then you're aware of what a powerful asset he is to the Autumn Court." There was rage in the Queen's eyes, and she glared over at Salvatore. "I would not have minded your death if it ensured Arlo's return."

Acacia's body tensed, her breath hitching slightly. Salvatore kept his head bowed, avoiding the Queen's stare. He wasn't going to argue with her because even he believed Arlo's life was more valuable than his own. He agreed with her. While the Fey had Glamour and useful weapons that could be manipulated by its users, no one's abilities came close to what Arlo was capable of. He may not be able to use traditional Fey powers without his suit, but his healing abilities were arguably far more monumental.

"My Queen," said Commander Kall-An, cutting in. The Queen bristled slightly at Kall-An's voice. He did not have the same charisma as Lord Bane. In comparison, his voice was rough and aggressive, almost disrespectful next to Bane's smooth confidence. "The Imps were closing in on us. If we didn't leave when we did, they would have come through to Fae, and we couldn't let that happen, not with what's already going on with the Winter Court. Arlo understood the risks of the mission. We had to leave him behind to ensure the safety of Fae, and to avoid possible danger upon the other Courts. Spring and Summer don't deserve—" He took a bold step forward.

"I don't care about the other Courts," the Autumn Queen snapped, waving her hand as if to push Kall-An back into his place. He stepped back quickly, his face slightly flushed with embarrassment. "So what of Zaria then? From what I can see, she is not present either. The information she was sent to Terra for is extremely vital to ensure our victory against the Winter Court. I will not start a war I am not certain I can finish."

Acacia, who stood off to the side to Salvatore's right, slowly shut her eyes at the mention of her sister's name. Her head fell forward a little more, causing a few strands of stray blonde hair to curtain her face. What dishonor Zaria was bringing upon the Aster family. She felt shame cover every inch of her skin like hot wax. She felt Salvatore reach back, slipping his cold hand into hers, and she squeezed it tightly. Her face felt hot with rage, but she swallowed it as best she could. The Autumn Queen already didn't take kindly to the other Fey women in the Autumn Court as it was.

Even Kall-An stayed silent at the mention of Zaria.

"Did you forget we are at the beginning of a brewing war with the Winter Court?" The Autumn Queen hissed at the FeyForce in her presence. She rose abruptly. The FeyForce flinched as a group. "We need Arlo. And we need him to get to the Book of Fate to make sure we win. Do you all not remember when we found him? Did you forget Zaria's mission?"

Acacia scrunched her eyes tightly shut as if to wince at the mention of the Book of Fate. She should have known better. Her lips parted as she opened her eyes again, vision slightly blurred from the pressure of having her eyes closed so tightly.

The Autumn Queen's guard swam back into focus as they stood shirtless on either side of her throne, all wearing intricately beaded masks to conceal their identities. Acacia eyed each of them individually from behind her thin curtain of hair. She kept her head bowed as the Autumn Queen continued to scream at them. The guards' masks were large enough to cover the top half of their faces, from their foreheads to just above their lips. They all wore a different color though each mask stayed in the general rainbow of autumn shades. It was strange to consider that Arlo almost ended up with that fate. He could have been standing, masked and half-clothed at the Queen's side. Instead, he was on Terra. Maybe dead.

*Of course*, they all remembered when they'd first found him.

Nearly a hundred years ago, rumors had spread like wildfire throughout all of the realms of the universe that the Book of Fate had been stolen. After being with the Elves for thousands of years, it went missing—and *of course*, every being who knew of its existence went looking for it. *Of course*, as soon as rumors surfaced of its supposed location, all the realms had converged, racing to be the ones to recover it. And, *of course*, the Elves had set fire to the theater where everyone thought the Book might be.

But no one had found the remnants of the Book of Fate in the wreckage.

No one could be quite certain it had been destroyed.

Many, including the Autumn Queen, believed it was still out there somewhere.

Acacia stiffened as she squeezed Salvatore's hand. She had been on the mission to Terra, and she remembered the Iroquois Theater fire. Her nose twitched at the memory as the smells of charred wood and burned human flesh invaded her senses, blocking out the ordinarily peaceful smell of trees and dirt. Acacia tilted her head down and shut her eyes again. Salvatore's thumb ran over the back of Acacia's hand. He'd been there too. They both remembered. She peeked to look at him, but he wasn't looking at her. His focus was alert and directed towards the Autumn Queen, but his eyes remained lowered. Acacia squeezed his hand again, and his gaze shifted toward her without turning his head. The corner of his mouth twitched into a small smile, and she nodded subtly in return.

***

The Iroquois Theater was badly damaged when they arrived. Far too many patrons had found themselves locked inside when the fire began. People had leaped from balconies down to the orchestra to avoid perishing in flames or dying from poisonous smoke inhalation. Or, at least, they'd leaped hoping they would avoid death. Most of them hadn't been so fortunate.

Acacia vividly remembered walking through the wasteland of broken bodies with necks bent in ways they should never be and dead skin flaking off in black pieces. Their beacons had indicated that the Book of Fate would be there, and the FeyForce arrived in full volume. They knew beings from a multitude of realms would be there to search. The Autumn Court *believed* they were the first on-site, but even they couldn't be sure.

Time seemed to be at a standstill when they arrived. The fire still burned hot, though the blaze seemed to have stabilized. As the FeyForce picked their way through the carnage, stepping over stinking bodies and pools of boiled blood, they searched for any evidence of the Book of Fate. As they made their way towards the front of the theater, sifting through crumbling purses, nudging open the flaps of men's jackets, trying not to gouge the charred flesh, Acacia remembered Zaria yelling.

"Hey! He's still alive!"

Arlo was still breathing when Lord Bane and Commander Kall-An reached Zaria as she hovered over his body. His skin seemed to emit a strange silvery light. The FeyForce squad turned to each other, exchanging wide-eyed glances.

They'd all heard the rumors: the Book of Fate glowed slightly like a lake during the full moon.

There were burn marks on Arlo's hands, on his inner forearms, nearly up to his elbows, but they didn't seem like they were from the fire. The marks were too regular. They snaked around his body like spiderwebs, not like the ravaging walls of fire that had claimed the crowds around him.

Lord Bane and Commander Kall-An exchanged glances. It was a curious thing, one man living among all of those corpses. Lord Bane knelt beside Zaria, who had her hand pressed to Arlo's chest as she flowed oxygen to his lungs.

"We're going to take him back to Fae," Lord Bane said as he looked up at Commander Kall-An. "He's the key. Look at this nether energy—if the Book of Fate is still out there—he's connected to it now."

"How can we be sure he'll help us?" the Commander asked. He stood resolutely next to Arlo's body, his brow furrowed. "I don't want to bring a Terran to Fae. Surely he poses a greater threat to our security than any potential good he might do for us."

"We can use Glamour on his memories."

"Is that possible?"

Lord Bane slipped his hand into Arlo's jacket pocket, retrieving a wallet. He riffled through it until he found what he was searching for. He read off of the small card. "*Arlo Jäger*. He is only human. It'll be even easier than using Glamour on another Fey."

Acacia remembered watching them all decide his fate as she stood off on the side, trying to avoid the fumes of the dead bodies surrounding her. She had looked at her partners, trying to gauge their reactions. She saw the Sanguine brothers whispering to each other quietly, Salvatore's face creased. When he saw her looking, he smiled slightly. She scowled. She'd had no interest in him then.

As her eyes fell back to Arlo, she saw Zaria's hands hovering over Arlo's forehead. She paused.

"Where should we place him?" Zaria asked, cradling Arlo's head in her hands.

"Ambrose?" someone on the FeyForce suggested. "He hasn't been the same since he lost his son. Maybe someone can Glamour him into thinking Arlo's his son?"

Commander Kall-An raised his eyebrows at the suggestion. "That's a good one," he said before turning to Lord Bane. "Do you think you could get close enough to him?"

Lord Bane nodded. "Anything for Fae."

Kall-An frowned, voicing his final misgiving. "We'll have to keep him close once he's in Fae. I don't like the idea of him wandering around with only a reclusive father to keep an eye on him. How do you propose making sure he is conditioned to take our side?"

Bane had looked at Arlo's unconscious form for a long time. Zaria still hovered over him, waiting for the all-clear to perform her duties. He sighed. "We'll recruit him to the FeyForce. It's the only place where we'll have absolute control over what he's told." He nodded to Zaria who focused her attention on the man before her. "Plus, if he's FeyForce, he'll have a distorted sense of his own understanding of Fae. And we can re-Glamour him the moment he starts asking too many questions." He rose. The plan was complete.

"A prisoner inside the FeyForce," Kall-An muttered, nodding slowly. "This could work."

Acacia watched as Zaria pressed her hands to Arlo's temples, speaking his name, using her Glamour to manipulate his memories, making him forget an entire life on Terra.

***

Acacia was jolted from her memories by a crash, the sound of the Autumn Queen's further displeasure. The Queen was not at all pleased with the presence of Commander Kall-An's FeyForce, and they were about to feel the full weight of her disappointment.

When Acacia's gaze moved to the Autumn Queen again, she noticed her Queen was staring directly at her, not blinking. Their surroundings had quieted, and everyone seemed frozen, including her husband. Acacia pulled on Salvatore's arm, but he didn't move.

The Autumn Queen continued to stare at her.

"Acacia," she said, speaking to her directly.

"Your Majesty," she answered, bowing her head as she lowered her eyes. Her body was tense now, and she clenched her jaw, trying to steady her breathing.

She had heard the Queen had the power to hold the room still, as if freezing them in time. Of course, time didn't actually stop. But, there in the throne room, Acacia could see that only the Queen and herself were moving. Only the two of them were conscious of their conversation, as if it were slipped into a pocket of existence utterly inaccessible to anyone else. It felt claustrophobically intimate. Acacia did her best to keep herself from trembling.

"The Imps ambushed you?" she asked. "Weren't you responsible for arranging a safe place to meet with Zaria? Did you assist them in this ambush?"

"No, no, of course not, Your Majesty." Acacia didn't dare look up at the Autumn Queen, whose stare could likely kill. "I would never disobey you or Lord Bane. You know my loyalty lies with the Autumn Court and with the FeyForce. I would never." She felt a panicked urge to explain. "My loyalty to you comes before any loyalty elsewhere, even to my blood family. I would never. I don't know what Zaria did, but I had nothing to do with betrayal. Please believe me!" Acacia briefly looked up in her panic, and the Autumn Queen's expression softened for a moment.

Acacia wasn't sure if it was out of empathy or the pity one might have for a whimpering dog. She decided on the latter, unsure if the Autumn Queen could feel empathy.

"I will let you prove your loyalty." The Autumn Queen inhaled deeply through her upturned nose and got up from her seat. She walked slowly towards Acacia. "You will fetch me Arlo and the Book of Fate. Should you fail, you will watch as I strip your husband of his autonomy and end his life. Then I will banish you from the Autumn Court. If you try to disobey me, I will kill you both. Am I making myself clear?"

Acacia began shaking her head. "No—" her mouth formed the word, but barely a whisper left her throat. She tried again, pleading, begging. "No, please! Your Majesty, I will do anything else. Please! You're asking for the impossible."

"Then we have a deal." The Autumn Queen sat back down in her seat. "This is not open for negotiation," she said and waved her hand.

The room returned to motion. No one seemed to notice that Acacia now stood a few steps further forward, her face a mask of horror.

The Queen's eyes ran over the assembled squad. "I will call for each of you for your punishment," she declared, waving her hand. "Until then, you're free to go."

*Punishment.*

Acacia was shaken from her moment with the Autumn Queen. She looked at Lord Bane, then at Commander Kall-An. She knew, deep down, that the two of them would conveniently skip out on any punishments the team would be forced to endure at the Queen's hand or at the hands of her guards. This assumption was reinforced when the rest of the team was dismissed while the two of them were asked to stay.

As the FeyForce filed out, they seemed relieved to have survived a meeting with the Queen, even with the promise of punishment hanging over them. And why shouldn't they be relieved? They were entirely unaware of the impossible task the Queen had laid upon Acacia's shoulders. They weren't feeling the brunt of the Queen's wrath for Zaria's betrayal.

The Sanguines walked quietly back to their home, not saying a word to each other, nor did they even glance in each other's direction. Acacia thought about her sisters and the demands the Autumn Queen made of her, and Salvatore thought of his brother and of Arlo. Their minds both wandered as they approached the rushing waterfall that shielded their door.

Acacia led her husband inside the home, and the two remained quiet still. There were no words to say.

It took them almost an hour after being home to speak to one another, still coming down from the awe and dread of being with the Autumn Queen.

"Perhaps we *should* look for him," Acacia suggested, once she and Salvatore were alone in their homes. She reflected on the Autumn Queen's words, though didn't mention them to her husband. How could she? Salvatore sat at the counter, tired from being in the presence of the Queen. His eyebrows furrowed at Acacia's words as he turned to face her.

"I thought you didn't care?"

Acacia dragged her index finger along the counter as she walked over to him.

"I don't care about my sister. She is a traitor. I care about Arlo—I care—I fear what the Autumn Queen might do to *you* if he doesn't return. If he hadn't healed you, he wouldn't have been blinded and would've seen the portal. He would have returned with us."

Salvatore tilted his head up, watching as Acacia came closer, towering over him from where he sat. "Are you blaming me, my love?"

Acacia ran her fingers through his brown locks before she cupped his face from where she stood and looked down into his eyes. "Never," she said softly, gently shaking her head. "But she will." Her expression was soft, almost sad. Salvatore's own face eased. He had rarely ever seen Acacia show any weakness. She was cold, calculating, and often unloving. But she was tender at that moment. The look in her eyes reflected her words.

"You're proposing going against a direct order from our commanding officers," Salvatore said gently. "What's gotten into you? You were against this when I suggested it."

"The Queen wants him back though," Acacia argued, trying not to reveal too much. She couldn't bear to see his face if he learned what the Queen had told her. She felt she had a better chance at succeeding with Salvatore, as he would also question her disappearance had she gone to Terra without him. "I think that goes over what they have to say, doesn't it?" she asked. "Arlo may not be one of us—but this is where he belongs. He's lost, and we have to find him. He still holds the key to a book we haven't yet found. I mean, think about it. He changed the Autumn Queen's fate. He changed yours when he saved you. We can't just leave him there. Maybe he can lead us to it. Maybe we can be responsible for bringing both him and the Book of Fate back to Fae."

"What's gotten into you?" Salvatore asked. He pulled away slightly, searching his wife's face.

"I don't want to be punished," she said. It was barely a whisper. She took a deep breath, steadying herself, looking into her husband's eyes. She knew she didn't want to lose him, nor could she bear the thought of being banished from Fae. "At least not by someone else's hands." Acacia ran her slender fingers down his veiny arms and toward his strong hands. Her palms covered the backs of his as she put them on her waist. "I think we should go to Terra together."

"Hopefully, you don't mean right *now*," he said, just as he pressed his lips against hers. Acacia smirked playfully into the kiss and pulled him closer to her.

# CHAPTER TEN

*10*

Arlo stared at the apparition standing in front of the Oriental Theater. He furrowed his eyebrows and rubbed his eyes, unsure if he was seeing what he thought he was seeing. He knew he desperately needed sleep, but no amount of rubbing made her disappear.

He shouted at the girl, but she only beckoned to him. Arlo stepped out onto the busy Chicago road and stalked across the street, forcing several cars to come to a screeching halt as drivers slammed on their brakes to avoid hitting him. The girl stood motionless, waiting for him, loose strands of her translucent dark brown hair that had freed themselves from her bun blowing gently in the breeze.

"Who are you?" he shouted as soon as he got closer, ignoring the voices of the drivers behind him who were shouting expletives at him for walking across a busy street with no warning. Arlo was too focused on the girl to care. An angry man grabbed his wrist, and instinctively, Arlo threw him off. The man's body sailed across four lanes of traffic before smashing into the window of the Tashtegos cafe. Through the smashed glass, Arlo saw Agent Harpy's jaw fall open. He ignored her. His eyes fell to the body on the ground. The Terran he'd thrown away from him didn't appear to be moving. Arlo spun around as angry shouts gathered around him. He put his hands to his ears, trying to block out the noise.

*How fragile were Terrans?* Had he just accidentally killed one? Arlo turned away from the crowd angrily. *He wasn't even supposed to be there!*

Arlo's eyes raked the front of the theater, searching for the ghostly girl through the waving arms of shouting pedestrians. He briefly glanced over his shoulder to see a few pedestrians who had stopped to see if the man he had thrown was fine—or at least alive.

Arlo felt overwhelmed. Everything about the mission had gone wrong. He let out a frustrated growl before his eyes locked back onto the transparent girl, halfway into the building now. She peeked out of it, her large eyes still locked on him, before disappearing inside.

Arlo ducked his head, pushing his way through the mass of angry Terrans, careful to use only a necessary level of force, and followed her inside.

As soon as Arlo entered the theater, he was greeted with unwelcoming darkness and chilled air that summoned bumps across every inch of his skin. The lights flickered on, and he looked up at the soaring ceilings and extravagant amounts of polished mahogany trim. There were marble staircases and iron gates pushed up against the walls.

It was something out of his nightmares.

"Arlo?"

The girl from outside had taken a solid form. Her hair was no longer messy but neatly pulled into a bun. Her outfit was no longer charred and damaged from a fire. She was beautiful, and she was the same girl from his nightmares. She looked just like him—it was almost like looking into a mirror.

"Where have you been?" she asked eagerly. "The show's about to start!"

He took a step back. As he did so, he caught sight of his own attire in a nearby ornate mirror that took up an entire wall. The man who stared back at him wore a tailored black suit. Arlo looked down at his hands, scanning his arms, his chest, his legs. Instead of the FeyForce uniform he'd been wearing moments before, he now was dressed smartly in a black wool suit, complete with a buttoned vest and thick tie. Arlo tugged at the sleeves and reached for the comm in his ear. It was gone.

"What's happening? Who are you?" he asked her in a bit of a panic, before looking down at his clothing again. "What is this magic? Where am I?"

"What are you talking about, Arlo?" she asked, her head tilted. She reached out to grab his wrist, but he pulled away from her. People began emerging all around them, and the once empty theater was now lively and packed full of an audience. "You're here to watch me dance in Mr. Bluebeard—"

"There you two are," a woman said as she approached the pair. Beautiful black hair and icy, ocean eyes, her skin was a pale porcelain. Arlo narrowed his eyes. He recognized her. He had seen her in one of the false memories when he had been captured by the Imps. She'd been crying because her father had said the two of them couldn't—

Arlo scowled. They weren't his true memories. They couldn't be.

He jumped back from the two women, standing defensively, his arms raised. As he moved, he crashed into other patrons who grumbled at him.

"Where am I?"

The two girls exchanged glances.

"Halina, do you think maybe he's sick?" the ballerina asked the other girl. Halina tilted her head sympathetically, not taking her blue-gray eyes off Arlo. "Do you have a fever, Arlo? Come here—" She reached out her hand towards him.

"Careful," she murmured. "Freya, do you think—"

Arlo was still defensive. With his arms out in front of him, fists made, he attempted to shove her away from him using the wind as a weapon—only nothing happened. He looked down at his hands, turning them over. He was no longer wearing his FeyForce uniform. The Fey, to some degree, could manipulate the elements and use them at will. He couldn't, not without his uniform. He cursed the incident that had taken his ears and his powers, doubly frustrated because he couldn't even remember it. There wasn't much he could do without his uniform.

Arlo took a deep breath. This had to be an illusion. He was still wearing his uniform in the real world. Arlo attempted to focus his energy into making himself invisible or using Glamour to confuse Halina and Freya. Something to shake him from this illusion—but nothing changed. The two girls just stared at him like he was some sort of circus freak.

"Arlo—" The one named Freya, the one who seemed to share his face, had her expression scrunched into a look of concern. "Are you okay?"

"You're scaring me," Halina added.

She really was so beautiful, Arlo had trouble not simply just staring at her in a daze. The longer he kept his gaze on her, the more flashes of her came to his mind. More memories of her. Caressing her face, his lips pressed against hers.

Arlo shut his eyes and took another step back, his palms pressing against his temples. This couldn't be real. These memories couldn't be his. It had to be Imp manipulation. Did the Imps even have that kind of ability? He couldn't think straight. He beelined his way through the other guests in the theater until he reached the exit door where he nearly slammed into Agent Harpy.

"You ditched me!" she shouted.

"I'm sorry," he said quickly, looking down at his clothing. He was back in his original FeyForce uniform. He balled his hands into fists and quickly walked away from the theater, not looking back. He had to get home. Lord Bane would know what to do.

Agent Harpy followed.

"I bought you your bruschetta and you ditched me! These are expensive, you know!"

"I said I was sorry! Can we not talk about this right now?"

"You threw a man through the window, so yes, we're going to talk about this right now." Agent Harpy almost felt like stomping her foot to grab his attention. His mind was clearly elsewhere. "Where are you going? Arlo!"

The commotion with the Terrans had mostly cleared since he had last been outside, but before he could answer Agent Harpy's question, Arlo was knocked to the ground by an Imp. He couldn't catch a break. He quickly got back to his feet, not taking his eyes off of the small, mischievous creature.

Imps were *thought* to be the attendants of the devil, and from afar, they looked like bats. Up close, they were little gargoyle-looking creatures. They had horns coming out of their heads, razor-sharp teeth, claws, and boney wings. Some were red, some were black. Arlo pushed the air toward the Imp and knocked the wind right out of its lungs. It tumbled away from him. He turned around and used Glamour, altering his own hair and his facial structure, hoping to conceal himself from the Imps.

Agent Harpy narrowed her eyes, but she had seen stranger things. The Imps being one of them. "Why are they after you?" Agent Harpy asked, looking back in the direction the Imp had tumbled away to. Her eyes widened, and she started smacking the side of his arm with the back of her hand.

"I don't know—" he started as he turned to look at what she had already seen.

A whole flock of Imps were headed their way.

"We have to go—" he said, looking back at the doors of the Oriental Theater. He didn't want to go back inside, but he didn't think he had a choice. He let out something that sounded a bit like an angry groan. "Follow me."

"Would you believe me if I told you it might have to do with the Book of Fate?" Agent Harpy asked, slightly out of breath as she followed him back into the Oriental Theater—the place he had been in such a hurry to flee from only moments ago.

Arlo furrowed his brows as he pushed his now long, blond hair out of his face. He quickly tied it back into a small bun on his head as he shut the door behind them. Standing against it, he pulled a small bottle from his belt and poured it on the handle of the door. The silvery liquid circled the knob before seeping into the lock. It traveled along the cracks of the door and frame, sealing it shut.

"The what?" he asked as he capped the bottle. Her words had stirred something in his memory. Where had he heard of the Book of Fate? Hadn't Marigold mentioned something? She'd said it was a myth. Agent Harpy was still staring at the door. "It's not going to hold forever—" he said, testing the handle and motioning for her to move further into the theater as his Glamour began to fade and his appearance returned to normal. But just as he turned to descend further into the hall, he stopped.

Zaria stood in front of a door at the far end.

Arlo felt his whole body tense with shock. The shock soon disintegrated into a mixture of anger and confusion.

"You!" he shouted. He was seething at the sight of her. "You're a traitor!" His hands balled into fists again. "You betrayed us, your own family?" his voice sounded uncertain now, even hurt as he raised his hands and opened them.

"Arlo—" Zaria began.

"No." He shoved the wind toward her, and Zaria crashed into the wall behind her. She struggled to her knees, her hands raised as if in surrender.

"Arlo—I know you're angry, but—"

He didn't respond. Instead, he attacked her again—this time pulling fire from the illuminated light above. He cracked the bulb and sent a stream of flame toward her.

She only barely extinguished it. Her eyes were wide, but it was clear she wasn't going to fight back. Her chest heaved. "Arlo, you need to let me speak. I want you to know the truth."

"The truth?" Arlo yelled as he made a slashing motion with his hand. Zaria fell back to her knees as the air hit her. He heard her back snap, but he knew he hadn't hit her hard enough to cause lasting damage. Even as he thought it, he felt ashamed for holding back.

"Please," Zaria pleaded. "I'm just asking you to listen." She raised her eyes to look at Arlo. He towered above her, his arm cocked as if to punch her.

He paused.

"If you don't like what I say, you can try to kill me then. But, please, listen to me first. I've never given you any reason not to trust me." She slowly lowered her hands. Arlo did the same. She took a deep breath and placed her hand on her back before she cracked her spine back into place, exhaling as she did so. "Your whole life in Fae was a lie. You're not even *Fey*, Arlo. You're *human*. And you were supposed to die here in that fire a hundred years ago. I know. I was there. We all were."

Arlo took a step back from her. "Wha… What…" His face was blank as his brain spun desperately, trying to take in the words she'd said. Seeing Zaria at all had been a shock, but what did she mean he was *human? His life in Fae was a lie?*

"I don't believe you," he managed to whisper.

But he didn't really mean it. Something about her words had stirred something in Arlo's heart—not a memory per se, but a feeling of truth, of fact.

Were those memories really his? Those two women—Halina? Freya?

He frowned and took another step back as he looked away. Arlo looked down at his hands, covered in the gloves he got while in Fae. He then reached to his ears. He thought about being rendered powerless when he was just trapped in an illusion less than an hour ago. He closed his eyes, still tugging at his ear.

"Your ears were never damaged in a fight, Arlo," Zaria noted quietly, watching him touch his ears, only he moved his hand at her mention and crossed his arms instead as he looked over at her. "The Autumn Court mutilated you. You had normal, human ears. They just wanted you to believe yours had been cut and that you'd lost your ordinary Fae powers. They wanted you to be on their side. They were using you this whole time."

He still didn't look at her. "I don't believe you." It was only a whisper now. Is this why he had no memories of his childhood? "Why?" he asked, despite knowing he didn't want to know the truth.

"The Autumn Court..." Her voice was so soft, Arlo wouldn't have heard her if it hadn't been for the sternness in her delivery. Zaria bowed her head, ashamed. "They—we—the Autumn Court—aren't as good as you think."

Arlo had his own reservations about the Court, but even he had decided long ago that you can't choose your family—the Autumn Court was just that: his family. His brows furrowed then. "What about my dad—what about Ambrose? How can you say I'm not Fey? My dad—" But even as he said it, he felt a sinking weight in his stomach.

"He's not your father," Zaria said remorsefully. "Ambrose lost his son tragically many years ago. On a mission." She waved her hand toward him, indicating Arlo. "The Autumn Court simply gave Ambrose a new one. You're not his true son. Not really. But Fey magic makes him believe that you are. Prior to your arrival, he was a very broken man. It is likely he'll return that way soon." Her brow furrowed. "You never wondered why there was nothing of you as a child in his home? No evidence or pictures? Nothing?"

Arlo stood so still, he might have been made of stone. He did notice, but he never really questioned it. "Ambrose isn't exactly the sentimental type—" his voice trailed off. He was only making excuses. Excuses he had told himself in attempts to lick his wounds.

"I know it's a lot to take in, and I understand that you're probably very confused right now." Zaria placed her palm against her chest. "I wouldn't believe it if I hadn't been there when it all happened. But something has happened now, and you need to know. I would never betray my home—my people—my family unless they were in even greater danger if I didn't. You know me." While Zaria spoke, Arlo continued to look away from her. He desperately wanted her to be lying, but something in his heart knew that hope was in vain. Why would she be bothering with him right now if she weren't telling the truth? If she was a traitor, she would have killed him, wouldn't she? She would have put up more of a fight, but she didn't fight him at all.

Zaria pursed her lips together as she looked over at Agent Harpy. "I think we need to bring him to the S.M.O.K.E. & M.I.R.R.O.R.S. office."

Agent Harpy turned her head and cocked a brow at Zaria's suggestion. She had been watching the proceedings from the background, but now she stepped forward. "We need to do what?"

"I think he needs to meet Director Quartermaine. He'll be able to give Arlo more information."

Agent Harpy stared in disbelief. She shook her head as if shaking water from her ears. "*Excuse me*? I'm sorry, *what*?" Director Quartermaine? She knew Director Quartermaine? She knew about the organization? Harpy looked the Fey up and down. "Who even are you?"

Agent Harpy had always known that Director Finn Quartermaine was a secretive man. He had seen things in his lifetime that she couldn't even begin to imagine, and he could do even more things than she could fathom. When he spoke, he rarely gave away more information than strictly necessary, but this, something apparently so tightly connected to her own mission, had completely blindsided her. She stared blankly back at Zaria, her mind utterly frozen in disbelief.

Is this what it felt like to realize you truly know nothing?

She was shaken from her thoughts by Arlo's hiss.

"You're working with them?" Arlo was pointing from Zaria to an Imp that had landed on her shoulder. It was the size of a pigeon. Arlo's eyebrows nearly disappeared into his hair, which was now damp and matted from his sweat. His curls hung loosely around his face, and he quickly swept the hair back. His chest heaved as he tried to steady his breathing.

Zaria could understand his concern and hesitation. She glanced at the little Imp on her shoulder. It nodded at her. "They won't cause any further harm to you, Arlo."

"They've caused plenty already," he grumbled, almost in a daze. He was still in disbelief, staring at the small Imp sitting on her shoulder, playing around with the loose strands of Zaria's brown hair. He didn't notice until then just how human she looked. Zaria was still ethereally beautiful like many of the Fey were, but she was dressed so plainly. He could have walked right past her on the street and not have given her a second glance.

"And for that, I am sorry," she said earnestly, placing her hand over her heart. "I never meant to scare you or harm you. I just wanted to get you away from Fae. It was imperative." She looked at the ground, "I'm sorry we couldn't speak sooner, Arlo. I'm sorry."

Arlo didn't answer. His eyes stared blankly at the ground beside his boots. He didn't know what to say. He was at a loss for words, trying to make sense of everything that had happened in the week alone. In the day alone.

Zaria turned to Agent Harpy. "I will meet you there? Back at the office?"

Agent Harpy was still trying to accept that Zaria knew Director Quartermaine, but rather than ask questions, she simply nodded. Questions could be asked at another time.

"I'll see you in a bit," Zaria said to the two of them before walking back down the dark hallway as though to walk further into the theater rather than out of it.

Arlo continued to watch her until her presence became nothing but a memory. He forced himself to look at Harpy. "She knows your people?" he asked.

Agent Harpy lifted her shoulders. "That was just as much a surprise to me as it was to you," she said. "Truthfully, I've never seen her before in my life."

"That you can remember," Arlo muttered under his breath. Agent Harpy only just barely heard him as he followed her outside the Oriental Theater. All of the Imps they had run from were gone.

Arlo massaged his temples.

"Are you alright?" Harpy asked.

"I feel like I'm trapped in one of my nightmares," he said quietly. "I barely understand what's going on. I'm even starting to see ghosts." He began walking toward the busy street, but Agent Harpy quickly grabbed hold of his sleeve to stop him before he got hit by a car. The last thing she needed was for him to die or cause a car accident. He swiftly went into defensive mode almost immediately out of instinct but checked himself when he realized it was only Agent Harpy. She quickly let him go. "I'm sorry for that, by the way," he said, acknowledging her bandaged hand.

Agent Harpy shrugged.

"You weren't the one who gave it to me," she said.

"I could heal it if you'd like," he offered, and she shook her head.

"Let me suffer a little," she said with a small smile before nodding her head toward the Tashtegos cafe. "Come on, let's go see what Director Quartermaine has to say about all of this. My car's over there."

"Car?" Arlo asked, frowning slightly as he looked back at the busy road. "You mean, like one of these death traps that keep trying to run me over?"

"Well, they wouldn't try to run you over if you stayed off the street when you're supposed to." Agent Harpy pointed at the pedestrian walk sign as the cars came to a stop at the red lights. "See?" she said as the red hand turned into a symbol of a walking person. "Now you can cross. You're not scared of getting *into* a car, are you?"

"No," Arlo said. Vaguely, an image of a much older car, black with thin wheels, drifted through his mind.

He closed his eyes. "Maybe just a bit of your driving, perhaps." His lame attempt at easing the situation at least got Agent Harpy to chuckle. "Did you by chance save my bruschetta?" She glared at him. "What? I'm still hungry," he muttered.

"Maybe you shouldn't have wandered off then."

"I'm sure you would have too if you saw a ghost."

For a moment, Agent Harpy considered this as she walked beside him on the sidewalk toward her car. Given her line of work, she couldn't exactly argue with him. The paranormal had become her life. She, too, would run toward it, not away from it. Agent Harpy glanced over at Arlo and decided against giving him the satisfaction of being right.

When they approached her car, Agent Harpy unlocked her door. Arlo had trouble with his car handle and struggled to release the latch.

"My door won't open," he said. He looked up to see Agent Harpy staring at him.

"I believe you have something of mine." She extended her arm out over the hood of her car.

Arlo frowned at her. "I don't know what you're talking about," he said innocently and shook his head.

"Don't give me that look," she said. "Give me my *Faerie Tales* book back. Ruthie will kill me if I don't give it back to her."

Arlo was fumbling with his vest when he caught wind of the name.

"Ruthie?" he repeated after her, pulling the book out of his vest. "Daughter of Erik?" Agent Harpy froze. Names were valuable, he'd said. Her lips pressed firmly together as her expression turned to worry. Arlo then shook his head. "I won't do anything to her," he said and placed the book in her hand. "I can't, anyway. Even if I wanted to. Apparently, I'm not Fey." He shrugged just as Agent Harpy unlocked his side of the car. He got in without another word.

Agent Harpy couldn't help but pity him. Though he sounded sarcastic and appeared to try to make light of the situation, it bothered him, and for good reason. Poor kid had been lied to about his identity.

# CHAPTER ELEVEN

*11*

The S.M.O.K.E. & M.I.R.R.O.R.S. office in Chicago looked like any other old office building, easily blending in with its surroundings. The gray stone sign read S.M.O.K.E. & M.I.R.R.O.R.S. with no further information that might indicate what either acronym meant.

"It was originally supposed to be two separate sectors," Agent Harpy said, as if reading Arlo's mind. She followed his gaze as it passed over the letters on the large sign out front. She pointed as she spoke. "The Sector of Managing Obscure Knowledge and Eccentricities is *S.M.O.K.E.*, and Maneuvering Irregular Rehabilitations, Removals, Obliterations, and Regulations Subdivision is *M.I.R.R.O.R.S.*"

"That's a mouthful," Arlo said, still working his way through each of the words Agent Harpy had just told him. He wasn't even sure he knew what it all meant. He recalled her mentioning it the first time they'd met, but even then, it all just sounded like gibberish so he hadn't really paid attention to it. In fact, it still sounded like gibberish.

"Hence S.M.O.K.E. & M.I.R.R.O.R.S. One of the founders clearly liked acronyms."

"*Clearly*," he repeated quietly.

Agent Harpy led Arlo inside the building. His eyes darted around the office. It was an incredibly bland space, filled exclusively with shades of gray, black, and white. Arlo's eyes were drawn to the only area of color in the room. On the far wall, pictures hung showing people shaking hands with Government leaders or posing in front of major landmarks. Even the occasional front page of a newspaper hung, neatly framed, preserved behind the glass. Arlo read the names under each picture as he walked past; he hadn't heard of any of them.

The receptionist nodded at Agent Harpy and pressed a button to allow entry through the thick glass door. Arlo followed, though hesitantly. She led him down a narrow hallway and wrapped her hand around the door handle.

The thin nameplate across the gray door read *Director Finley Quartermaine*.

"Are you ready?" Agent Harpy asked.

Arlo barely moved a muscle. He wasn't sure what he should be ready for or what to expect. Agent Harpy tilted her head and opened the door, not waiting for a response.

Zaria was already there. The Imp still perched on her shoulder like a little devil. A man sat behind the desk. He looked tall and lean, his hair revealing his age. Arlo assumed this was the Director whose name was on the door. Arlo looked at Agent Harpy before his eyes moved to Zaria again and finally back to the man seated.

Director Quartermaine stood up. His blond hair was graying, giving off a very sandy appearance. "You must be Arlo," he said. His voice was gruff.

Arlo nodded. "Director Quartermaine," he said, acknowledging the nameplate located on the desk that separated the two of them. He wasn't sure how to do it properly. Bowing seemed too formal, but this man certainly was important. He settled for a curt nod.

"You must be wondering why you're here," Director Quartermaine said. "I'm sure you must have a lot of questions."

"More or less," Arlo said. His eyes wandered around the room before landing on the Director's wall of recognition. His focus returned to the Director. "Mostly just a lot of disbelief."

"Because you were living a lie?" he asked. His voice sounded almost kind, but Arlo kept his stare locked with the Director, unsure how to respond. "No one's going to hurt you, Arlo," the Director reassured. His gaze fell to Arlo's hands. Arlo hadn't realized he had balled them into fists. "You can relax."

The Director motioned to a seat in front of his desk next to Zaria. Arlo looked suspiciously around, but his exhausted body eventually gave in. He sat gratefully, though he did his best to keep his body alert.

He cleared his throat. "Why am I here?"

The Director nodded at Zaria.

"I questioned my mission," Zaria admitted. "I looked into the burning of the Iroquois Theater because I wanted to know why it was so important to Fae and why it was dividing the Courts. Something about the whole thing—the night we found you, the random intelligence missions to Terra since then—something wasn't adding up." She looked at Arlo. "You know that Autumn Queen wants to attack the Winter Court." Arlo nodded. "I didn't understand what she was waiting for and why she kept sending us to Terra since she clearly didn't care about Terrans at all. My mission was—"

Arlo closed his eyes and shook his head. "We're not supposed to be told—"

"—to capture Imps and torture them for information," she finished, even with Arlo's interruption. "We are told, actually, the details of each other's missions." She looked down at her hands. "You're the only one purposely left out. It was part of the arrangement after you were taken. You're not Fey, Arlo. There's a lot you haven't been told."

He stiffened at her words and averted his eyes to stare at the small Imp still perched on Zaria's shoulder like a parrot. "I was FeyForce. Just like you, Zaria."

She shook her head. "Not like me. You were FeyForce because Lord Bane figured it was the best way to make you think you were on our side, sharing the cause, fighting for your family. You were FeyForce so they could keep strict control of you without you realizing you were…" her voice trailed off, but Arlo knew what she was going to say.

"...a prisoner."

Zaria nodded. Arlo glanced again at the Imp, avoiding eye contact with everyone else. It was one of the smallest Imps he had seen from all of the attacks. The small creature gave him an evil grin. Arlo rolled his eyes at the foul creature and averted his gaze.

"I came across this photograph," Zaria said, placing the picture on the Director's desk for Arlo to see. "It's you." She pointed at him in the photo. "And the cast of Mr. Bluebeard, the ballet that was playing that night." Her finger then slid to the young woman to his left. He recognized her from his dreams. "This is your twin sister, Freya, a ballerina in the show, and this girl," she said, moving her hand again to the young woman on his right. "This is the lost Elven princess, Halina. She stole the Book of Fate and ran away to be with the man she loved—" her finger slid back to Arlo, "—when she was told she couldn't be with him because *Destiny* wouldn't allow it. So she took Fate into her own hands. Literally. She stole the *Book of Fate* to be with *you*."

Arlo scoffed and shook his head. He tried to make himself laugh at the tale they were trying to tell him. Trying to get him to believe.

"I've never seen her before. I've never seen either of them before." Even as he spoke the words, he felt his face flush. It wasn't true. He'd seen them hundreds of times in his dreams.

"Well, it has been nearly a hundred years."

Arlo's eyebrows shot up. As his brain processed her words, his mouth began to twitch. He began to chuckle, and soon, his chuckle broke out into a forced yet uncontrollable laughter. Relief washed over him like a wave. It was impossible, all of this was a lie. A trick. He laughed at himself for doubting himself. Of course, this was the real lie. He was Fey, and everything would go back to normal as soon as the FeyForce came to rescue him. "You can't be serious," he finally managed after some composure. "Do you hear yourself, Zaria? Do I look over a hundred years old to you? That's impossible. I don't know what lies they've been telling you, Zaria, but even you should be able to tell this is a heap of beetle dung."

"Time works differently in Fae, or did no one ever mention that to you?" she said. Arlo winced, and his laughter caught sharply in his throat. Zaria leaned forward. "How old do you think I really am?"

Arlo's chest felt tight. His breaths came shallow and fast. His eyes searched wildly around the room for a new lifeline that could pull him out of this nightmare. He rose shakily, shaking his head. He stepped away from them and the table.

"This is ridiculous." His hand shook slightly as he pointed to Zaria. "You're all full of dung. And you were my *friend*." He nearly spat the word. "How could you pretend now that my damaged memories are from anything other than a life of faithful service to the Autumn Court? How could you? I've been on the FeyForce for so many years." He waved his arms. "I saved the Queen, or are you going to tell me that was all a lie too?"

Zaria shook her head, interrupting. "You *have* been on the FeyForce for years. For many *Fey* years, which translates to nearly a hundred Terra years. And you've served loyally because we took the memories that might have made you want anything else."

"You mock me for my sacrifices and take advantage of my muddled memories."

Zaria sighed as she looked down at the photograph. "Arlo," she said quietly. "Your memory—it's my fault."

Arlo's eyes snapped back to her face. "What? Are you going to tell me more lies?"

Zaria glanced up at him, her eyes oddly reflective. She took a deep breath, and Arlo was surprised to see her shoulders tremble slightly. "Lord Bane and Commander Kall-An took the credit for finding you in the wreckage of the theater that night, but I'm the one who found your body first, Arlo—and I was the one who suggested we use Glamour to manipulate your memories. Unfortunately, Glamour can only do so much, and your nightmares were breaking down the walls we—the walls that I—built to keep them in." Zaria's eyes focused on the photograph. "You don't remember them because of what I did to you." Zaria parted her lips slightly as she sighed. "I never forgave myself for what I did to you—your memories, and I couldn't apologize for it. Not without you thinking I was crazy, or ruining everything the Fey had done, betraying my people."

Arlo stared wide-eyed at his friend. They'd survived countless missions together, and all this time, she was the reason he had no childhood, no life before the FeyForce. The room felt uncomfortably small, yet Arlo also had no awareness of his surroundings. His eyes were glued to Zaria.

She looked up at him, and Arlo saw the glistening trail of a tear on her cheek.

"I'm so sorry," she whispered.

Arlo stood frozen for a few more moments. Director Quartermaine watched Arlo thoughtfully, but Agent Harpy's jaw hung wide open. Arlo rubbed his temples and took a step back to lean against the wall. He wasn't sure what to believe, or how to feel. He clenched his jaw, mixed with feelings of anger and remorse. Arlo glanced at the photograph, feeling a pain in his chest. He stared at the two women in the photograph. Survivor's guilt, maybe. He instinctively rubbed at his sternum and looked away.

Zaria broke the silence. "I didn't know how important you were until recently. The Autumn Queen was still at the beginning of her plans to take over all of Fae when she started sending 'intelligence missions' to Terra…" Zaria closed her eyes and sighed. "She wants the Book of Fate to tell her she'll succeed. That she'll be the one and only ruler of all of the Courts."

"It's not as though the delay has stopped her plans," Arlo said, struggling to focus on the conversation.

"Sure, but it's a lot easier to go to war when you know you'll win because Fate wills it to be. The Autumn Queen is too much of a coward to actually die—but the Winter Court doesn't fear death. They're surrounded by it. Imagine where she would be—where Fae would be—if she knew she would be successful?"

"Will she be successful?" he asked. He shook his head. He was asking questions in all the wrong order. "Did you find the Book?"

Zaria shrugged. "I don't know if she'll be successful." She paused, glancing at Director Quartermaine. "But yes. In a way, we found the book, but it can't exactly be read right now."

Arlo felt an uncomfortable squirm in his stomach. He had hoped that the Book of Fate was a myth. And, if it had to be real, he had begun to hope it truly had been destroyed.

"The book saved you," Zaria added, as if she could read his mind.

"Why?" he asked, slightly agitated. He looked up at Zaria, still unsure how to feel about her after her claims of using Glamour on him.

"We don't know yet," she said softly and looked away.

"Something's coming," Director Quartermaine cut in. Arlo jumped, hearing his voice. He'd almost forgotten that others were in the room with him and Zaria. "This is much bigger than Terra, or Fae, or any of the other Realms. Something is coming, and the *Infernals* knew it. They were preparing, long before our own discovery of their artifacts."

Director Quartermaine got up from his desk to look out of the nearby window. "Fate's design…" he muttered to himself. "The Book of Fate is an *Infernal Artifact*. The Infernals are the eldest beings in the universe, thought to be the sons of the Creator himself."

Arlo raised his eyebrows. "Infernals?"

The Director waved his hand. "Right now, they're not nearly as important as the items they've left behind." He nodded to Arlo. "You've touched the Book of Fate, and look what it did to you. I once held an artifact in my hands as a child. It changed me too."

Arlo took one last look at the photograph.

"This is too much," he said quickly. He began backing out of the room and quickly left before anyone could stop him.

Agent Harpy looked at the door that slammed shut behind him. She started for the handle, but Director Quartermaine stopped her.

"Let him go," Director Quartermaine said. "I'm sure he needs to clear his head. This was a lot to take in. To find out your life is a lie? All an illusion."

"But that went better than expected," Zaria added with a sigh. She looked over at the Imp on her shoulder, who just shrugged and continued to play with Zaria's hair.

"He said he saw a ghost?" Director Quartermaine asked Agent Harpy.

Agent Harpy nodded, looking down at the photograph. "I'm assuming it must be one of these two women. I'd like to think there aren't just random ghosts hanging around Chicago."

"It's her," Zaria answered, pointing at Freya, the ballerina. "His sister. It has to be. The same one that Echo sees."

"How do you know?" Agent Harpy asked. "And Echo? Who sees her?"

Zaria ignored her later questions about Echo. "Halina is the Elven princess. Her soul wouldn't have stayed in this realm. It would have stayed with her body when her people came to collect it. It would have returned to her home for her final rest." She looked over at Director Quartermaine for validation of her claims, and he nodded. "Echo, on the other hand," Zaria began, "is top secret. Need to know. Unfortunately, you don't need to know. Not yet."

Agent Harpy's eyes moved back and forth between Director Quartermaine and Zaria. So, apparently, this random FeyForce traitor had the security clearance to know about this Echo, but she, one of the highest-ranking S.M.O.K.E. & M.I.R.R.O.R.S. agents, didn't. Rubbing at her throat, she still had her hand on the door handle.

"I think I need some water," she said. "My throat is scratchy."

She didn't wait for permission from either of them and left before Director Quartermaine could stop her again. Agent Harpy shut the door behind her and fished her phone out of her pocket and went through her contacts. Pressing a few buttons, she put the phone to her ear. "Hey, where are you?" she asked once it stopped ringing.

"I'm eating—what's up?" Agent Eiríksdóttir answered.

"I need some information from the Republic of Letters. Remember Arlo—your convention man?"

"Yeah, of course. What do you need?"

Agent Harpy looked back at Director Quartermaine's closed office door as she quickly walked down the hallway.

"Do you know an Echo—" she cut herself off when she heard a noise coming from down the hallway. "Hang on, I'm still at the office," she said. "I'll call you back."

Agent Harpy hung up the phone and walked around the corner and nearly walked into two other people dressed for a convention, only they didn't look as welcoming as Arlo had—which was saying a lot. Agent Harpy took a step back, her hand automatically reaching for her gun.

"You won't be needing that," the tall, slender female said as she waved her hand. The gun disappeared from its holster. Agent Harpy frantically patted her body for another weapon. They were all gone.

"Who are you?" she asked. "Team Rocket?" Agent Harpy immediately closed her eyes and mentally slapped herself for the Pokémon reference. Agent Eiríksdóttir and her pop culture references were rubbing off on her. "My god…"

The blonde woman looked to the man next to her who towered over the both of them. Agent Harpy wasn't a short woman, but this man was ridiculously tall.

"We're friends of Arlo," she said coolly. "You're going to tell us where he is."

Agent Harpy scoffed as she subtly looked around at her surroundings to see what she could use as a weapon. The only thing within reach was a stack of boxes containing files to be uploaded into their recently updated computer system. "Or what?"

A small smile crawled across the woman's face, her lips curling. "I was hoping you would say that."

"Now, Acacia, behave," said the man, but his mouth twitched nonetheless.

"What's your name?" Acacia asked her.

"It's none of your business," she said. Agent Harpy quickly grabbed the box of file folders next to her and threw it at the woman. "Catch!" she shouted before quickly darting around the corner. But to her surprise, the man had met her on the other side somehow and took hold of her wrists.

"Leaving so soon?" he asked, pulling her close to him, and his grip tightened. Agent Harpy had no idea where he'd come from or how he'd appeared in front of her so quickly. "My wife and I just want to play."

"No offense, but I'm not into that kind of experience," Agent Harpy muttered, keeping her eyes locked with his.

"Your name?" he asked, tilting his head with his request.

Acacia dug into Agent Harpy's pockets from behind and found her wallet. She opened the leather and found the identification card.

"Terrans are so stupid," she said and held it up for Salvatore to see.

"Prudence Lian Harpy," he said, reading off of the card. "Three names—we can do a lot with a full name."

The handle of Director Quartermaine's door began to jiggle. The Fey couple exchanged glances with one another and disappeared into thin air, taking Agent Harpy with them.

"Yes, someone should check on Echo before—" Zaria began before frowning slightly as she exited the office. She quickly glanced around the hallway curiously as she narrowed her eyes. The Imp mirrored her, doing the exact same thing, glancing around the hall.

"What—" Director Quartermaine started, and Zaria quickly held up her hand.

"I'm not sure," she said. "Maybe it's nothing." Zaria quickly shook her head and redirected her attention onto

Director Quartermaine as she attempted to clear her thoughts. "All of this is just happening so fast—and it's been a long time since I used Glamour—it's surreal that I even told him. I dreamed of the day I would. It's haunted me for so long."

"Did you lift it?"

Zaria shook her head. "The Imps tried to break down some of the spell—the outer wall, if you will. Their power to undo magic is stronger than mine, but Arlo panicked. It triggered Freya, and someone," she looked pointedly at the Director, "must have forgotten to tell her what was happening and she interfered." Her shoulders fell, her eyes still gazing down the hallway. "I figured I would do it in fragments—I assumed Freya would help now. It seemed unfair to unleash all of that upon him at once. I'm not trying to break him. I thought the Imps would be the best way, but they were a little too rough, and Freya wasn't exactly fond of their methods."

Director Quartermaine nodded as he shut the office door behind him.

"She did mention that."

Zaria wrinkled her nose. "Sometimes I forget you can see her. Are you going to tell Arlo?"

"It's probably best if I don't acknowledge her in his presence. For now, anyway." He rubbed at his chin. "So, what were you saying about Echo—"

"Yes, I think it's time," Zaria agreed. "Once he returns, we'll figure something out. But until then, I think he needs some space." She glanced around the hallway. "Is Freya around here now or is she with him?"

"She has a plan." Director Quartermaine nodded and left Zaria alone in the hallway. She continued to look up at the walls and the ceiling as though searching for an answer she couldn't see. When she peered around the hallway, she noticed the stack of boxes full of file folders. Zaria frowned.

"You noticed it too, didn't you?" she asked her Imp friend, who nodded, even though it was evident that he didn't need to. "Glamour," she said in almost a whisper. Zaria furrowed her brows and stared at the boxes. She opened the top box, and the files were a mess. Placing it on the ground, she opened the one beneath it—much neater, organized. Zaria continued to frown, the crease in her forehead deepened. Closing both boxes, she stacked them back on top of one another again.

"There's more Fey here," she said softly to the Imp, quickening her pace down the hallway as she reached the receptionist's desk.

She had to find Arlo.

# CHAPTER TWELVE

## *12*

Outside the office building, Arlo descended the steps and took a sharp left turn to walk around the side of the building. He entered a narrow alley. The walls were tight, and bags of trash set at the bottom of steps that led into the alley from windowless side doors. He massaged his temples and pushed his unruly brown hair out of his face.

Freya appeared, and this time Arlo was more annoyed than startled.

"Go away!" he snapped.

"I can't," she said.

Arlo's head shot up so fast he heard his neck pop. He froze. He'd never heard the ghost speak. Well, he'd heard her in his dreams thousands of times, and he'd spoken to her in the theater. But that was different. She was solid, as if he was inside a memory. Her voice sounded exactly the same.

No, there was a very slight echo in it as if she were farther away than she looked. He stared.

"We're linked. Even if I wanted to leave you alone, I couldn't unless you leave this realm again. You're stuck with me."

"I don't even know who you are!" he nearly yelled. His voice was growing hoarse in his frustration. He turned away from her and groaned, yanking his gloves off of his hands. Arlo threw them on the ground. Not thinking about his actions, he walked towards the brick wall that made up the side of the building. He punched hard. Without his gloves, the hit left no mark on the red brick. He cried out as the skin on his knuckles broke.

He reeled back, mind spinning, trying to ignore the ghostly woman behind him. He didn't know what to think. Part of him was in denial. None of it could be true. He was Fey. His father was Ambrose. He'd suffered injuries in his loyal work for the Autumn Court's FeyForce.

And yet…

This girl was undeniably the one from his nightmares. This girl was the woman from those odd visions—*memories*, a voice in his head whispered—whatever they were. But he couldn't remember. She seemed familiar and unfamiliar all at once.

It was maddening.

"I can't believe you don't recognize me." The young woman wearing his exact face took a step back. Her fingers were laced together in front of her. "I've been stuck on this plane for a hundred years, waiting for you to come back. And you don't even know me."

The way she said it made Arlo stop in his tracks. Her voice sounded deeply hurt, almost hopeless. He sank down onto a dirty step, shoving aside a black trash bag. Pushing his curly brown hair out of his face, he began to shake his head as he looked back at the ground, kicking around a few rocks. He chuckled a little.

"This isn't possible," he said, lifting his gaze to meet hers. "I'm Fey."

Freya smiled weakly. "You are not Fey. You are Arlo Jäger. You're a human man—"

"No!" he snapped, raising his palms as if pushing any other thought away. "I am Arlo, son of Ambrose Rosier of the Autumn Court—"

She took a step towards him. "You are my twin brother," she said, her voice growing stern. "—Older by exactly twelve minutes. You like fresh baked blueberry muffins that are still warm, broiled veal cutlets, and chicken pot pie. If you could, you would eat pumpkin pie for breakfast every morning—" She took another step closer to him.

He jumped up from the step and backed away slightly.

"Don't come any closer," he said.

She didn't listen. "You hate when your food touches one another on your plate and won't eat a vegetable unless it's been roasted or fried—"

"I said don't come closer—"

"What are you going to do?" she asked, right in his face. She was barely two inches away from him. "You can't hurt me, Arlo. I'm already dead." Freya unclenched her jaw. "But you have no idea what I can do to you."

Her words felt cold in Arlo's ears. Although Freya was slightly blue and mostly translucent, he could still see the similarities in their appearances and in their manners. But even dead, she was more graceful than he was. Just then, she smiled. She reached for his throat and pushed him backward.

"Let me take you back a hundred years to Poland, in 1902."

Her voice erupted throughout his brain as though it were coming from his inner monologue. Except it wasn't his voice.

He shut his eyes.

"What are you doing to me?" he demanded, fingers pressed hard against his temples. Arlo shook his head and gasped for air, fighting against the immense pressure building in his skull.

"I'm not doing anything," her voice said in a gentle whisper. "I'm not the one who can travel to the past."

"What?"

"Don't open your eyes!" she shouted. "Not yet."

Arlo stumbled as his feet hit something roughly. He fell backward, landing hard on his tailbone. He turned to his side to take pressure off of it as he slowly opened his eyes. His eyelids fluttered, and everything started off blurry.

"Welcome home," Freya said, offering him a hand. She was a solid person now, the color of her skin matched his, and it was almost like looking into a mirror—only she was female. Her hair was long, brown, wavy. She had a pointed chin, just like his, and a small nose, with large, green eyes. Arlo quickly shuffled backward on the ground, trying to get away from her. She put her hands on her hips. "Where are you going?" she asked.

"What did you do to me?" he asked, looking around. They certainly were no longer in Chicago anymore.

"We're home—or what used to be our home."

"How did we get here?"

She pointed at his chest. "You."

"What?" he said, staring at her in disbelief. His eyebrows were raised.

She smiled.

He didn't like when she did that.

"What do you think your abilities are?"

Arlo paused before he spoke. "I can use my Fey abilities when I'm in my suit and—"

Freya shook her head. "No. It's not *your* ability if it comes from a suit."

He scowled. "I can heal others but—"

"But what?"

"It takes a lot out of me. It feels like I have to give part of myself. Whatever I give eventually comes back," he considered for a moment. "I've saved a lot of people." He wasn't sure why he was telling her this. Maybe it was thinly veiled narcissism, but he felt like he could trust the girl with his face.

She looked at him thoughtfully. Kindly. "You don't fully know what you can do, do you? Well, I suppose you wouldn't. You thought you were Fey for the last ninety-nine years. Healing is part of it—your real ability, but only a part." She took a seat on the handcrafted wooden chair. "While you were playing fantasyland with the Autumn Court, I was developing my abilities. I learned a lot about us—about what we might be able to do once we were together." She tilted her head as she tucked her long brown hair behind her ear. "Have you heard of Dioscuri?" she asked. Arlo remained sprawled on the ground. She was speaking so quickly and talking about things that were completely foreign to him. He shook his head. "The Dioscuri were known separately as Castor and

Pollux; they were semi-divine figures and were reunited in the sky as stars."

"What does that have to do with us?" he asked.

"That is us," she said simply. "Well, like us. The Dioscuri is more of a title. I've learned that the Dioscuri is picked by Destiny to become divine. To help those in trouble or grave danger. It's a position, I suppose. Like a job that needed to be filled. What is it you can do, Arlo?" she asked, though she wasn't really looking for an answer. "Heal others, but at a great cost to you, right? Yet you do it anyway."

"It's a temporary loss to save a life."

"But you can't help yourself, can you? Knowing you can help, even if you lose something to do so, you have to help. It's almost an instinct for you."

Arlo finally dragged himself up from the ground, feeling as though she were talking down to him, both literally and figuratively.

"Where are you going with this?" he asked, dusting himself off. It was then he noticed his clothing had changed again. He wore an unbuttoned grayish-white sukmana over a black vest and white shirt. Arlo pulled off the woolen coat to take a better look at it. He felt a sense of familiarity.

"When we're together, we become divine," she said, now looking up at him as he examined the outer garment.

"I thought you would have known when I rescued you from the Imps."

He lowered the sukmana. "When you what?"

"I guess you don't retain memories while you're out."

"What do you mean?"

"I can—take control of your body when you're unconscious—or when you're losing consciousness. If I'm feeling particularly strong—or you're particularly weak—I might even be able to force you into a sort of coma—I mean, I would never do that to you, not without your permission. I would never—" she continued, noticing his expression falter into a look of concern.

Arlo simply shook his head. "At least someone's looking out for me when I can't look out for myself," he said, hanging the sukmana up on the rack. "So what happened? With the Imps?"

"They were out of line," she said. "They weren't supposed to be probing your memories like that—breaking down the barrier that Zaria had built. But it clearly was more difficult than they'd planned, and they were being rough with your memories."

He tensed at the mention of Zaria using Glamour on him.

"I saw that you were in pain, and since you were out cold, I… took over. When we become one, your physicality changes to look more like me as I become apparent. But anything I do in your body, leaves with me." She glared meaningfully at him. "I might be able to finally get out of that ballerina outfit if you'd let me." Arlo frowned. "Your body isn't affected by anything that happens when I'm—using it."

"I'm not following."

"It's almost like you let me borrow the ability to take physical form while you go into a dormant state. But since I am also in possession of your energy, my pupils split, and I can't really pass for a normal person. You can alter someone's future when you save them—I have premonitions. I can travel to the spirit world—or the Underworld—but not the past—like you. I can't absorb energy, but I can redirect it, even though I don't have a physical form. You can absorb energy, you can pass it to someone else—that's why you can heal people, right?"

"But I lose at least one of my senses in the process," his mind was processing all of the information. "How do you know any of this?"

"The Book of Fate."

"You read it?"

"Well, no. It's not that *simple*..."

Arlo paced around the small cottage as he listened to Freya. For the most part, it sounded like nonsense, but ever since he returned to Terra, it had all been one long nightmare that seemed like it wasn't going to end any time soon. "Did you say I can travel to the past?" he asked, glancing her way. She nodded. "Is that—are we—"

Freya pursed her lips together; she didn't have to nod again.

"We are not in a memory. We've just returned to our life in another time. That's why we're alone. We're in 1902, before we left for America with Halina."

A chill ran down Arlo's spine. "We're *in* the past—"

"Well, it's technically the present now. For us, at least." He shot Freya a glare, and she smiled weakly. "Sorry," she said softly, even though she wasn't actually. "I know this is a lot to take in, but like Director Quartermaine mentioned, this is bigger than us. We're not just Freya and Arlo anymore."

Arlo turned around and noticed several photographs of the two of them, even as children. It was the exact presence that was missing from Ambrose's house, and though it never bothered him before, though he never thought anything of it, it made sense now why it never truly felt like a home. Arlo never truly belonged there. He picked up one of the photographs, and his eyes slowly glanced her way.

There was pain in his chest as the truth presented itself. He almost felt an actual thunk in his heart as the missing pieces of his life slid into place. How could he keep denying what was clearly staring at him in the face?

"I'm sorry I left you alone for so long," he said softly. Saying it out loud was strange. "A hundred years," he continued, looking back down at the photograph. "That's a long time to be by yourself."

A single tear slid down Arlo's long nose, falling on the glass that covered the photo. He wouldn't have noticed it if not for where it had landed.

"It was a long time," Freya said and nodded. "It felt like an eternity, trapped in an everlasting nightmare. But I wasn't alone," she said reassuringly. "Not the whole time, at least. I met someone who helped me." Freya got up from her chair and went to look at the photos with him. "I tried to dream-walk, to reach you in Fae, but I never quite got through."

"I think you did," he said, looking at her. He brushed his hand over his face. "I had a lot of nightmares about you. About the fire. I didn't really understand them, but I think I do now."

"And here I thought you didn't remember me," she chuckled and punched his arm playfully as she scrunched her nose. "I told you: We're linked."

Arlo nodded.

Beneath the pile of their photographs was another of him with Halina. She really was quite the beauty; the discolored photograph didn't fully capture it, nor did it do her justice. At least not from what he could recall from the recent memories he had of her.

"So about this girl," he said, pushing the other photos off of it.

"Halina," Freya said, nodding. "You were everything to her."

He could feel his arrogance taking over.

"Well, I am pretty great," he said, nodding as he glanced at his sister. Arlo furrowed his brows, thinking of Freya as his sister and not just as the ballerina from his nightmares. It began to feel natural and not forced. It was a strange feeling, to accept her as his family, but how could he not? With her in a living, solid form and color in her cheeks, she was calm, and welcoming. Not at all like the coolness her ghost gave off. Arlo knew he could trust her; his gut was telling him he could. His gut was telling him he had known her his whole life—even if he had spent most of his life away from her.

One hundred years.

A flood of guilt welled up inside his body.

He retained the color in his cheeks while she lost hers. While she died in that fire, strung up like a puppet.

He hadn't saved her. But he'd survived.

Arlo turned away from her.

"Don't do that," she said.

"Don't do what?" he asked, not turning back around.

"Don't feel guilty for being alive."

His expression hardened, and he crossed his arms over his vest. He tried to clear his mind, but he didn't know what to think or say.

"Halina," Freya said, changing the subject. "Would you like to visit her?"

Arlo wasn't sure he had it in him to visit her. If this was how he felt as Freya gained familiarity, how would he feel being around Halina? Especially knowing it was all in the past—and what would become of her future?

Arlo clenched his jaw and slowly turned around to face Freya.

"I'm not sure I'm ready for that," he admitted. While he faced her, he didn't meet her gaze. He knew if he looked at her right then, he wouldn't be able to hold back the emotion that struggled just below the surface.

"We can wait here," she said, taking a seat again. "We have all the time in the world here. That's the beauty of time travel. We're not in a hurry anymore." She searched his face. "But I do believe it is imperative you see her before we go back."

Arlo looked at the wooden table and chairs as he walked around to take a seat and join her at the table. He ran his fingers along the handcrafted markings as he pulled out the chair across from Freya. In another lightning bolt of intuition—or, he reminded himself—actual memory, he felt that his father made it.

"Tato made this, didn't he?"

Freya smiled, a real broad smile as she sat back in her chair. Her large, green eyes were beginning to redden as they watered. "You remember?" she asked.

Arlo's brows furrowed as he nodded slowly, finally taking a seat. He pressed his palms flat against the surface of the table. "And he got upset when Mama tested whether or not it was straight with a marble and—"

"The marble rolled right off and onto the floor." She began laughing. "He was so mad," Freya said, clasping her hands together. "He was so proud, and she destroyed it just like that!" She snapped her fingers.

Arlo looked thoughtfully into the worn surface of the table. His mind felt like it was fighting a battle through fog, slowly claiming victory as memories returned home.

"It's still a good table though," he said, his hand still feeling the edges. "It's so smooth."

"Mama loved it, even if it wasn't as perfect as Tato wanted it to be. We had every meal at this table."

"Every meal," Arlo said, nodding. He could see that too now, the four of them sitting there and eating their meals. While his parents were still a bit of a blur, he could remember their presence all around the table. The quiet meals, the happy ones. So many memories had happened there, so many memories shared at mealtime with loved ones.

He even remembered telling his parents about Halina for the first time.

Arlo continued to etch his thumbnail against the edge of the table. He stared at his nail, scratching against it for a moment before his lips parted to speak.

"I think I'm ready," he said finally, looking up at Freya. "I think I'm ready to see Halina."

***

Everything blurred from his vision. When things came into focus, he was standing in a palace. Arlo frowned slightly, confused by the rush of familiarity. He was standing in the Wilanów Palace—one of the first public museums in Poland. The design was a unique collaboration of different building traditions, inspired by Polish aristocratic mansions with side towers, Italian suburban villas, and French palaces with two oblong wings on each side projecting forward from the main black. He stood in the central part that displayed a commemoration of King John III Sobieski, and to his left stood a young woman with raven-black hair. She was looking up at a few paintings but at the same time, seemed to be staring at nothing.

"I thought I might find you here," Arlo said, the words coming out of his mouth before he even thought to say them.

She didn't look at him, but he knew in his stomach this was Halina. He recognized her from the resurfacing memories and old nightmares. She subtly wiped her cheek with her hand and turned away.

"Hey," he said softly, reaching for the crook of her elbow. "What's wrong?" He gently tried to coax her into looking at him, but she continued to turn away in the other direction. "Halina—"

She finally turned to him. Her eyes were bloodshot, and her blue irises seemed cold and distant. Not the cool ocean he knew they usually were. "We have to run away. Now." She spoke quickly and grabbed hold of his sleeve, dragging him toward the door.

"Halina, what's wrong?"

"We're going to go to America," she said hurriedly. "We have to. I—"

"Not without me, you're not!" Freya popped up from the two of them. Halina smiled a little, and Freya's eyes widened once she noticed Halina had been crying. "Halina! Oh, what's wrong?" she asked quickly. She pulled the small girl into a hug and held her tightly, only making Halina sob further. Halina let go of Arlo's sleeve and wrapped her arms around Freya as she cried into her shoulder. Freya looked up at Arlo, and Arlo only shrugged and shook his head.

"I don't know what happened," he mouthed the words to his sister, who fondly stroked Halina's long, black hair.

Everything blurred again.

***

"I've always wanted to go to America," Freya declared as she started to pack her bag. "Maybe I'll meet a cute American boy—" Arlo rolled his eyes. Freya chuckled as she folded another garment. "You know, I don't even care about that. I just—the American dream always sounded so nice, and now it's within reach."

"Which is what?" Arlo asked.

"Freedom?" Freya wasn't sure if she was telling or asking. "Find meaning and purpose for my life. I want to dance."

"And you're amazing at it," Arlo said, shuffling through some of his things.

"I know," Freya declared happily, just as things became hazy once more.

***

It was a cool night, and Arlo walked hand in hand with Halina, who kept her focus ahead. Her slender fingers were cold to the touch, and he moved his hand down to warm them, giving them a gentle squeeze. It was nearing their time to leave Poland, and he slowly came to a halt. Halina did the same.

"Are you sure this is what you want?" Arlo asked. "You've never wanted to leave Poland before," he noted. He tilted his head, and some of his curly brown hair fell against his forehead.

At first, Halina didn't look up at him. She chewed on her plump bottom lip as she considered what to say.

"I did something terrible, Arlo." Her eyes stared at the ground. "I can never go home." Arlo frowned at her words, and Halina's gaze slowly rose to meet his. Her eyes were watering again. "I want to be with you. I'd give up everything to be with you."

As he reached out to wrap his arms around her, pulling her tightly against his chest, the haze overtook him once more.

***

His ears rang with the screaming of guests. Sweat beaded on his forehead as panic erupted throughout the Iroquois Theater. He looked one way, then another, frantically searching for Halina in the unruly crowd of people.

"Halina!" he shouted. "Halina!" Arlo put his hands up to cup the sides of his mouth as he shouted for Halina until his voice grew hoarse. Guests were running into him one way, then another, as they all tried to find their way out of the burning theater. He choked on smoke and his eyes burned, but he kept looking.

"Arlo!" he heard someone scream.

He turned around and saw Freya dangling from the ceiling, tangled in ropes. She fumbled with her harness as she looked at him in the crowd. Her hand reached out to him, before the fire claimed her.

"Freya!" He heard an unfamiliar roar erupt from his throat. He was only vaguely aware of the dampness on his face—tears and sweat—as he struggled to make his way toward the stage even as he knew he was too late. Her body lay limp, hanging from the ropes like an abandoned puppet.

Arlo dropped to his knees as his body lost the will to walk. His lungs burned as he panted, unable to process the horror, eyes still glued to where his sister's body swung in the billowing heat.

He was kicked several times as guests stumbled over him, but he didn't move.

After what might have been seconds or hours, his eyes fell from Freya's body, landing on Halina's bag. He wasn't sure why he felt drawn to it, perhaps it was the only thing he had left to cling to from either of the women he'd held so dear. Quickly, he crawled over to it and looked inside. It contained a large, old book with a very subtle, faint white glow.

Arlo looked up for Halina, just as an explosion erupted.

His spirit rose from his body, and he stared at himself. His limp body lay on the ground, deathly still. He looked at his ghostly hands. In the flickering firelight, his translucent fingers appeared amber, almost fleshy.

Then the Fey warriors arrived. Glancing back at the book, he watched it disappear—it just dissolved in his hands.

Arlo noticed Salvatore and Acacia—and then Zaria who approached him and knelt down beside his body. He watched as she alerted Commander Kall-An and Lord Bane that he was still alive.

"Did we—did Fey start the fire?" Arlo asked, his first attempt at separating himself from the Fey. Supposedly, he wasn't Fey. He didn't know how he knew, but he knew Freya's spirit had manifested behind him.

"It wasn't the Fey—but it wasn't the Imps either," she answered softly, just barely loud enough for him to hear. Arlo didn't turn around to face her. "The Imps weren't even here until the forties when the Japanese Demon ripped open a portal." Freya looked around the theater for Halina. "It was the Elven King." She chewed on her bottom lip. "The Book of Fate couldn't fall into the wrong hands—and he sacrificed his only daughter, Halina, to keep it safe."

*I did something terrible, Arlo. I can never go home.*

Halina's voice haunted him.

"What was the point in that?" Arlo asked while the theater burned around them before he turned to look at Freya, who was still tinted blue in the orange light—perhaps because she was actually dead, and he wasn't. "It's still lost, isn't it? I just watched it disappear."

Freya's lips parted for a moment as she struggled to find the right words. He watched as her translucent form walked over to the stage and looked up at her limp body, still strung up by the ropes she dangled from.

Arlo looked up at her body too—he could tell she was mourning her life. He took a step toward her to stand beside her.

"I'm sorry I couldn't save you," he said softly.

Freya only shook her head.

"It was Fate for me to die here."

Arlo felt anger rising within himself at that word: Fate.

He clenched his fists for a second before releasing the hold.

*Fate*, he thought to himself. *Were they all just pawns in a game?*

What a *cruel* game it was.

# CHAPTER THIRTEEN

## *13*

The two of them returned to the alley beside the S.M.O.K.E. & M.I.R.R.O.R.S. building in 2002 Chicago, Illinois. Arlo stared at the ground, brows furrowing into a frown as he seemed to search for answers in the grass beneath his feet.

"Do you remember?" Freya asked.

Everything seemed both hazy and clear all at once. Everything conflicted, and yet everything made sense. He wasn't sure what to think, but memories began pouring back in and flooding his brain. Wherever they had been locked away—the seal had been broken.

Slowly, he nodded. "I remember enough," he answered quietly, slowly looking up at her. It was harder now to see her in her translucent form after reliving memories of her alive. After experiencing the life and joy that was his sister. His expression softened.

Freya pursed her lips together empathetically and tilted her head.

"Don't feel sad for me," she said with a sullen smile. "I still managed to live some kind of an American dream," she continued with a shrug. "Even if it wasn't the one I had been anticipating." She tilted her head, Arlo was looking at her, but he didn't say anything. "Are you ready to go back inside?" she asked.

He hesitated.

"What of Zaria?" he asked.

Freya tilted her chin down. "You can trust her," she said. "She's a good one."

"And the others?"

"I've been watching Director Quartermaine for the last forty or so years. I met him when he first got here and this establishment went up. You can trust him. If there's anyone here—aside from me—who has any semblance of what you might be feeling, it's him. The artifact that affected him as a child? It was Death's Scythe. He's a nice man."

"Can he see you?"

Freya nodded. "The only one aside from you and—" Her voice trailed off.

Arlo didn't notice, still considering his newfound memories. "The book is lost," he said, shaking his head. "I saw it. It's lost. It disappeared from the theater when the Fey arrived. I don't know where it is—I don't know—what happened—I don't know why we're like this—"

The side door of the alley opened, and Director Quartermaine stepped outside.

He first looked at Freya before his gaze settled on Arlo.

"Fine day, isn't it?" Director Quartermaine asked, looking up at the sky, just visible in the crack between the two buildings. Arlo frowned at him, while Freya only smiled. He exhaled deeply and stuck his hands into his pockets. "The book was lost," he said, nodding. In response to Arlo's face, he shrugged, "I could hear you. But uh—the book was also—found, for lack of better word. Stumbled across—I'm not sure how to phrase it, really."

Arlo frowned. "What does that mean?"

Director Quartermaine smiled, which made Arlo uneasy. The Director didn't answer right away and took a deep breath. Taking a minute, he admired his surroundings. He glanced at Freya and winked.

"You should come with us," he said finally, as his gaze returned to settle upon Arlo.

Arlo looked at his sister and she nodded.

"Go with him," Freya encouraged. "There's something you have to see."

"You guys have it, don't you? You guys have the Book of Fate."

It wasn't a question, as much as it was a statement.

Director Quartermaine closed one eye as he tilted his head.

"Kind of," he said, speaking out of the corner of his mouth.

"Kind of?" Arlo frowned. "What does that mean?"

"Come, and you'll see." Director Quartermaine kept his hands in his pockets as he turned around to walk back into the building.

Arlo looked at his sister again.

"I don't like this. I don't like being left in the dark."

She chuckled softly to herself. "Some things never change."

Director Quartermaine led Arlo and Freya back into the building to a room that resembled a security control office. It was in the basement where only a few had the clearance to enter. There were several television screens all stacked and lined against the wall farthest from the door showing black and white footage from different cameras. Most of the screens had nothing in particular happening, just the scenery or the hallways, with nothing out of the ordinary. Director Quartermaine pointed Arlo's attention to a screen toward the bottom. A young girl was laying in a bed, hands clasped over her ears, and her body scrunched together in the fetal position. Her white dress was drenched in blood.

Arlo stared at the girl on the screen.

"How old is she?" he asked, not taking his eyes off her.

"She turned eleven this year," Director Quartermaine answered.

"What's wrong with her? She looks like she's in pain."

He nodded. "She is." He cleared his throat as his attention moved from Arlo and onto the girl on the screen. "Two of the Infernal Artifacts almost fell into the wrong hands. Once in 1903 and once in the forties during World War II. We think—given our research and work with the Republic of Letters—that maybe the Infernals, as *beings*—chose to give life to their artifacts in hopes they'll be able to defend themselves."

Arlo's brows furrowed as he frowned. He shook his head and looked from the screen to Director Quartermaine and Zaria. "You think she's—she's the Book of Fate? So they've taken on human form?"

Freya exchanged a glance with Director Quartermaine, who nodded.

"How many are there?" Arlo asked.

"Infernal Artifacts? In total? We're not *entirely* sure," Freya said. "Three that we know of for certain: Destiny, Death, and Dream. But we don't know how many there are of *us*."

"What do you mean?"

Freya looked to the Director, and he nodded. "People who've had contact with an Artifact. Exposure during distress—the Infernal Artifacts seem to protect those they deem worthy." She pointed at Arlo and herself. "Like what it did for us—and Director Quartermaine and his older brother."

"Your brother?" Arlo asked curiously, looking at Director Quartermaine. "Who's your brother?"

"A war hero," Director Quartermaine answered quietly before shifting his focus away from him. "During World War II, we almost saw the end of humanity when an artifact fell into the wrong hands." His eyes turned black. "Not everyone walked away from it unscathed."

Arlo tensed at the sight of Director Quartermaine's black eyes. His own did something of the same, only Arlo's turned white—and he expended a tremendous amount of energy to do so. Director Quartermaine seemed to be able to do it with ease. Like flicking on a light switch.

"I lost my brother," Director Quartermaine continued, his eyes returning to their normal hazel color. "I remember the exact moment I knew he was gone. The energy we give off—the energy the artifacts give off—I can feel it. I can detect it. It's comforting, almost, to know you're not alone in this madness, and when you lose it—you feel empty. I spent a long time searching for that feeling again. I dedicated my life to it. I've seen many things, come across many strange creatures, but I could never detect him again. You're lucky that even in death, you have your sister." Director Quartermaine looked over at Freya. "I would give anything to have had my brother's guidance all these years."

"I was only just reunited with her—" Arlo began.

"And now she'll always be with you." Director Quartermaine's voice was low, his gaze remained on Freya who looked at him with empathy. A small, genuine smile appeared across her lips. "I admit, I'm envious." Freya looked down and crossed her arms.

"So they really did lie to me." Arlo thought of Salvatore and Acacia, and all of the Fey as he looked back at the screen of the young girl who kept in the same position. "All of them. About the Imps—about me—about everything."

"I'm sorry you had to find out this way," Director Quartermaine said. "I was hoping it would be gentler. Zaria did her best, but we underestimated how deeply your memories had been buried."

"Are you sorry?" Arlo asked with more aggression in his voice than he intended, but to a certain degree, he was angry. The life he knew and lived for a century had been a lie—whether it felt like a century or not, it was all he had known for a long time.

As if reading his thoughts, Director Quartermaine only sighed.

"Zaria was lied to, too." He looked at the young girl on the screen. "Who knows how many of the Fey know the truth and how many don't. Our intelligence has confirmed that the Winter Court doesn't even want to be at war with your Court—they want peace among Fae as much as the other Courts—and yet the Autumn Queen fills her FeyForce with nonsense about them." He sighed again and looked over at Arlo. "Everyone gets lied to about something at some point. Don't be too hard on her."

Arlo remained silent, his eyes glued to the girl on the screen. "It's not right," Arlo whispered eventually, looking back at Freya. He felt guilty for having been away from her for so long. Even if it hadn't been his own choice. The corner of her mouth twitched, as Arlo looked back at the girl on the screen. "The girl—" he started, "can I meet her?"

"Of course," Director Quartermaine said with a nod. Just as Arlo had spoken, the girl on the television looked directly at them—seemingly at Arlo—through the screen.

"Can she see us?" Arlo asked, slightly taken aback as she just stared at them. At him. She didn't blink. She just stared.

"No," Director Quartermaine said, furrowing his brows as he took a closer look at the screen. "But this is the first time she's done this. We believe that you and your sister are both connected to her in some way. After all, she is the Artifact that did this to both of you. That saved you."

"What's her name?" Arlo asked.

"Arlo!"

They all spun around as Zaria crashed through the door, clutching her side.

"I've been looking everywhere for you!" she said, breathing heavily.

"What's wrong?"

"There's Fey—there's Fey here."

His face paled. "Who? What do they want?"

"The same thing they've wanted since they took you."

"Who?" Director Quartermaine asked.

"I don't know where they are—" Zaria continued as she gathered her hair with her hands to put it up. "I'm pretty sure it's Acacia, at the very least. Probably sent to deal with her traitor sister. I'm pretty sure she isn't going to listen to reason."

"She cares about me—" Arlo began.

"She cares about Fae more, Arlo. Between the Fey and you, guess who she'll choose?" Zaria snapped. "Who would you have chosen if you had the choice?" she asked Arlo.

Arlo looked back at his sister, who only lowered her gaze. Before all of this, he would have chosen the Fey.

Now everything was broken. Everything was confusing. Ignorance was its own matter.

Director Quartermaine was already in motion. He was tearing cables out of the wall, their fraying fibers sparking in the dark room. He continued to smash computers with an iron bar he'd seemed to pull from somewhere in his jacket. "What are you doing?"

"The Fey are here," he said, sparks flying as he continued to rip through the hard drive of the security system. "I don't want any links to the girl. I don't want them to be able to trace her—or to find out we know where she is." He looked between Arlo and Zaria. "None of this happened—you hear me?" His eyes were pitch black again. The sight of the cold, black eyes made Arlo's skin crawl.

Arlo nodded immediately. Arlo had his own unique abilities, but something about Director Quartermaine made him uneasy to the point where he was almost scared of him—or at least on edge around him. While he knew Director Quartermaine wasn't exactly a normal Terran, he was still Terran—one who displayed amazing abilities. Arlo supposed he was the same. Terran. He needed to stop thinking he was Fey.

He was Terran.

He was human.

He had to start remembering that.

He had to focus.

"Has anyone seen Harpy?" Arlo asked, looking around the assembled group.

The blood seemed to drain instantly from Zaria's face. "Oh, no."

"What?" Arlo asked. "You don't think she took her? Why would she take Harpy? Why would they even come back?" Even as he said the words, he knew Harpy would be the perfect target for Acacia.

And, if Acacia took Harpy, then there were a lot of reasons for the blood to drain from Arlo's face too, his skin tone now matching that of Zaria's. Zaria knew Acacia better than most people, and she could be ruthless.

"I'm trying to fill in a lot of blanks here, but the Autumn Queen has been after the Book of Fate for a long time, Arlo. The FeyForce returned to Fae without you. You were their only link to it. I'm guessing the Queen wants you back. You're a valuable asset—to any team you side with. They're going to come for you."

Arlo looked back at Freya. Only hours before, he'd longed for any evidence that Fae cared enough about him to mount a rescue mission. Now, the prospect made his hands feel icy cold.

"We'll be ready," he said, and Freya nodded.

***

Just as the three of them headed toward the elevator, the elevator doors opened to reveal Harpy, standing alone.

She raised her eyebrows while the three of them stared at her.

"Are you guys okay?" she asked. At first, her focus was on Arlo, but then she spotted Zaria. Harpy clenched her fists for a moment before releasing her hands. She gently dusted the sides of her pants with her palms and pressed the 'door open' elevator button. "Well, are you guys coming in or not?" she asked the three of them.

Zaria looked at Arlo, who didn't take his eyes off Harpy.

"Yes," Director Quartermaine said as he pushed past the two of them and was the first to enter the elevator. Zaria went next, though she remained aware of Harpy, and openly stared at her curiously.

Arlo looked at Freya.

"What are you looking at?" Harpy asked.

Arlo glanced at Harpy and frowned.

"Nothing," he said and got in the elevator. "Where were you?"

"Distracted," Harpy said as the elevator doors closed. "A lot of things have been happening since you arrived here."

Director Quartermaine noticed that no floor buttons of the elevator had been pushed. The elevator remained still. "Harpy?" he said.

"There are other Fey here," she said quietly. Her focus remained ahead on the steel doors of the elevator as if someone would hear or see her spilling a secret she wasn't supposed to say. She sounded scared.

"Did you see them?" Zaria asked. When Harpy didn't turn to face her, she moved to stand in front of her. Still, Harpy didn't lift her gaze.

"What's wrong with her?" Director Quartermaine asked.

"I think they took some of her memories," Zaria said quietly, trying to get Agent Harpy's attention. "Hello?"

But she seemed to be slipping further from them the longer they stayed in the elevator.

Zaria looked up.

"Now I'm not entirely sure what's waiting for us up there," she said softly.

Arlo and Freya both exchanged glances before nodding.

"We're prepared," he said reassuringly, even if he wasn't entirely sure himself. He hadn't yet used Freya's abilities with his own, and he wasn't at all sure how it worked—but she seemed confident, and her assurance soothed his worry.

"You should be worried about what's in here with you," Agent Harpy said, finally looking at Zaria.

Zaria took a step back as if slapped.

"You know I'm not on their side," she said. "I'm Fey, but I don't agree with them or what they're doing. I never did. I was fed lies."

Harpy narrowed her eyes and nodded, though she didn't appear convinced. As she looked away from Zaria, the look in her eyes grew distant again. She finally reached out to press the button for the eighth floor of the building.

"What's on the eighth floor?" Arlo asked, looking at Director Quartermaine.

"You're asking the wrong person," he said sternly, not taking his eyes off of Harpy. "Harpy?" he said, but she didn't acknowledge him.

"The eighth floor just has offices," Zaria said in confusion. "Records and whatnot."

"Records of what?"

"You ask too many questions, Arlo." Agent Harpy didn't turn around as she spoke and kept her gaze locked on the doors. "Just be quiet."

"You asked me quite a few yourself," he said. "If you don't remember."

"I don't."

Zaria tensed and took a step back from Harpy. She was in line with both Director Quartermaine and Arlo now. Freya stood on the other side of Arlo, invisible to everyone but Arlo and Director Quartermaine.

"They really did a number on her," Zaria noted, staring at the back of Harpy's head.

"Is she going to be alright?" Director Quartermaine asked.

"She has the chance to return to normal, assuming they give the memories back—or maybe the Imps can trigger something." She glanced at Arlo. "Like what they did with him."

"I didn't exactly enjoy that," he muttered while Freya huffed. She didn't enjoy it either.

"No one ever does," Zaria said. "It's not meant to be enjoyable."

The creaky, slow elevator came to a halt, and the doors opened.

"Well, well, well," Salvatore said, standing on the other side of the elevator doors. "Zaria—what a pleasant surprise." His gaze then shifted over to Arlo. Something that looked like relief melted over his face. "You found her," he said, almost surprised.

Arlo frowned slightly, unsure how to respond. He then grabbed hold of Zaria's sleeve and moved forward, pulling her with him. "She found me, actually. But, it's not quite what you—"

"What are you—?" Zaria began to say, but Salvatore slashed his arm and her mouth disappeared.

Salvatore reached out and hugged Arlo, clapping him on the back. "We were so worried about you. With the comms not working..." His eyes rose to scan the other people in the elevator.

Agent Harpy began to walk forward. She turned into the dark hallway.

"Harpy!" Director Quartermaine yelled. "Stop! That's an order!"

But she didn't seem to hear him as she continued on into the darkness, dragging her left foot in a limp. He looked down and noticed a blood trail she left behind as she hobbled away.

Director Quartermaine looked up at Salvatore again—and his eyes turned black.

"I don't like when people fuck with my friends," he said.

"We didn't fuck with her," Salvatore said, releasing Arlo. "She's just fine. Just a little—tired, maybe." The corner of his lips twitched as he took hold of Zaria's arm, pulling her hand down away from her face as she struggled to use her own Glamour to bring her mouth back. She looked over at Arlo with her eyes wide, but he kept his gaze away from her. He avoided looking at Freya too, who was constantly prodding at him, wondering what it was he was doing.

He wasn't quite sure either.

Black smoke surrounded Director Quartermaine as he stepped out of the elevator. Black veins moved up his cheeks and toward his eyes as he reached to grab hold of Salvatore himself. The moment Director Quartermaine came into touch with him, Salvatore's life began to drain from his body. His skin began to gray, and his throat closed up. He began to suffocate.

"Director, stop." Arlo snapped out of his confusion, spurred to action as Salvatore—his best friend for, until moments ago, his whole life—began to disintegrate right in front of him.

Salvatore let go of Zaria, and her mouth came back.

"Director!" she gasped.

Director Quartermaine blinked several times, his eyes returning to their hazel color, and the black smoke dissipated.

"Sorry, I—Fey are different, it seems—" He stepped back, his palms raised as if preparing to negotiate.

Zaria screamed.

Arlo heard his voice yell, "*No!*"

A sickening, slicing squelch cut the air.

Director Quartermaine gasped and looked down—staring at the blade that had punctured through the front of his body. Blood quickly drenched the front of his shirt as he stumbled backward.

Agent Harpy ripped the blade out of his body, and Director Quartermaine dropped to the ground.

Freya's large green eyes were the last thing he saw.

# CHAPTER FOURTEEN

*14*

Finn Quartermaine was assigned to Chicago in the sixties when he was twenty-seven years old. Now thirty-two, he had been at his post for five years and was no closer to finding the Book of Fate than when he had first arrived. Occasionally, he'd sense a strange source of nether energy, but most of those ended up being dead ends.

He was a frequent visitor of the Oriental Theater, which had been built in the twenties after the Iroquois burned down. Many spirits still lingered there. Every time he was inside, he could see them frantic, appearing and disappearing as they struggled to find an escape. It was like an echo they were trapped in. Reliving their last moments, again and again. While Finn sympathized, he knew better than to interfere.

"Do not interfere with the Vestiges," Dr. Stolly had told him over the phone once. Dr. Stolly was a respected member of the Republic of Letters, and a good friend to Dorothea Sharp and Finn's older brother. "I understand wanting to free them, but they are not ghosts, nor souls or spirits. They're echoes trapped in a moment. Freeing them will do more harm to the world than good to them."

*Vestiges*, he called them. *A trace of something that was disappearing.*

Finn kept his focus on the Vestiges whenever he went to that theater, watching as they reenacted their final moments in an infinite loop. He felt comforted, or at least consoled to a certain degree, that they weren't aware. Still, it was hard not to feel bad knowing this was their Fate. He wondered about his brother's Fate—what became of him.

That was when he met *her*.

Freya.

She was not a vestige stuck in a moment, nor did she wander aimlessly. She lingered. She lurked, she followed.

While he focused on the replay before him, Freya lingered in the background, watching him. She had a pale blue tinge which made her stick out from the white translucent figures. However, she had grown reckless.

"Who are you?" Finn asked. He didn't turn around. Freya blinked in confusion before stepping back to sink into the wall behind her. "You can hide if you want, but I know you're there."

Hesitantly, Freya moved closer to him till she was at his side.

Finn turned his head and looked directly at the ghostly ballerina.

"You can see me?" she asked. He stared right at her.

For a moment, Finn didn't say anything. He couldn't find the words. She was so young. So beautiful, and doomed. But somehow, even in death, her large eyes still glistened.

"I can see you," he said quietly.

They'd looked at each other for a long while.

"Do you know where my brother might be?" she asked. "He was here, but then there were these people—not people—" she frowned. "They took him."

"Who's your brother?"

"Arlo," she said. "Arlo Jäger."

***

Everything was dark.

Wet.

Cold.

Finn looked around. *Was this the Underworld?*

His eyelids fluttered as he regained consciousness.

Arlo dropped to his knees, his hands pressing against the wound in Director Quartermaine's chest. Arlo's dark eyes turned white as a faint glow came from his palms. The strong stench of iron no longer stung his nose as he lost his sense of smell. His eyesight began to go—but the Director wasn't healing. As Arlo pressed down on the wound, he continued to feel the blood gushing through his fingers. His vision was blurring. It wasn't working.

"Stop, Arlo." Director Quartermaine tightened his grip on the young man's wrist. The Director's voice was faint. Arlo was losing his hearing. All of his senses were beginning to fade, but there seemed to be no slowing the flood of blood pouring from his chest.

"But you're dying—I can help—this is what I do—"

"No." Director Quartermaine tried to breathe deeply, his breath jagged. "You can't risk yourself to save me—you'll lose all your senses in the process. Perhaps even your life. And even that probably wouldn't do any good for me—we're different. We don't heal the same as others." Director Quartermaine smiled. "I knew I was too old for field work," he muttered.

Arlo refused to move his hands, but the corner of his mouth lifted a little.

"No offense, but I think I have you beat by a few decades, Director."

Director Quartermaine chuckled. "Well, you look good for your age." His body spasmed slightly, and he coughed, flecks of blood speckling his chin.

Just as Arlo looked up, the Glamour lifted, and Agent Harpy turned into Acacia. It was the last thing Arlo saw before he went entirely blind.

"It was *you*," Arlo said as he felt someone grab hold of him. He felt his mouth form the words, "*How could you*?" but Arlo couldn't hear anything happening around him, deaf to the noise, deaf to his own voice. He struggled against the grip, but it was useless. He was still too weakened from trying to heal Director Quartermaine.

Director Quartermaine. Arlo's heart beat rapidly in his chest at the thought of him. He had no idea if he was even still alive. He couldn't hear anything, he couldn't see, he couldn't smell. He felt trapped by his own body, betrayed, and useless.

"It's okay, Arlo. We're bringing you back to Fae," Salvatore said, not realizing Arlo couldn't hear him. He looked over at Acacia before glancing down at Zaria, who was hunched over Director Quartermaine, her arms spread protectively across his chest. "What about her?" he asked his wife.

"We don't need her," Acacia spat, not bothering to look at her sister. "She's a traitor. We have who the Autumn Queen wants—now let's go."

"Where's Harpy?" Zaria yelled as Acacia reopened a portal.

Acacia glanced back over her shoulder. She narrowed her eyes and sneered.

"Hmm—I do hope you find her—before it's too late."

Freya locked eyes with Director Quartermaine as she walked toward the portal. Her bottom lip quivered as her translucent eyes watered. He nodded at her, and she nodded back. She touched Arlo's arm and quickly faded from Director Quartermaine's sight.

The Sanguines disappeared through the portal with Arlo, leaving Zaria with Director Quartermaine. As the portal closed, his eyes dissolved back to their usual kind, hazel. His hands remained firmly pressed against his stab wound, with the added pressure of Zaria's hands on top of them.

"I can ease the pain," Zaria admitted softly, "but I can't save you."

Director Quartermaine only shook his head.

"I don't wish to be saved," he said. His breathing was jagged, and every breath hurt his body. Zaria pressed her bloodied hand to the side of his face, gently touching his temple with the tips of her fingers. "Death is not the end, Zaria."

Director Quartermaine closed his eyes.

Zaria closed hers as well.

"*Finn Quartermaine*," she whispered.

Finn Quartermaine was twenty-seven years old again, standing at the Pearl Harbor Memorial in Hawai'i with Miss Sharp. She had just given him his assignment in Chicago in the sixties. He was dressed in a white suit tailored to fit his body perfectly, and he held the briefcase tightly at his side with one hand. With the other, he flipped through the file containing what they knew of the Book of Fate, another of the Infernal Artifacts.

"Finn?"

The familiarity of the voice caught Finn off guard. He froze. *It couldn't be.* The young man with sandy blond hair and clear hazel eyes turned around. His face was scruffy, and just before him—stood his brother.

"Hayden?"

It was as though the marble statue of the famed Corpse Walker had taken on a life of its own as Hayden appeared in the flesh, looking exactly as he had the last time Finn saw him as a child. Hayden's eyes were a brighter shade of blue than Finn remembered, clear and sparkling. They reminded Finn of their mother.

"I'm really proud of you," Hayden said gently as he came closer. Finn clenched his jaw tightly as tears threatened to spill from his eyes. He had wanted to see his brother again for so long. "I'm so *proud* of you."

Finn's eyes welled and the dam finally broke. Tears rolled down his reddened cheeks as Hayden pulled his younger brother into a tight hug. It was an embrace he didn't realize just how much he had missed. Since Hayden left, Finn had spent every night sleeping in his older brother's bed.

He wrapped his arms around his older brother, holding on for dear life.

Zaria stood off to the side, watching as the two brothers reunited. A small smile peeked at the corner of her lips before her eyes wandered around the memorial and landed on the section dedicated to the famed *Corpse Walker.*

Her Glamour had created this false memory for the Director to slip into, one that would put him at ease as he faded from her quickly. She only blinked once or twice before the memory gently dissolved. In only a breath, she went from standing at the memorial to sitting in the office building, with her bloodied hands pressed against the Director's body. Director Quartermaine's heartbeat beneath her hand was barely a flutter, slowing until it stopped altogether.

She sat back on her shins, pulling her bloodied hands into her lap.

"I'm sorry, Director," Zaria uttered softly. "I'm so sorry."

The elevator doors opened and Agent Eiríksdóttir emerged holding a file in her hands. Her eyes widened as she spotted Director Quartermaine on the ground. Immediately, she dropped to her knees beside Zaria.

"What happened?" she asked as her eyes began to water. She turned her head, expecting to see Harpy. Agent Eiríksdóttir frowned and jumped back, hand reaching towards her hip. "Who the hell are you?"

"Zaria Aster," she said softly. "I'm Fey."

Agent Eiríksdóttir leaped another step away from her, causing herself to trip as she scrambled into the corner. Zaria wiped the tears from her cheeks, smearing the Director's blood on her face. She then used her sleeve.

"I don't mean any harm," Zaria said quietly.

"You're standing over the dead body of my boss," Agent Eiríksdóttir said as she pulled out her revolver and pointed it at Zaria. Her hands were shaking, and her eyes were beginning to water. Mentally, Agent Eiríksdóttir had to keep telling her to pull herself together. Now was not the time to cry. "I have iron frangible bullets."

"I didn't do this," Zaria said softly. She started wiping her hands on her clothes as she got to her feet, not paying much attention to the revolver in Agent Eiríksdóttir's hands. She was fully aware that if Agent Eiríksdóttir did have iron frangible bullets—and Zaria wouldn't be surprised if she did—they would definitely hurt her and potentially kill her. But there were more important things to worry about. "I know you probably won't believe me. You have no reason to—you don't know me—I don't have a lot of time to explain, but we have to find Agent Harpy."

"What happened to Harpy?"

"I don't know. But she's here somewhere," she said. "I'll explain what I know, but can we at least start looking?" Agent Eiríksdóttir took a moment to consider her options. She then lowered her revolver, but Zaria shook her head. "Keep it out," Zaria said as she noticed the agent move to put it away.

"Why?"

"Just in case," Zaria said, looking down. "Fey did this. Fey killed your boss. Fey kidnapped Harpy. Fey took Arlo."

"Took him back to—"

"Yeah. The Fae Realm."

"This would be cool in other circumstances." Agent Eiríksdóttir sighed, cautiously moving towards Zaria and beginning to follow her. "I have a question."

"Just one?" Zaria asked, somewhat sarcastically as the two of them walked down the hall, looking down every aisle and in every cubicle for Agent Harpy.

"Who is Echo-01?" Agent Eiríksdóttir held up a picture of a young girl. Zaria stared at the picture for a moment before lifting her gaze to meet the agent's.

She then sighed.

"She's what they're after," Zaria said with a very gentle shrug of her shoulders as though she had given up. "She's the *Book of Fate*. And we can't let them get to her."

# CHAPTER FIFTEEN

*15*

Even though he was completely blind to his surroundings, Arlo knew the Sanguines brought him back to Fae. He could feel it. The air was different. The temperature was different. Still, he couldn't help but think of Director Quartermaine. His hands were still damp with the Director's blood. He curled his fingers over the wetness on his palms. His fingers were beginning to feel sticky as the blood congealed.

*'Go to sleep,'* Arlo heard a whisper coming from inside of his own head. It was Freya. *'Go to sleep, Arlo. I'll handle it.'*

He couldn't. Arlo shook his head. *No*, he thought.

*'What do you mean 'no'?'*

*No*, he thought again.

Arlo couldn't see, hear, or smell, but Freya could.

She pulled herself away from Arlo's body, following him like an echo rather than fully immersed in his physical form. No one there could see her anyway. Fae was unlike anything she had ever seen or could have imagined. They were surrounded by the beauty of autumn, but the trees remained full of crunchy orange leaves, and the ground was coated with just as many. They floated across the sky in the wind like music notes. She could understand why, even if Arlo had known who he really was, he might have wanted to stay. Freya couldn't deny that she likely would have stayed too. Squinting in the distance, she could almost swear she could see winter ahead. A chill ran down her spine when she thought of the war the Autumn Queen wanted to wage against the Winter Court. Had she still had a beating heart, it would have fallen to the pit of her stomach.

Freya frowned, wondering what would happen if the Autumn Queen got her hands on the book as she was now. She wondered what the Queen would do to the little girl. It made Freya sick to even think about.

***

When you spend such a long time alone, ten years ago could feel like yesterday. Freya could recall clearly when Finn Quartermaine returned from his trip to Hawai'i in

1992 when Mrs. Sharp had called him and requested he visit immediately. Freya had stood patiently in his office, waiting for him to speak as he continued to pace the room. Her large eyes watched as he walked back and forth in the small area between his desk and the door.

"Finn," she said softly. He stopped in his tracks. Slowly, he turned to look at Freya. He was fifty-seven years old. His dark blond hair was beginning to salt into a sandy color, and wear from the job tugged at his hazel eyes. "What happened?" she asked.

"It doesn't make any sense," he said.

"What happened?" Freya asked again, her voice remaining calm and soothing.

At first, he hesitated, and Freya had wondered if, at last, he'd found something he would not confide to her.

Ever since that first day in the theater, she had wandered through her death beside him as he navigated his life. He'd sought solace from her when complications arose with his missions or when he felt isolated from his past, from the world. For Finn, Freya was his most trusted friend, his truest ally in a world of unknown treachery and darkness.

In return, he provided Freya with the only companionship she'd had for nearly a century. The two of them, separated by the very plane of the material world, had found a crack, reached out, and found each other even as the abyss of loneliness threatened to engulf them.

"It's a girl," he said finally. She didn't know what to make of his words, and it was clear that he didn't either. Freya noticed his hands were shaking slightly as he ran them through his hair. "She had these red markings all over her body, but they weren't just markings. They were—they were like—runes carved in her skin. And the nether energy she gave off—I've never felt anything so strong, not since I had Death's Scythe in my hands. When I got close and touched her arm," Finn stopped and looked down at his hands. "My fingers turned black. The same thing happened when I was a kid. It was something I'll never forget. It's the girl, Freya. The Book of Fate is a human girl."

"So what does this mean?" she asked, though she could guess based simply on the look in Finn's eyes. There were a lot of things she didn't have to worry about, being dead and all. But Finn wasn't dead.

"I'm scared," he whispered. He took a deep breath before continuing. "I'm scared for the Fate of humanity. If the Infernals decided they needed their artifacts to become human, then something a lot worse than demons is coming."

"Is she going to be okay?"

"I couldn't tell you."

Freya watched as Director Quartermaine slumped down into his chair. He had never looked so small. Not in the twenty-five years she had spent learning every facial expression and tick. The imposing presence of Director Finn Quartermaine had gone. He was just Finn. Finley. A scared boy from a small town in Pennsylvania.

"Finn," she said softly. "Are you going to be okay?" Freya had learned much about Finn during their time together. He was her only friend. No one else could see her, or if they could, they never made it known. Only him, when he found her in the Oriental Theater with the Vestiges. That moment changed both of them forever.

***

"Where are we going?"

Freya was pulled from her memory by the sound of Acacia's screeching voice.

"We're bringing him to Bane," Salvatore answered.

"We should bring him to the Queen," she said sharply.

"Look at him, Acacia. He's not in any shape to be seen by the Queen right now. We need to take him to Bane first. That's protocol. Why would we bring him to the Queen like this?"

Acacia sighed, but she knew he was right. She was just itching to bring him to the Queen for a huge reason that was standing right beside her.

Arlo made absolutely no noise. He didn't utter a sound. He walked with the Sanguines only because he was being directed to, and Salvatore's grip was so tight around Arlo's arm that even Freya felt uncomfortable under his hold. She pulled herself fully back into his body.

*'Arlo,'* Freya said again in thought.

Her voice was loud in his head, as he was still deaf to all other noises.

Arlo very subtly shook his head.

*No,* he thought again.

*'Why not?'*

*I can't.*

He could hear her sigh. Having Freya also occupy his body while he was conscious was an unusual sensation because the sigh sounded to him the way it would if he sighed. He could hear the whistling of the air in his mind. It was strange and confusing.

*I couldn't save him,* Arlo thought. His mind was still trying to grasp the shock of letting Director Quartermaine die. *I save everyone, and I couldn't…*

*'Is that what this is about?'* Freya questioned.

Arlo turned his head to the side as if to look away from her, forgetting for a moment that they were communicating inside of his mind.

Salvatore noticed the movement and tried to speak to him. Acacia raised her eyebrows. Salvatore shrugged. "Either he's still deaf or his acting skills have improved significantly during his time on Terra."

Acacia rolled her eyes at his comment.

*'You can't save everybody, Arlo. It's just not possible.'*

*But I made him stop,* Arlo thought. *He was caught off guard. He was confused—if I had just let him kill Salvatore, he'd probably still—*

*'I'm pretty sure this Fey lady would have killed Finn anyway if that happened. With much more savagery than she did.'* She paused. *'I think he would have been okay with how his life ended, working to protect the people he cared about. Working to protect the future of the world…'* her voice sounded like it caught in her throat slightly. *'He always said that death sounded like such a peaceful adventure. Maybe he even found his brother on the other side.'*

Arlo sighed.

*You care about him a lot, don't you?*

*'I do. He was all I had for a long time.'*

*I'm sorry.*

Arlo heard a shaky breath in his ears as Freya steeled herself.

*'We don't have time for this, Arlo. You need to pull yourself together—or let me.'*

*Are you going to kill them?*

*'I don't want to kill anyone, Arlo. But it's dangerous here. We don't belong here. Something bad is going to happen, and we need to get back to Terra. Quickly.'*

*Where are we going right now?*

*'They're bringing you to someone named Bane,'* Freya answered.

*Okay,* Arlo thought. He knew that he would be subjected to Glamour as soon as Lord Bane heard he'd spent time on Terra with Zaria. *Here's what we're going to do—*

***

Salvatore dragged Arlo to the FeyForce headquarters where Lord Bane sat with Commander Kall-An, both of whom immediately looked up at them from the noise and sudden disruption.

"What are you two—" Commander Kall-An's eyes fell onto Arlo as he sucked in air through his nose. "That was an order. You two disobeyed—"

"The Terrans are hiding something," Acacia interrupted. "Arlo's strong enough to heal our Queen, but he couldn't even heal a supposed Terran who almost killed Salvatore."

"It seems Salvatore's a weak link since this is the second time he almost died on Terra," Commander Kall-An sneered. "Maybe we should reconsider the position he holds on this team."

"You're not listening to me," Acacia said, actually stomping her foot. "That man—something was wrong with him. It was like he was draining Salvatore's life force. What kind of Terran does that?" She glanced at Arlo. "Except his kind."

"So you think this man had exposure to the Book of Fate as well?" Lord Bane asked as he slowly stood up from the chair.

Acacia lowered her gaze.

"I don't know what to think. But if there's more like him, maybe we don't even need the Book," she said. "If we can find other Terrans who can do what Arlo did—"

"Well we would've had another if you hadn't killed him," Salvatore muttered.

"I didn't have a choice," Acacia snapped at her husband. "He would have never helped us anyway."

"You killed him?"

"With the 'Weapon of Death' meant for a Samoan goddess." Acacia fished it from her cloak and threw it on the table. The weapon was shaped like a spear with teeth on both sides, and it was caked with Director Quartermaine's drying blood. "An agent led me to it. They had it in their facility. They have all kinds of weapons there, Lord Bane. I don't trust their organization. What is a *human* organization doing with the weapon of a *goddess*? What are they doing? I have a lot of questions and zero answers."

Lord Bane opened his mouth to answer, but Arlo suddenly collapsed before Salvatore could steady him. "What's wrong with him?"

"He tried to save him, and he couldn't. Like I said," Acacia grumbled as she crossed her slender arms over her chest. "If anyone was listening to me—"

Arlo's eyes suddenly shot open. His pupils had split as Freya's features began to emerge through his own. His body slowly rose from the ground, and levitated about a foot from the floor. His hair grew longer and waved rapidly in a wind that wasn't there.

"What's happening?" Commander Kall-An demanded as Salvatore moved away from Arlo and closer to Acacia. Acacia's eyes darted between Arlo's body and the weapon she had thrown onto the table. Salvatore noticed and slowly shook his head, warning her not to try. She couldn't kill Arlo; she must know that.

Freya's possession of Arlo threw their hands in the air. Every time their body moved, there was a strange myriad of layered colors that followed every movement like a visible echo of each limb. Instantly, Freya rose her right arm up in the air, and all three of the Fey flew backward, knocking into different walls of the room, leaving only Acacia standing.

"Acacia Aster," the voice said, loud and booming. "You deserve to be punished for your crimes."

Arlo's right arm shot out toward her, and Freya gripped the air. Acacia rose from the ground and gripped at her neck. Despite nothing being pressed against her throat, she felt like she was suffocating. She kicked at the air, trying to find footing. Arlo's left arm aimed at the wall. His palm faced out, and Freya turned his hand slowly, first clockwise, then counter-clockwise as though she were opening a safe.

Slowly, a portal began to open right there in their headquarters.

"Impossible..." Commander Kall-An whispered from the ground as his eyes grew wide, staring at the opening into Terra.

While Arlo was distracted with Acacia, Lord Bane quickly got to his feet and rushed to another door in the room to the left of the entryway near the closet. When he returned a moment later, Freya's hands were still raised, holding Acacia and controlling the portal. But now Bane also held something in his arms. He shoved the petite blonde girl ahead of him, firmly grasping her shoulders. She had a thick vine wrapped around her head and through her mouth that muffled her voice. Her eyes were wide and terrified.

"Leave, and I'll kill her," he threatened.

Acacia struggled to breathe.

"Is she supposed to mean something to me?" the voice boomed from Arlo's mouth as frightened tears flowed from the blonde girl's eyes. As Freya didn't know who she was, she felt invincible to whatever leverage they were trying to use against her.

"Your Bride-To-Be doesn't mean anything to you?"

"*Bride—*?"

Freya began to lose hold on Arlo's body as he stirred. Clearly, the girl meant something to Arlo if she could shock him out of his stupor. The portal she had opened slowly started closing on itself as Arlo fought to regain his consciousness. She was only fully in control when Arlo was asleep or unconscious.

Freya released Acacia, who quickly dropped down to the ground. Acacia gasped for air, wheezing thickly, filling her lungs that had been absent of air for much longer than she liked. Freya used her Nether energy to rip the vine from Marigold's mouth and shove Lord Bane away from her. Before Freya could do anything else, Arlo completely awoke. Arlo's body fell to the ground in a heap, and Freya's spirit tumbled out of his body as if she'd been kicked.

Arlo began to regain his hearing, and although he was still blind, he could feel Marigold rush toward him. He could hear her sobbing, her hands grabbing at his clothes.

"Come on, Arlo!" Freya shouted at him. "Follow my voice!"

Arlo grabbed Marigold by the wrist and quickly scrambled to his feet as he ran toward Freya's voice. She was standing in the center of the portal, her arms and feet braced against the edges to keep it from collapsing.

Lord Bane watched as Arlo passed through the portal. He could have sworn that for a second, he saw a translucent outline of a young woman.

"*Dioscuri*..." Ignatius Bane muttered quietly as the portal shut before him, and Arlo's body disappeared from sight.

Something they had only believed to be a myth was real.

Dioscuri.

The Divine Twins.

"How dare you threaten my sister!" Acacia snapped as she got up from the ground and stalked toward Lord Bane. Salvatore wasn't quick enough to catch her wrist. "How dare you bring her into this!" She raised her hand to slap

Lord Bane across the face, but he stopped her. Using her wrist, he yanked her toward him and tightened his grip.

"What has gotten into you, Acacia? Stand down. Now!" he snarled.

"What did you call Arlo?" Salvatore asked as Lord Bane released Acacia and shoved her so hard she fell back onto the ground. She didn't immediately get back up this time.

"Dioscuri," Lord Bane said, looking back at the wall where the portal had opened. "I don't know what you brought back to Fae, but that wasn't just Arlo."

"What are we dealing with?"

"I don't know," Lord Bane admitted. He looked down at Acacia who remained on the ground. He offered her his hand, but she ignored it. Lord Bane rolled his eyes and stepped away from her. "But I intend to find out."

"What is Dioscuri?"

"The Greeks believed the Dioscuri were star-crowned, semi-divine twins known as protectors. They were believed to save those in trouble or grave danger." Lord Bane moved to examine where the portal opened. "Was Arlo a twin?" he asked without turning around.

Salvatore and Acacia exchanged glances.

When no answer came, Lord Bane turned his direction to Commander Kall-An, who was also just getting to his feet.

"We're going back to Terra. Suit up," he instructed. He passed a calculating glance over the Sanguines before he and Kall-An exited.

Salvatore strolled toward Acacia and pulled her to her feet slightly more roughly than usual.

"What's gotten into you?"

Acacia turned away from him and looked down at the Weapon of Death still laying flat on the table. The voice of the Autumn Queen echoed in her head as she slowly looked back up at Salvatore.

"What if we went back there and… stayed there?" she asked.

"On Terra? Are you insane? We can't stay on Terra, Acacia. We're Fey. What's wrong?"

She quickly closed her eyes, lashes fluttering.

"You're right," she said, as if to blink away the thoughts. "Just, both of my sisters and everything… and you being in danger," she said, barely whispering the only part that wasn't a lie. "I don't know. It's just been a long day."

Salvatore lifted Acacia's chin with his finger. "Are you going to be okay seeing Zaria again?" he asked. "You know she's going to be there."

"I'll be okay," Acacia whispered in reassurance.

# CHAPTER SIXTEEN

*16*

Beside Poland, in another realm, the Elven King stood in front of a mirror that stretched nearly as high as the ceiling. The mirror was narrow, only two feet in width, with an intricate white design along the edges and a saying that wrapped around the entire perimeter written in old Elvish. The Elven King was a tall man, nearly seven feet in height, and his blackened fingertips pressed together while he stood in observation. His skin was porcelain white, and his long, pale hair flowed over his shoulders to his waist. He wore a regal crown of gold embedded with nothing short of the finest jewels. He tilted his head back slightly, staring at the figures in the mirror. Instead of his own face staring back through the glass, he watched as Salvatore wrapped his arm around Acacia, both staring at the spot where Arlo and Marigold had recently exited through a portal.

"And so the Dioscuri is coming to power," he declared out loud. His bright yellow eyes looked up at the moving portrait hanging on the wall adjacent to the extraordinary mirror. It had a beautiful silver frame, and its delicate, detailed design could have been made only by the Elves. The painting was of a beautiful young woman with porcelain white skin that matched his, only she had black raven hair and piercing blue eyes. His daughter, *Halina*. Her icy eyes were also fixed on the looking glass, purposefully avoiding the King.

"He clearly never loved you," he continued, hand moving toward the mirror, which now showed Arlo with Marigold, her hand clutched tightly in his as he guided her through the other end of the portal. The Elven King's blackened fingertips were almost close enough to graze the silver surface. "Look how quickly he's moved on to that Fey girl."

"It took him a hundred years to even consider it," Halina muttered softly. "I'm not sure I would call that *quick* for a human." Her thin brows were scrunched together, large eyes wider than usual. She appeared almost doll-like as she peered through her frame. Her dress was immaculate even as her face struggled to hide her emotion: heartbreak. Even after a century.

The Elven King cocked a brow at her words as he turned his body to face her portrait entirely. Even as an old oil painting, Halina was just as beautiful as she had been in life. Sometimes it pained him to see her that way, hanging on his wall and tugging at his heartstrings, reminding him every day of what had happened all those years ago. Knowing what caused it. Elves preserved the dead in paintings. The process was rather grueling and somewhat disgusting but well worth it. It was a traditional practice for them, and one the Elven King himself did not directly partake in. Still, he was well aware of what went on to have her painting hanging before him.

She still loved Arlo, even now.

"It wasn't a hundred years for *him*," the Elven King said in reminder. "He spent most of it in Fae. Their time works differently. You know that." He wasn't sure why he said it. His daughter's pain was written on her face, yet he felt compelled to remind her again of her role in history. Perhaps he did it to deflect from his own sense of guilt. Perhaps he was simply Fated to cause his daughter pain. His gaze lowered at the thought, but only for a moment. He was quick not to let her notice.

Halina only shook her head. She avoided looking at her father, even while she had his full attention. She could feel his stare watching her every movement. "I can't believe I caused all of this." She looked down at her hands, her own palms and fingertips were blackened. "I shouldn't have stolen it."

The Elven King turned away from her to walk back toward the looking glass as it faded back into a mirror image of the room they stood in. He set his jaw, staring sightlessly at his reflection. "This was Fated to happen, Halina."

"Humanity has its own free will," she argued.

"That is a myth, my child. Everyone has a part to play."

"Did you know?" she asked, her eyes finally moving to look up at her father. He turned around to face her, his fingertips pressed together before him. The Elven King did that often when he was focused, and sometimes when he was worried.

However, things rarely worried him.

"Did I know *what*?" he asked, though he had a feeling at what her question would be. He tried to still the flash of anger in his stomach—though it wasn't directed at his daughter. He'd always known this question would come. In truth, he was surprised she hadn't asked sooner. She hadn't once brought it up previously—but he'd always known that seeing Arlo again might trigger it.

"That you were going to kill me?" While she looked in the direction of her father, it took Halina a long time for her eyes to finally lift high enough to meet his.

"I knew before you were born." The Elven King turned away from her and glanced at the mirror. "That was my curse."

Halina tilted her head, going over his words in her mind. His curse. Before she could open her mouth to speak again, he continued quietly, slowly at first.

"When I was just a child, the Infernal known as Destiny trusted my father with the Book of Fate. The Infernals are an interesting sort—Destiny appeared as a small boy with black hair and pearl white eyes. He looked no older than a child. He told my father never to open it because he would not like what it said. He would not like knowing." The Elven King sighed as he looked up at the mirror. He pressed his fingers against the glass. "Knowledge is power—but it can also be damning."

"You opened it?" Halina's voice was shaky as she asked.

The Elven King turned his head to face Halina again. Slowly, he nodded.

"I opened it."

He added pressure to his fingers pressing against the mirror, and the image began to change to reflect the memory he recalled. It showed him as a much younger man, his hair tied back neatly, though even if loose, it would have been far shorter then than it was now. The Elven King pulled his hand away from the mirror as he looked at his younger self in the looking glass, running to find where his father had stored the book.

"We were in the middle of a war with another kingdom, and I wanted to know what would become of it," he continued, still watching himself. "We were losing. I didn't understand. What good was having the Book of Fate if we weren't going to use it to our advantage and learn the outcome?" His voice had grown louder as he spoke. Now he paused. Halina waited silently. The King took a deep, shuddering breath before whispering, "We would be victorious, I would learn, but at a price. I became King later that same week when my father was murdered. I learned that it didn't matter what I did to try to change the outcomes of what I had read. It all ended the same. It all funneled down to one path." The Elven King watched as his younger self flipped through those golden pages of a very white and pristine book that seemed to blacken with his touch, just as his fingers did. The Elven King looked down at his large, slender hands. The tips of his fingers were still black—a reminder, and a curse.

"I learned that I would also have a beautiful bride who would provide me with three children, but only two of which would outlive me." He watched as his younger self continued to flip through the pages, drunk on the knowledge. "I learned that I would be the reason you died—and the loss of you would be too much for my beautiful bride to bear. I learned so much that day, and I hadn't even met your mother yet." The Elven King stepped away from the mirror as his younger self grew stricken with grief, longing for a love he hadn't yet felt.

"I was worried to love, I was worried to have you—but then I became King, and everything the book had told me was pushed to the back of my mind. Too many things to worry about. Too many things to do. When I met your mother, I didn't think of the curse—nor did I think of it when she had your brothers. It was only when you arrived—my daughter, Halina. Everything the Book had said would happen, happened. It was inevitable."

"You should have just let me be with Arlo," Halina said softly. "You wouldn't have had to lose either of us." She glanced over at her mother's portrait. While her mother sat in her frame, her head hung, and her half-closed eyes stared unseeing at her empty hands. She never moved or spoke anymore. She had clearly retreated to a space in this life where Fate could no longer touch her.

The Elven King shook his head, and the memory of his younger self faded from the mirror.

"It was *Fate*, Halina. Fate unravels exactly as it should. I tried to change it once to save my father, and he died anyway. You cannot stop it. I would have let you be with a Terran boy if I knew you would be alive—but it wouldn't work that way. It doesn't work that way. The theater had to be set ablaze."

She huffed, displeased with her father's response. But she didn't know what else to say. He watched as Halina's gaze dropped to her father's hands before looking at her own blackened fingertips. "Well it wasn't very big," she muttered, "considering it's supposed to have the Fate of all. It was actually small when you consider the scale of the universe and the beings within it."

"It only shows the Fate of those who are in possession of it. You cannot see the Fate of someone else."

"You saw mine—"

"Because it was my fault. It was always going to be my fault." He slowly returned to stand in front of Halina's portrait. "But the Book had an ending—"

"Your death, right?" she asked. "I assume it would end with your death based on what you said. For the reader, at least."

"I thought that too—but it stopped eleven years ago. In 1991." The Elven King glanced at the looking glass again. "And now I know why."

"I'm not following," Halina admitted softly.

"The Book became a living, Terran girl. *Human.* I suppose she's technically an artifact still—in 1991—when she was born. The book ended in 1991 because it changed forms." The King frowned at the thought. "It was always going to change forms. It always knew."

Halina tilted her head. "What's coming, father? What will happen to Arlo—and all of them? What's going to happen to the world?"

The Elven King shook his head. "I do not know." He gently touched the front of the portrait, and she lifted her hand to line her fingers with his. "But you are safe, my daughter."

"Because I'm already dead."

"Death is not the end, Halina. Surely you know that by now."

"But this is not what I wanted, either." She looked over at the portrait of her mother on the opposing wall. It was still and lifeless. Her mother rarely made what the Elven King would refer to as 'appearances,' because seeing Halina hanging across from her was often too much for her to handle. "Where does mother go? When she's not here?"

The two considered the motionless woman on the opposing wall.

"Probably the Underworld," he said eventually. "But I can't be certain. She might just be present with us, but also not. She was really lost when you died. I never found her again—not really, at least." He glanced over at the portrait. Halina's mother was beautiful, an older, more elegant version of Halina. She had the same raven-black hair and pale porcelain skin. But unlike Halina's painting, there was a very distant and cold look in her mother's blue eyes. They were clouded over, vacant. "Our kind don't belong there though," the Elven King continued. "In the Underworld. It's best to stay here—because you may never find your way back."

Halina remained staring at her mother's painting sympathetically, but she nodded. She couldn't help but think of searching for her. She wondered if she could speak with her mother's soul, or perhaps bring her back and end the pained emptiness of her gaze. She kept her eyes locked on her mother's painting while her father nodded his goodbye and left for supper. Halina inhaled deeply and sighed. Her hands fumbled with the cloth laying on the table next to her.

The Portrait Dimension connected paintings, and she could travel from one to another if there was one nearby, but she never went to her mother's. Not since the last time.

Part of her was afraid of her.

She could recall so vividly the way her living mother had looked at her when her portrait had first been hung. The grief on her face. The pain in her blue eyes. Halina's mother had gripped the edges of her frame so tightly in her hands that its intricate details cut into her palms and drew blood from her hands. But her mother didn't care. All the Elven Queen cared about was that her youngest child and only daughter was dead.

"You're dead, Halina! You're dead," she shrieked at the painting and collapsed to the floor. It was all her mother could make herself say. Halina couldn't comfort her. She could only sit and watch from behind the canvas as her mother slipped into an abyss of anguish and grief before her eyes. Halina sat on the floor of her painting, watching as the light in her mother's eyes clouded and dimmed with each passing day. The kindness of her blue eyes turned to a cold gray, and not long after that, she became unresponsive. A shell of her former self. There was no longer any life in her, no longer any spirit.

Eventually, the Queen stopped visiting Halina's painting. Halina had slipped through different portraits of their palace, trying to find her mother. Instead, she heard her father's voice echoing through the hall.

"That is not my wife," said the Elven King. "She died long before her body. It was only a matter of time. I'm sure you will be able to make the necessary funeral arrangements…"

Halina had clapped her hands over her mouth as she ran back to her own portrait in the mirror room and collapsed to the floor in agony. Though her mother had not been herself for some time, the pain of truly losing her broke her heart, or what was left of it.

It was a bittersweet moment for her painting to be brought in and hung across from Halina's. Her mother cried, and she cried, as the two were able to embrace for the first time in years. But it took mere weeks for her mother to grow distant again, as if the vacancy that had claimed her life still gripped her in death.

Her pupils constricted, and her hands gripped Halina's arms too tightly.

"You're not my daughter! My daughter is dead!"

The Elven Queen had not comprehended that she, herself, was also dead.

Halina continued to stare at the portrait of the woman who sat in the painting across from hers. Most days, her mother didn't do anything. She didn't look at anything, she didn't say anything, she barely moved, appearing as any ordinary painting in the world. She just sat there, lifeless. Other times, she would briefly come back, her eyes a crystal blue, and she would flash her beautiful and welcoming smile at Halina.

But those moments didn't last very long.

While Halina sat there and waited for one, it never came. Not tonight. Halina parted her lips as she sighed and took one last look at the mirror.

# CHAPTER SEVENTEEN

*17*

The S.M.O.K.E. & M.I.R.R.O.R.S. building was unusually quiet as Arlo, Marigold, and Freya stepped through the portal. Arlo's vision was beginning to come back and he squinted as if trying to see in a dimly lit room. The portal had reopened to the same spot they had left, and Marigold's breath caught sharply when she saw the large pool of congealing blood on the floor. Arlo's heart sank again when he thought of Director Quartermaine, but the Director's body was gone, and Zaria was nowhere to be found.

Marigold swayed and her knees buckled, her hand pulling from Arlo's as she sank to the ground. Her breath came in short gasps and tears spilled unbidden from her terrified eyes. She instinctively wrapped her arms around her legs as her mind processed the situation: She was no longer in Fae, there was blood everywhere—a lot of blood, Lord Bane had threatened to kill her, and Arlo was—he was—

Arlo dropped down onto one knee next to her, automatically resting his hands on her shoulders in a comforting gesture.

"Are you alright?" he asked. Marigold reacted as if she'd been hit. She scooted back from him, her body trembling in panic. Arlo's face furrowed with concern. He slowly raised his hands in surrender. "I don't mean any harm to you, Marigold."

"What are you?" she asked, her voice was small and shaky.

Arlo inhaled deeply and sat down on the floor before her. He passed a hand over his face, and Marigold was surprised to see that he also looked overwhelmed, even exhausted.

There was a long, drawn-out moment of silence between them as he thought over how to phrase it. There weren't exactly multiple ways to say what he needed to say. There was only one way to say it. Admittance. Complete disclosure. He sighed as he glanced over at Freya, who nodded. Marigold followed the direction of Arlo's eyes and furrowed her brows when she saw nothing there.

"What are you looking at?" she asked sharply, but he didn't answer. That was something that he could tell her at another time. The last thing he wanted to do was overwhelm her further. She was already clearly frightened, and with good reason. Arlo was sure she had never left Fae, and now, within moments, she'd been used as a hostage and dragged into an unfamiliar realm with someone—something—she'd never seen before.

"I'm not Fey," he finally admitted. "I'm not like you, or your kind. I'm not from Fae. Everything I had known, and probably everything you were told about me, none of it was true. It was all a lie." He leaned back against the wall next to her. She kept her eyes fixed on his face even as he stared into the middle distance of the office, occasionally glancing at a fixed point somewhere between them and the pool of blood. "It was all fake. It was all pretend." He sighed, thinking over the words that had come out of his mouth. It was still weird to say it all out loud. "I'm human."

Marigold's thin eyebrows scrunched together in a frown before a small, forced smile began to spread across her face. Then she laughed, but it sounded unnatural. "Is this a joke? How could you be human? You healed the Queen. Mortals can't do that."

"I said I was *human*, Marigold. I never said I was mortal."

"What does that even mean?"

"It's hard to explain," he said, glancing at Freya.

"And what do you keep looking at?" she asked as she once more tried to follow the direction of his eyes as they landed on that fixed point in space.

"I have a sister—Freya—she's dead—" he said plainly, and rather bluntly.

"Arlo!" Freya snapped, not liking or appreciating his delivery.

"Sorry," he said to Freya with a shrug, though to Marigold he appeared to be talking to nothing. "There's not exactly another way to phrase that." He returned his focus to Marigold whose large eyes were quickly moving from him to a space just to the left of Freya's head.

She forced herself to take a few slow breaths before raising her hands to rub her temples. Arlo smiled a little to himself. He knew he was doing a terrible job explaining, but this was the first time he'd ever tried. He scanned her face. In his few days on Terra, he'd forgotten how beautiful Marigold was. Now he was also struck by her confused, tear-stained face, and he felt a twinge of pain in his chest as her eyes searched his, clearly seeking a lifeline in the chaos.

He fumbled for words, trying to continue his bumbling explanation. "Um, I went to Fae in 1903—when I was supposed to die in a fire—but was saved by the Book of Fate. Unfortunately, my sister did die, but she kind of haunts me."

"I don't *haunt* you, we're linked."

"Whatever you want to call it," he said, mindlessly waving his hand at his sister, keeping his eyes on Marigold. "She doesn't care about the technicalities, Freya." Arlo started to get back to his feet and dusted off his uniform before reaching his hand out to Marigold. "Honestly, this is all still new to me too. I don't blame you for being scared and overwhelmed. Zaria could explain better than I could."

Marigold stared at his hand for a moment before looking up at him.

"You found Zaria?"

He nodded, and his heart spasmed embarrassingly as Marigold's eyes lit up. He shrugged. "Well, I *did* find her. I have to find her again. I have no idea where everyone went." He wiggled the fingers of his outstretched hand. "Come on. It'll be alright." Marigold finally took his hand, and he helped her to her feet as he turned to Freya. "Can you find them?"

She nodded and vanished.

Marigold crossed her arms over her chest and averted her gaze as she looked around. The two stood awkwardly next to each other, unsure exactly what to do.

"I've never been to Terra," she said quietly.

"Don't worry," Arlo reassured. He hesitated before gently touching her arm, just under the elbow. "I'm still me—Arlo—you know. I've learned more about myself, but it's still me. I won't let anyone hurt you. I promise."

Marigold looked up at him, her eyes meeting his. She finally nodded.

Freya reappeared, and Arlo quickly shoved his hands into his pockets.

"They're at the hospital," she said to Arlo. "Some of the agents on the first floor were talking about it. Agent Harpy is in pretty bad condition. We should go. I'm sure you can help her better than they can. If you let me, I can get us there quickly."

Arlo nodded. His sense of smell still hadn't entirely come back yet, but it was faint, and he could smell the lingering scent of blood on the floor.

He turned to Marigold.

"Will you trust me?" he asked.

Marigold narrowed her eyes. She inhaled sharply through her nose and let out a small breath through her parted lips. Finally, she nodded.

Freya touched Arlo's shoulder and slipped into his body just as he closed his eyes.

When they opened again, his pupils split.

Marigold's eyes widened, and she took an involuntary step back before forcing herself to stop. Freya used Arlo's hand again, outstretching his left. His hand turned clockwise then counterclockwise. A small flicker of fire sparked as a portal grew out of thin air. The sharp smell of hospital disinfectant wafted through.

"For the love of gourd," Marigold whispered softly.

"After you," the voice said from Arlo's mouth, though it wasn't Arlo's. It was a mixture of his with an echo of femininity attached to it. It was unique, loud, and commanding. Marigold jumped a little at the sound of it before nodding. She stepped through the portal, and the Dioscuri followed. With a wave of their right hand, the portal disappeared.

They had stepped into a custodial closet in the nearest county hospital. The Dioscuri opened the door and peered into the hallway. Their split pupils scanned the rooms as they walked down the hall, looking through each window for Zaria and Agent Harpy, with Marigold trailing closely behind.

"Can I help you?" a nurse said, nearly bumping into the Dioscuri.

"No," their voice said in unison as they continued down the hallway. Marigold apologized and quickly ran after them. They stopped at one of the patient doors and flung it open without touching it.

Agent Eiríksdóttir and Zaria both jumped up defensively. Agent Eiríksdóttir's hand flew to her gun, but she hesitated at the sight of Arlo. She squinted at his split pupils, glancing at Zaria for help. Zaria had also risen in shock when the Dioscuri stepped through the door, but her eyes were now glued to her younger sister, her expression confused but also slightly relieved.

"Arlo? You scared the shit out of me," Agent Eiríksdóttir exclaimed. "I almost shot you." She wiped her forehead and put her gun away, taking Zaria's relief as a sign of safety. "What is wrong with your eyes?"

"Lord Bane called them the Dioscuri," Marigold said as she closed the door behind them. She met her older sister's eyes as she chewed on her bottom lip.

Agent Eiríksdóttir frowned at the mention of Dioscuri, and she stared at Arlo curiously, not quite sure which pupil to focus on. "Freya?"

They nodded.

"Terrifying," Agent Eiríksdóttir admitted, "but so cool."

"Marigold?" Zaria said softly, blinking her eyes rapidly. "What are you doing here?"

"Lord Bane threatened me—the Dioscuri saved me."

The Dioscuri turned around at the mention. They closed their eyes and nodded their head as Freya left the body. Arlo's head rolled forward and quickly jolted up as he blinked several times, his pupils returning to normal. He rubbed at his temples. "That's going to take some getting used to."

Agent Eiríksdóttir stared at him. "What the hell, Arlo?"

He only shrugged. "She's strong," he said, looking at Freya.

Freya shook her head. "No, *we're* strong," she corrected before nodding toward Agent Harpy who lay unconscious in the hospital bed. "You're needed."

Arlo forced himself to look away from where Zaria had wrapped Marigold in a warm embrace. He turned to focus on the figure in the bed behind Agent Eiríksdóttir.

"What happened to her?" he asked, acknowledging Agent Harpy as he looked at her bandages. He clenched his jaw.

"Acacia cut off her arm and nearly blinded her in one eye."

Arlo's mouth fell open. It felt so senseless. Harpy had already been in fairly bad condition when she'd been used to lure him and Director Quartermaine to the eighth floor. Acacia must have cut off her arm in the few minutes before she'd come back disguised as Harpy. Unless it had been Acacia pretending to be her the entire time. He frowned, lost in his thoughts.

"I took her pain away," Zaria mentioned, still hugging her younger sister. "But—" she shrugged. "Obviously I can't heal her."

Arlo lifted the soaked bandages covering the stub of Harpy's left arm. The flesh was partially blackened as if it had been burned by the Acacia's knife. Arlo's hand hovered over the exposed muscle and bone. “If she used the same weapon she used to kill Director Quartermaine, I’m not sure I can heal her either,” Arlo admitted as he stepped back slightly from the hospital bed. “Harpy led her to a Samoan spear known as the Weapon of Death,” he said, looking over at Agent Eiríksdóttir. A shudder ran through his body as he considered the injury.

He knew FeyForce training strongly discouraged using unknown weapons in combat. Acacia would have been well-familiar with this directive, yet she’d purposefully sought out a new weapon and tested it liberally on an already tortured Terran. Maiming the face and cutting off an arm were good tests for a weapon. By doing so, Acacia would have been able to assess both its agility and its power against sinew and bone. She would know whether the blade caused immediate death or whether the process was slow, agonizing. Clearly she’d been pleased with her initial experiments or she wouldn’t have used it against Director Quartermaine.

Arlo shook himself back to the present moment. “Do you know anything about that weapon?”

Agent Eiríksdóttir paled. “It’s called Fa’amategataua, and it’s believed to be able to kill anything. Nafanua never had to use it, so we never knew exactly if the myths were true.”

"I think it's safe to just assume that *all* mythology is true at this point," Arlo said.

Agent Eiríksdóttir laughed even though Arlo wasn't trying to be funny. She knew deep down he was right. They were cautious, but perhaps not enough. There was still too much doubt, too much incredulity. Maybe if there hadn't been, Finn Quartermaine would still be alive.

Arlo approached the bed again and began to unwrap the bandages over Agent Harpy's face, revealing a very graphic slice through her face down her right eye. A triage nurse had clearly done their best to close the gaping wound, but medical staples could only do so much. Arlo inhaled deeply and put his hand over her wound. He closed his eyes and focused his energy. A faint light flowed from his hand in a thin strand that began to sew her wound back together. When the faint glow had stopped, there was still a very thick scar running the length of her face, and he was frustrated to see that her eye remained clouded and milky. He sighed and briefly let his head hang forward. Healing was something that could only move forward. He could not reach back and reverse the damage to her eye.

He then unwrapped her arm and repeated the process. He managed to regrow a little bit past her elbow, but even as he tried, he couldn't do any more. Arlo still retained most of his senses, only losing sight. Though he kept trying, it still wouldn't work. It was as though something was blocking him. Agent Eiríksdóttir grabbed the bloodied bandages and discarded them.

"Why is it always sight?" he groaned.

"Do you want me to—" Freya started, and Arlo quickly shook his head.

"Not right now," he told Freya. Arlo then turned toward the direction he remembered Zaria had been standing in last. "Can you wake her?" he asked.

It took Zaria a moment to realize he was addressing her. She was still getting used to Arlo talking to Freya, and it was especially confusing without his eyes able to lock their focus onto anyone. Zaria nodded before saying yes.

She finally let go of Marigold and walked over to the hospital bed. Zaria sat down on the other side of Agent Harpy and gently tapped the side of her temple. Agent Harpy's eyes immediately began to flutter as she slowly blinked. Her vision through her damaged eye was blurry at best, with a few dark shadows that she couldn't seem to blink away. But, given that it was a miracle she could see out of the eye at all, she counted herself incredibly lucky. Harpy blinked several times as Arlo slowly came into view.

"Arlo?" she said quietly, unsure if she was really seeing him.

"Welcome back, Agent Harpy." He smiled. "I'm sorry I can't see you, but I'm sure you're as beautiful as I remember."

She laughed a little, before looking down at her arm sympathetically. She raised the nub and sighed. "I'm alive," she said finally. "I can't ask for more than that."

At those words, Arlo immediately got up from the bed and turned away from her.

Zaria hung her head and Agent Eiríksdóttir cleared her throat uncomfortably.

"What?" Agent Harpy said. There was an eerie silence in the hospital room that made a chill run down Harpy's back.

"Director Quartermaine is dead," Arlo said, not turning around. "Acacia killed him. I tried to heal him, but she used a weapon older than me—older than all of us. Probably given to a goddess by Death himself."

The room hung suspended in the silence. Marigold lowered her gaze, feeling out of place in the intimacy of this grief.

Agent Harpy slowly sank back into the mattress of her hospital bed. She was at a loss for words. "A weapon I led her to," she muttered softly.

"It wasn't your fault," Zaria said. "Glamour is powerful, and if Acacia knew your full name, there was no way you could have stopped her. We're lucky she left you alive."

Suddenly, Agent Harpy didn't feel so lucky. She touched the scar on her face. It was nearly three inches long. "I'm sure she wasn't expecting you to find me. She just wanted me to suffer."

"Perhaps," Zaria said quietly.

Agent Harpy's eyes wandered toward the other Fey girl in the room. "What about her?" she asked curiously. "Can we trust her?"

"Marigold's harmless," Zaria said. "She's not a warrior. She never wanted to be." She looked at her hands in her lap. "Honestly, she's probably a better person than all of us in this room. She truly believes people can be—and often are—good."

"This is true." Arlo's voice sounded constricted, and his eyes were closed. "You can trust her."

The blonde Fey girl took a hesitant step toward the hospital bed. Marigold's eyes were glistening with tears. "Acacia did this? I'm so sorry," she uttered. Her mouth hung open slightly as she surveyed Harpy's injuries in a new light. She whispered again, "I'm so sorry."

Agent Harpy closed her eyes and shook her head. She couldn't bring herself to look at her. Marigold looked too much like Acacia.

"We have to go," Arlo said as he turned back around. "If we stay here, we're just going to draw Bane to us. We can't put all these Terrans in danger."

"The Imps are amalgamating," Zaria said. "They'll be ready should Ignatius return."

"Good, because he will." He turned his head in the direction he sensed Freya was in, just beginning to make out hazy shapes in the room. "Freya and I will go back to S.M.O.K.E. & M.I.R.R.O.R.S."

"You should stay here," Zaria told Marigold. "Keep Harpy company. She'll need it."

"But I want to help—" she started to protest. She wasn't sure exactly how she would be helpful in a fight between the Autumn Court and these Terrans, but she felt a responsibility to help. Her sister had caused these people so much pain, and she wanted to help set it right.

Zaria shook her head. "It's too dangerous."

"Acacia won't hurt me." Marigold spoke with conviction, but she wasn't sure how well she actually knew Acacia anymore.

Zaria set her jaw. "Maybe not, but she won't be the only one there. You have to trust me, Marigold. I've only ever had your best interest at heart."

Marigold sighed and nodded as she finally yielded.

As Arlo walked by her, preparing to leave, she reached out and grabbed his hand. Without thinking, she threw her arms around his neck and whispered, "Please be safe." She wasn't sure how much family she'd have at the end of this mess, but she was suddenly certain that she didn't want to lose him.

Slowly, he wrapped his arms around her small frame and pulled her close to him. He could feel her heart beating wildly in her chest, and he raised one hand to the back of her head, gently brushing her satin hair.

"I will," he said quietly, tilting his head down. He could smell her hair—sunshine and leaves. He turned to kiss her cheek just as she turned toward him and his lips brushed up against hers. Arlo pulled back a little, muttering an apology.

The two awkwardly stepped away from each other, Marigold blushing deeply and Arlo blinking as his vision slowly gathered detail.

"Um, Marigold," he began, ignoring the bustle in the room as the group prepared to leave. She raised her eyebrows at him. "I don't know what's going to happen, and I know you didn't ask to get dragged into it, but I just want you to know that I really did mean everything I said to you back in Fae. Back before," he gestured vaguely at the room before taking her hands in his. "And, I know I told you my life was a lie, but I wasn't lying when I told you that… When I told you I…" He drifted off.

Marigold smiled and stood on her tiptoes. She leaned into the kiss. A small smile tugged at the corner of Arlo's lips as he kissed her back.

"Alright, lovebirds. What happened to the urgency?" Agent Eiríksdóttir asked as she clapped her hands. "Let's go!" Agent Eiríksdóttir turned her attention to Agent Harpy and tapped her sock-covered foot with her finger. "You take care, okay? I need my partner back, and we still have to watch the new Star Wars movie. Don't think you're getting out of it."

Agent Harpy's face scrunched into confusion.

"We're in a fight with the Fey and you're worried about Star Wars."

"Damn right," Agent Eiríksdóttir said, glancing over as the Dioscuri opened a portal back to the S.M.O.K.E. & M.I.R.R.O.R.S. office. "What good would it do for me to worry about the Fey?" she asked sincerely, not taking her eyes off the portal as she yanked a mobile privacy curtain to hide the portal from view of the windows.

Agent Harpy tilted her head. She had a point.

Worrying about the Fey wasn't going to do any good.

"Be safe," Agent Harpy said. "Who else is going to force me to go to the movies?"

Agent Eiríksdóttir grinned. "Count on it!"

Agent Harpy sighed to herself once the portal closed. She looked over at Marigold, who was still staring at where the opening had been. She observed the blonde Fey girl. She seemed relatively small in comparison to the other Fey she had encountered, Salvatore in particular. Marigold's hands were tightly clasped together, and she appeared to be massaging her fingers out of nerves. Her gaze remained locked on the portal that was no longer there.

Harpy figured she should say something. Offer some kind of reassurance to the young Fey girl that everything would be okay. But she wasn't certain that it would be. She wasn't certain of anything at this point. Her mind crossed to Director Quartermaine, and she closed her eyes to focus on steadying her breathing. Agent Harpy wasn't going to cry in front of Marigold, but she couldn't believe he was gone.

Director Quartermaine was always there.

He always had the answers. He was always steps ahead of everyone. Agent Harpy thought fondly back to how he'd welcomed her into the organization all those years ago. Now he was just—gone. A pillar of S.M.O.K.E. & M.I.R.R.O.R.S. whose office now sat empty, cold.

She exhaled deeply through her mouth and opened her eyes again. She had to stop thinking about it. The more she thought, the sadder she got. Harpy reached for her glass, only to grab nothing. She looked down at where her hand used to be. It was such a strange sensation. It felt as though she still had her hand and her fingers, but it wasn't there. A phantom.

"Here, let me." Marigold had turned around and walked over to the tray. She got the water for Agent Harpy and extended her hand to her.

"Thank you," Agent Harpy said softly as she took the water with her right hand.

"It's the least I can do."

Agent Harpy took a sip but kept the glass in her hand as she lowered it to her lap. She studied Marigold for a moment. Her vision was still blurry in her left eye, but she could see her well enough. "So you're the youngest of the Aster girls?" Marigold nodded as she took a seat on the chair nearby. "Do you know much about this Lord Bane?"

"I know enough," she said quietly.

"Are you worried?"

"Most of the FeyForce under him and Commander Kall-An are still in the infirmary from the rescue mission." She paused. "The one when they were ambushed by the Imps and left Arlo behind."

Harpy nodded. "I am familiar." She considered. "If they're still injured, we might have an advantage."

"Maybe," Marigold said quietly. "Or they might be more ruthless this time around. They have too much to lose now."

Just then, the door to the room slowly opened.

Marigold froze at the sound of the creaking noise of the door's hinges. The door was still hidden by the mobile privacy curtain Agent Eiríksdóttir had used to conceal their departure.

"Are you expecting a visitor, Agent Harpy?" she whispered quietly, her eyes moving to meet Agent Harpy's, who sat perched up in her bed now, attentive.

Agent Harpy furrowed her brows and shook her head in a 'no.' Perhaps it was no one, maybe just a doctor or nurse. But wouldn't they have announced their presence upon entry rather than remain quiet like they had all the other times?

Marigold curled her small hands into fists as she slowly got up from her chair with her back still facing the door. While she wasn't a combative Fey, she had abilities like all the rest. She just wasn't well-versed in using them and would definitely be useless against a member of the FeyForce. Especially her oldest sister.

She inhaled deeply and slowly turned around, one foot leading the other. Her stomach twisted, and she felt like she was going to throw up. Marigold's bottom lip quivered as the door swung closed.

Marigold reached for the curtain and ripped it back.

Her heart nearly stopped.

There, standing in the room with them, was a tall girl who, despite her height, appeared to be no older than eleven years old. Her hospital gown was soaked in fresh, bright red blood, and the metallic smell tickled Marigold's nose. Marigold opened her mouth, wanting to ask the child if she was alright, but as Marigold's gaze slowly rose to the girl's face, she couldn't find the words to say. Instead, she gasped.

The young girl had three eyes, one of which was in the dead center of her forehead. Though, upon closer inspection, the one on her forehead wasn't a true eye, but an eye-shaped symbol that glowed white on her skin. Shimmering white strings were wrapped around her hands and fingers, and a pair of long, rusty scissors hung from the pinky finger of her right hand.

"For the love of gourd," Marigold uttered as she took a step back toward the hospital bed. Agent Harpy got up from the bed and defensively stood in front of Marigold. She held out her hand.

"Please stay back," Agent Harpy said, warning.

"Dioscuri," the young girl said, not taking her eyes off them. "Where are they?" Her voice was surprisingly loud and had a slight rasp to it, as though she were sick or losing her voice.

Marigold and Agent Harpy exchanged glances.

"She's looking for Arlo?" Marigold asked in a whisper, before looking back at the girl. Her eyes widened. "Fate," she said softly, pointing to the symbol on the girl's forehead. "That's—you're—" she stepped back, eyes wide.

"What do you know about the Book of Fate?" Agent Harpy asked her.

"I know—I've read about that symbol. That eye has been the consistent insignia of Fate throughout history. It marked the Book of Fate." She hesitated. "And I know that the Autumn Queen wants it badly," Marigold said softly, now keeping her gaze on the young girl. She didn't know which of her eyes to look at, but the one on her forehead continued to draw her attention. "She was upset with the FeyForce when they returned without Arlo, and Lord Bane, he took me and he—" her sentence dropped, and she never finished what she was going to say.

Agent Harpy didn't press.

"There are dangerous beings looking for you," Agent Harpy said to the girl. "Why don't we get you cleaned up, and we can—"

"No!" she roared at them, her voice loud enough that it rattled the windows.

Marigold screamed, and Agent Harpy jumped.

The nurse tending to Agent Harpy burst through the door to see if everything was okay. Marigold quickly cupped her small hands over her mouth after the sudden outburst. She looked from Agent Harpy to the nurse to the three-eyed child and back to the nurse. She apologetically lifted her shoulders.

"Are you alright, Ms. Harpy?" the nurse asked again, completely ignoring the girl standing there in a bloodied hospital gown.

"Um, I'm not the one you should be asking?" Agent Harpy replied, looking over at the girl who stood there still, staring her down. "I'm not the one covered in blood."

The nurse looked behind her before returning her gaze back to Agent Harpy.

"Are you alright, Ms. Harpy?"

"You don't see her?"

The nurse turned around again. "Who?"

Agent Harpy looked over at Marigold, who only shrugged her shoulders.

"I'm fine," Harpy said quickly. "I almost fell out of the bed," she quickly leaned against Marigold, and Marigold was quick to catch her in her arms. "My niece here, she freaked out and thought I was going to hurt myself. You guys are efficient." She regained her composure and took a seat back down on her hospital bed.

The nurse smiled meekly. "Okay, well, if you need anything, just press the call button, okay?"

The two of them nodded, and the nurse quickly left the room.

"She can't see you." Harpy stared at the child. She turned her attention to Marigold. "So, this Book of Fate. It's obviously important."

Marigold nodded.

"Powerful?"

Marigold glanced at the bloody girl and nodded again.

"Dioscuri," the girl repeated.

Agent Harpy considered. "I don't know what's going on, but if you're this Book of Fate, it seems too dangerous to bring you to the Dioscuri," she protested.

"They're in danger," she replied monotonously.

# CHAPTER EIGHTEEN

*18*

Acacia Sanguine was running out of time.

The Autumn Queen commanded her to retrieve Arlo and the Book of Fate, and she was farther from her goal now than she had been when she was first given the assignment. Arlo had slipped right through her fingers, and she had absolutely no lead on the Book of Fate whatsoever. Acacia wasn't even sure if it still existed, if it hadn't been destroyed in the fire long ago. The agent they cornered, Agent Prudence Harpy, didn't seem to have any idea where it was or if it existed at all, and Acacia and Salvatore certainly did a number on her. For a brief moment, Acacia wondered if the agent was still alive as she cleaned the Weapon of Death. S.M.O.K.E. & M.I.R.R.O.R.S. had a whole gallery full of unique weapons, but Acacia hadn't had the time to linger and admire them all.

She tucked the jagged knife back into her cloak as the remaining members of the FeyForce prepared for their mission back to Terra. Their numbers were pathetic as many of their team were still recovering in the hospital wing.

Acacia walked over to Salvatore who stood cleaning a weapon of his own. She rested her temple against his shoulder and looked up at him.

"Yes, darling?" he asked, not looking down at her but keeping focused on the task in his hands.

Acacia sucked in air sharply through her nose and exhaled through her parted lips as she leaned closer toward him. "Everything's just been so chaotic," she said quietly. Acacia normally wasn't very affectionate in front of other people, but she had grown tired over the last few days. It had been one fight after another, and it wasn't as though she lacked a soul. She still longed for comfort from her husband. "I'm just tired, I think." She thought over her words after she said them. They weren't necessarily a lie, but at the same time, not the whole truth. She nestled against her husband.

She needed to succeed. *For him.* This might be her last chance. She inhaled his warm scent, trying not to think too hard about memorizing it, unsure how much longer she would be able to press her face against his skin.

Salvatore put the weapon on the table and turned his body to face his wife. He tilted his head, trying to meet her gaze, but Acacia kept shifting her focus and averting her eyes.

"You sure you're just *tired*?" he asked. "You're not acting like yourself."

"Beings act silly when they've passed the point of exhaustion," she said quickly in defense, finally looking up at him with tired eyes. "I just want to survive this mission and maybe take leave for a little while. Together. We can go somewhere nice."

"Where will we go, Acacia? When would we go? We survive if we succeed, and then we'll likely go straight to war with the Winter Court. There's not much space for time off."

Acacia sighed and leaned her forehead against his chest, fully knowing he was right.

"I love you," she said, wrapping her arms around his waist.

Salvatore frowned and mimicked her motions. "Not as much as I love you." He moved one hand to stroke her blonde hair. "What is it you aren't telling me?" he asked.

"Can't a woman just tell her husband she loves him?" Acacia asked defensively, pulling back just enough to look up at him.

"A woman can, but you aren't that type of woman."

Acacia sighed. "You almost died twice on Terra. I just—"

"I assure you, there won't be a third time."

But it wasn't Terra she was worried about. It wasn't the Imps or the agents. It was the Autumn Queen. She wanted to tell him. There was a slight look of desperation in her eyes, but when she opened her mouth to speak, she felt a small prick at the corner of her lips, as if there was a needle and thread waiting to sew her mouth shut. Acacia instead forced herself to smile reassuringly, as if his answer would suffice. She really needed to pull herself together if they were going to succeed.

***

Upon returning to S.M.O.K.E. & M.I.R.R.O.R.S., Arlo found himself staring at the Fey ear cuffs and communication earpiece he had in the palm of his hand. There were so many things running through his mind about his life in Fae, and his identity. He was overwhelmed by the mixture of emotions and thoughts of Ambrose, his supposed father. The Fey man had lost his real son and wasn't even given the opportunity to grieve. He was just Glamoured. They took that from him. One of their own.

One of their decorated and well-respected veterans. If they could do that to him, what else could they do without remorse? What else could they do without a care? Arlo considered for a moment what they had done to him too, but he was just a human man. A mortal—at least, he was. They wouldn't have kept him alive if they didn't think he was useful. It was all selfishness.

He sighed, curling his fingers over the earpieces in his hand.

"You have no reason to be nervous," Zaria said as she started to put up her brown hair.

"I'm not nervous," he said, and that was true. He wasn't. Irritated, would be the word he would use, but not nervous. "It's not like I haven't encountered them before." He'd even fought them in training before, many, many times.

"Well, I haven't." Agent Eiríksdóttir was sitting in the corner, her leg bouncing with anxiety now despite saying earlier she wasn't worried about the Fey. Her arms were crossed tightly over her chest, and she was staring straight ahead at nothing in particular. "I've seen what they did to Harpy." Perhaps it had been her adrenaline speaking beforehand, or perhaps Eiríksdóttir had feigned strength so that Harpy wouldn't worry. Whatever the reasoning was for her previous behavior, it was certainly gone now.

Zaria tilted her head as Arlo tucked the pieces into his pocket. They clicked against something else in the depths of the pocket, and Arlo removed the broken cell phone that he'd picked up behind the dumpster on his first day on Terra. He smiled at the memory before slipping it into his other pocket where it wouldn't jostle the FeyForce earpieces.

"You don't need to be nervous. Agent Harpy wasn't prepared, which was our mistake." Zaria walked over to Agent Eiríksdóttir and took a seat beside her. "The Imps will help us. They're going to interrupt interdimensional travel. They typically exist between realms, so if they know someone is coming or going, they can sometimes slow them down, even stop them if they're prepared. They've agreed to do their best to keep the Fae stuck here," she smiled encouragingly. "So even if things don't go exactly according to plan, they can't just escape back to Fae with Arlo or… anything else."

"I don't want *them* stuck here!" Agent Eiríksdóttir rubbed at her temples. "I am not cut out for this. I should have stayed with the Republic of Letters. I don't want to do fieldwork. I've changed my mind. I'm resigning. I'll send my letter to—" she paused once it dawned on her that she could not send Director Quartermaine anything. Her expression sank with her heart. "We don't have a director. I don't even know who's in charge in an emergency like this." She wished Harpy was there. Eiríksdóttir couldn't help feeling like she'd know what to do.

Zaria looked over at Arlo who only shrugged and looked down. He didn't want to be reminded of Finn Quartermaine's death. When he looked up again, Zaria was still staring at him. She raised her eyebrows and tilted her head toward Agent Eiríksdóttir. Arlo wrinkled his nose as he took a hesitant step forward. He supposed she was expecting him to comfort her.

"So you're with the Republic of Letters, right?" he started and scratched at his ear. "That makes you a—what? Do they call them agents too?"

"An Intellectual," Agent Eiríksdóttir answered in a matter-of-fact tone. "We're called Intellectuals. I only became an agent when I joined S.M.O.K.E. & M.I.R.R.O.R.S."

"And what do you folks do, exactly?" Arlo inquired further. Agent Eiríksdóttir stared at him like he had grown another head. Arlo simply shrugged. "Cut me some slack, I haven't been in Terra for a hundred years."

"It's an intellectual community that transcends space and time. Dedicated to the research and understanding of all that we do not know," she informed him as she straightened her posture. "We seek knowledge and comprehension. Potential integration of other types of benevolent beings."

Arlo glanced down and noticed Agent Eiríksdóttir had stopped shaking her leg.

"And what do you know about Fey? I could be wrong, but I think you know quite a lot. I saw the book you gave Harpy."

Agent Eiríksdóttir tilted her head and narrowed her eyes.

"You're right," she said with a bit more confidence, nodding as she stood up. "I know all about Fey. I have iron frangible bullets for my revolver." She walked to the desk in the corner and began shuffling papers.

"Good job. I'm impressed how you did that." Zaria said to Arlo. She nodded towards where Agent Eiríksdóttir now stood loading her revolver.

"Nerves can make people so anxious they seemingly forget everything. Getting them to talk about something they know usually brings them down from that. Like anchoring a balloon that's trying to float away." He considered Agent Eiríksdóttir for a moment. "Oddly enough, that was something I learned in FeyForce training. To manage civilian trauma responses in times of crisis."

"It's still a good method," Zaria said, wondering why she hadn't thought of it. However, Arlo's training had been much more recent than hers was.

"I'm surprised you didn't just use Glamour on her," Arlo said, raising his eyebrows. Zaria narrowed her eyes as she tilted her head.

"Are you going to hold that against me? I had a job to do."

Arlo opened his mouth to speak just when a portal opened behind him. He turned around, swinging his dagger keychain around his finger.

"You really don't need that," Freya said from beside him.

"I don't need you to fight all of my battles for me," Arlo argued as the dagger became full size when he caught it in his hand.

"Arlo!" Lord Bane shouted just as Arlo turned toward the portal to face him. He pointed his sword at Arlo as he stepped toward him. "I know what you are." He glanced around the room, and his nose wrinkled. "And from the looks of it, so do you."

Arlo furrowed his brows as he paced the floor. He stood just a little in front of everyone else, including Freya, who tilted her head in observation, wondering what it was he was doing.

"That I'm human? Apparently you've known this whole time." Arlo pointed at the center of his own chest. "I'm the one who didn't know."

Lord Bane scowled at his mockery. "Not that you're *human*," he spat.

"But I *am*," Arlo said, raising his eyebrows. "I am *human*. And you knew all this time, and you kept it from me."

"You're more than that," Lord Bane growled under his breath. "And you know it."

"What am I then?" Arlo asked. He still paced the floor. He didn't bother to look at Salvatore or Acacia, Commander Kall-An, or any of what was left of their FeyForce after they had been ambushed by the Imps. He felt their eyes burning into him—he was their former friend.

It hadn't even been that long ago, but it felt like an eternity after all that he had learned. The Fey standing before him weren't the family and friends he had grown to love. He didn't really know them at all. While heartbreaking, he glanced at Freya. She was his family. That was real.

"Lead us to the Book, Arlo!" Lord Bane demanded. A vein in his forehead stuck out prominently in his tense stance. "I know you know where it is."

A small grin peeked at the corner of Arlo's lips. Small, but enough for Lord Bane to notice. Lord Bane narrowed his eyes.

"It's *me*," Arlo said, taunting Lord Bane. "I *am* the Book of Fate. That's why I didn't die in the fire. It bound itself to *me*. All this time, for a century, it was right under all of your noses," he said, Arlo's eyes moving to each of the FeyForce that stood in front of him, "and you had no clue."

A murmur rose up behind Lord Bane as the FeyForce squad exchanged shocked glances.

"The Book of Fate is a…person?" Salvatore asked, looking over at Lord Bane. He was puzzled by the possibility. Frowning, he then directed his attention back onto Arlo as he shook his head. "Arlo, don't make this difficult. Tell us the truth, and then we can all go home. Stop lying. "

"Am I lying?" Arlo tilted his head in consideration. "How do you know?"

"We just know," Lord Bane snapped.

A small smirk peeked at the corner of his lips. "But you're not entirely sure, are you?"

"Stop playing games with me, Arlo!" Lord Bane demanded as he reached for his weapon.

Acacia came out of nowhere and slashed his left cheek with the Weapon of Death. Arlo stumbled backward from the sudden attack and tripped over his own feet. His hand quickly moved to touch his bleeding face. His eyes glowed a faint white color as he glared up at Acacia.

"If you *are* what you say you are," Acacia started, circling Arlo like a shark, "then the Queen requests your presence. *Immediately*." She twirled the Weapon of Death in her hand. He looked away from her, and his eyes scanned his surroundings while counting her steps. Just when she was about to take another, Arlo's arm shot out and grabbed her ankle, forcing her to lose her balance.

Acacia landed hard on her back. She raised her weapon, but he blocked her with his dagger. His grip on her ankle tightened, and the slash in his face began to sew itself back up with the energy he started to drain from her. He let go of her only once he was fully healed. Acacia groaned.

The healing had taken no more than a few seconds, but the FeyForce had stayed dutifully behind Lord Bane, awaiting orders. Acacia's groan, however, broke Salvatore's focus. Salvatore lunged at Arlo just as he was getting up from the ground, but Zaria was quick to block his attack. Zaria shoved him backward and into the opposing wall before she turned around to offer Arlo a hand. But, even as Arlo was about to grasp her, another member of the FeyForce attacked her from behind.

Arlo scrambled to his feet. Acacia was dizzy from the energy Arlo had drained from her to heal himself. She held her head in her hands and blinked several times, trying to see straight, but everything was a blur. Acacia clicked on the comm on her wrist four times before dragging herself toward the wall.

Agent Eiríksdóttir fired at the FeyForce, but only managed to graze a few of them, none of which were fatal shots. Still, the iron frangible bullets were enough to cause more than just irritation. The Imps were protecting her from the Fey who cornered her as she tried to reload her revolver.

Zaria and Salvatore were fighting in close proximity, their knives creating sparks as they sliced and parried. While Salvatore was much taller than Zaria and towered over her small frame, her stature made her far faster, and she used her abilities well. Still, Salvatore was a well-trained fighter. Even as Zaria ducked under another swing, Salvatore began predicting and anticipating her moves until he was able to knock her down. She fell to her knees, trying to block his next lunge. But even as he swung, she knew her weight was off and she wouldn't be able to hold off his blade.

Salvatore felt a flash of victory as he swung his dagger toward his sister-in-law. "Traitor," he hissed. A searing pain shot through his shoulder and blood spattered Zaria's upturned face. Salvatore dropped his knife and grabbed his shoulder. Even as he spun in fury to see Agent Eiríksdóttir's raised gun, Zaria grabbed his dagger and backed away.

Arlo saw Salvatore get shot. Even as he focused on the trio of FeyForce officers who'd been sent to fight him by Lord Bane, he felt the familiar lurch in his stomach. It had become an all-too-familiar feeling over the past few fights he'd been in with Salvatore. It was the feeling of watching your best friend face death.

Arlo grunted loudly as he disarmed two of the Fey. *Salvatore isn't on your side anymore*, he reminded himself. He glanced up again. His eyes landed on Freya. She raised her eyebrows.

"Just let me know when you're finished showing off," she called over the pandemonium.

In the midst of the chaos, the door behind them was blasted open. A young girl stood there in her bloodied hospital gown. Arlo recognized her immediately, even though she was a mere shadow of what he remembered from the security camera. She was no longer the tame, innocent-looking young girl who was suffering. Her light brown hair ruffled without wind and her eyes glowed a bright, almost blinding white. Two extra ghostly and transparent arms appeared out of her body; one held unusually large rusty scissors and the other a spool of thread. Her real hands were tangled in the glowing white string itself. Her face appeared to glitch, as it inhumanely turned one way, then the other, yet she continued looking straight ahead with her three eyes. She was such a terrifying sight, Arlo had barely noticed she was accompanied by Agent Harpy and—Arlo felt a tug on his heart—Marigold. Marigold wasn't a fighter. This was the last place she should be.

He heard shouts behind him and spun around to see a glowing circle opening behind Lord Bane.

The Autumn Queen stepped into the room.

# CHAPTER NINETEEN

*19*

The fighting ceased immediately upon her arrival.

The Autumn Queen was accompanied by her male slaves, who were all still masked and stood around her like bodyguards. She was dressed in golden silk with leaves patterned across her large chest in a way that barely concealed her breasts, leaving little for the imagination. A thorny woven crown sat upon her fiery red hair that fell in beautiful ringlets against her shoulders. One couldn't argue that the Autumn Queen wasn't beautiful. She was dazzling, but her beauty stopped skin deep, and the diamond sparkle of her eyes betrayed her cruelty.

The Autumn Queen's sharp eyes first landed on Acacia. A terrifying smirk passed over her blood-red lips. She then turned to Salvatore.

Salvatore stood frozen, his arm still outstretched as he'd begun to lunge for Agent Eiríksdóttir. Locking eyes with the young Fey man, the Autumn Queen tilted her head.

"Go on," she encouraged him before looking at Acacia. "Time's up, darling," she hissed.

Before anyone could move, Salvatore grabbed Agent Eiríksdóttir's revolver right out of her hands. Placing the barrel of the gun beneath his jaw, he pulled the trigger.

Time seemed to stand still as Arlo watched Salvatore's body hit the ground. He was deaf to Acacia's howls of agony as he stared at Salvatore's body, whose face was now unrecognizable, contorted, eyes blurred. Blood pooled on the ground, creating a red pillow that wove itself through Salvatore's hair.

Out of instinct, Arlo scrambled toward Salvatore. His own blood thundered in his ears, and he couldn't look away. Even after everything the Fey had done—all their lies and deception, even though Arlo was not Fey himself, Salvatore had been his friend. One of his dearest friends. For nearly a hundred Terran years.

Arlo pressed his palms to the sides of Salvatore's broken head, staring hopelessly into his shiny, glazed-over eyes. Salvatore stared openly at nothing while his blood began soaking through the knees of Arlo's pants.

Arlo felt his own body convulse with shock as he realized his power was refusing to flow into his friend. Salvatore was dead.

Arlo couldn't bring back the dead.

His heart pounded so loudly in his chest, he couldn't hear any of the commotion surrounding him. His focus was fixated on Salvatore. He reached for his wrist, and while there was still faint warmth to his skin, his body was quickly turning cold.

As if a faraway tunnel was opening up, allowing light into the oppressive darkness, sound slowly echoed through Arlo's shock, beginning with Acacia's violent grief.

Acacia's eyes were wild. Furious. Her face had frozen in a mask of hopeless rage as she rose to her feet. Still wielding the Weapon of Death, she boldly stalked toward the Autumn Queen whose focus had turned to the young girl in the bloodied gown.

Marigold stepped in front of her oldest sister, hands raised pleadingly.

"Acacia," she whispered, her own face streaked with tears.

"Get out of my way!" Acacia hissed at her youngest sister. Marigold's eyes were swollen and shiny. While she trembled with fear, she shook her head, causing her blonde hair to bounce.

"Acacia, don't do this," Zaria said softly from the sidelines. "She'll kill you."

Acacia looked back at Salvatore's dead body, her face was splotchy red and wet from her tears. She had the air of untouchable, perhaps invincible pain.

"She already has."

Acacia took one more look at Marigold and then Zaria. Zaria shook her head, and Marigold mouthed, "*please*."

Acacia stepped backward and vanished into thin air, using her Glamour to make her escape from the Autumn Court. Zaria looked over at Marigold, who had slumped back against the wall, still shaking in fear from standing up to her older sister. Tears were sliding down Marigold's face as she stared at nothing. Zaria turned her attention back to the Autumn Queen who had approached and was fixated on the child.

"How did *she* get through?" Agent Eiríksdóttir whispered to Zaria.

"The Imps could only block *outgoing* portals," Zaria said, looking to her right at the Imps fading in and out of sight.

"So she's *stuck* here?" Agent Harpy asked quietly as she slowly maneuvered her way over to Agent Eiríksdóttir while the Autumn Queen was distracted. "With us?"

Zaria nodded. "For now."

The two human agents exchanged glances with one another, sharing equal discontent with the Autumn Court's *Fey Queen* being trapped on Terra—especially after what they'd just witnessed her do to one of her own FeyForce officers.

The Autumn Queen had moved away from her guard and approached the strange, glowing young girl. She began circling her, eyeing the uniqueness of her appearance: the two phantom arms with the spool of thread and the scissors. She stopped in her tracks and closed her eyes, inhaling deeply as she took in her scent. A small smirk appeared across her thick lips as she dragged her tongue against the bottom one. The Autumn Queen opened her eyes again and looked at the young girl.

"*Book of Fate*," the Autumn Queen uttered softly, and the girl looked up at her. "May I have your name?" she asked the young girl, tilting her head down in consideration. The Autumn Queen smiled at her, but the young girl remained stone-faced.

"Don't! Don't give her your name!"

The Autumn Queen glared at him. "Arlo," she hissed as she sewed his mouth shut with Glamour with just a gaze of her eyes and a simple thought. Freya looked over at him anxiously and began to reach for him, but he shook his head.

*Not yet.*

Though he didn't say it aloud, Freya understood and yielded.

The Autumn Queen waved a hand at her guards and they leaped forward, grabbing Arlo's arms before he could react. He struggled, though more out of habit than fear. Freya stood by his side.

Two guards with thick, elbow-length gloves approached with large cuffs made of iron. They clasped Arlo's arms in the cuffs before spinning him around.

Arlo glanced at Freya. Were they stronger than the cuffs? He thought so but felt a flash of worry when he saw Freya also examining them.

The guards spun him around so he could watch as one of the Queen's slaves set a miniature brazen bull on the ground that was hardly bigger than an acorn. The guard then took a step back and rolled a tiny matching marble toward it. It knocked into the bull's small feet, not once but thrice, and the bull began to grow in size. Arlo clenched his jaw. He knew about this weapon. He'd seen it used before. He felt his heart quicken in his chest as the metal beast grew, but he also felt a light brush on his hand. Freya winked.

*'Just a little longer,'* she whispered. *'I have a plan.'*

Against the wall, out of the corner of his eye, he saw Agent Eiríksdóttir take an uncertain step forward. He shook his head determinedly at her.

"I'm tired of you," the Autumn Queen said to Arlo. "You used to be so—" her eyes swept over his body and licked her lips. "—enticing. But I guess I don't need you anymore," she added as she swept her gaze back toward the Book of Fate.

The young girl turned her head and watched as the guards shoved Arlo through a door in the side of the brazen beast, which had quickly grown to the size of a standard bull. They locked him inside, and the two gloved guards started a fire beneath it to roast him to death. Brazen bulls were designed in the form of the actual animal and had an apparatus that would transform screams into the sounds of a bellowing and infuriated bull.

"Now that he's out of the way," the Autumn Queen said, brushing her hands as if she'd had to do all the work herself. She leaned towards the young girl. "May I please have your name, my sweet child?"

The bull began to make muffled grunting noises, and the young girl tilted her head to the side, listening. The Autumn Queen gently reached out and hooked her chin with her finger, directing the girl to look up at her.

"Free him," the girl said, her voice raspy.

"We don't need him," the Autumn Queen assured gently.

"Free him!" she snapped.

The Autumn Queen stepped back as though she had just been slapped, her face suddenly devoid of any kindness she'd pretended towards the child. She waved her hand, and her guards leaped forward, arms outstretched towards the young girl.

The Book of Fate closed her eyes for a brief moment. Suddenly, she thrust open her arms, generating a force field that pushed away the Queen's guard.

The Autumn Queen's eyes lit up and her lips parted in awe.

"Such power," she admired. Her guards scrambled to their feet, and she halted them to stop where they were. One side of the Autumn Queen's mouth curled into a smile as she realized where she was standing.

She was inside the force field with the Book of Fate.

Just the two of them.

Wind seemed to blow around the young girl, tousling her light brown hair, and her phantom hands continued to unwind thread that seemingly led nowhere but the tangled mess in her real, solid hands. The Autumn Queen breathed deeply as she walked forward, slowly at first, as if testing her agency within the forcefield.

Outside, her guards were slowly getting to their feet. One attempted to touch the force field, and it seared his flesh, leaving a sizzling burn.

A loud noise erupted from the bull, almost a bovine chuckle. The Fey guards stood ready to stop anyone who dared try to get near it.

The Autumn Queen stroked the side of the young girl's cheek with the back of her hand.

"I don't mean any harm to you," she said in a gentle whisper. "I just want to know your name."

The brazen bull began to rattle.

Agent Harpy and Agent Eiríksdóttir exchanged glances with one another. Marigold leaped forward, arms outstretched, but Zaria was faster. She wrapped her arms around Marigold's body and pulled her backward. All four of them didn't take their focus away from the bull.

It was rocking from side to side, and an unmistakable clanking could be heard inside its body. The guards cautiously turned to look at the bull.

Marigold screamed when the door snapped off and flew across the room, wedging itself into the opposing wall.

The glowing Dioscuri emerged from the opening.

It still looked like Arlo, but Freya seemed to be glowing around him. They blinked, and their pupils split in two. The Dioscuri landed on their feet and touched the forcefield. The glowing perimeter crackled with energy, flexing briefly at the Dioscuri's touch before reinforcing itself. The Dioscuri was not burned, but neither could they force their way through.

"Zaria..." Marigold gasped, tugging on her sister's sleeve over the arm that was wrapped around Marigold's body. "She's dying." She pointed.

If the Book of Fate had been a horrifying sight before, it was nothing compared to what now stood in the forcefield with the Autumn Queen. The young girl's hospital gown was not only soaked in her blood, but blood now dripped down her legs, adding itself to a widening pool of red at the girl's feet. Small flecks of blood splattered the inside of the forcefield where her hands had pushed the air away from her. The force field was too much for her.

The Autumn Queen paid no attention to any of it.

"I must know," the Autumn Queen continued, stroking her cheek. "I must know the fate of Fae. Will I be Queen of the Fairies, my child?"

"How do we get inside?" the Dioscuri asked, talking amongst themselves.

"I don't know," they answered while moving around the force field, bulldozing over any Fey guard who tried to get in their way.

The young girl was struggling to keep her stance. She swayed where she stood, and the Autumn Queen began to smile. "Come, my child. Rest," she soothed. Her voice was calm.

The girl fainted, and the force field collapsed.

Immediately the Dioscuri went for the Queen, but she held the young girl's unconscious body in her arms.

"Do not come any closer," the Autumn Queen warned. "Or I will poison her." The Autumn Queen had her long, pointed fingernails pressed against the young girl's exposed neck.

The Dioscuri tilted their heads.

"You're bluffing. You need her."

"Unless she already told me what I needed to know," the Autumn Queen squealed in delight.

*'Take it back, Arlo. Pieces of your soul live within the Queen since you healed her.'*

*My soul?*

*'Your energy—your lifeforce—whatever it is, you've given it to her to make her stronger,'* Freya told him internally. *'Take them back,'* she urged.

*How?*

*'I can redirect your energy back into you.'* Her voice paused. *'But we'll need to split. Now!'*

Freya leaped from their bond. She went right and Arlo went left, going after the Autumn Queen from two different directions. Slamming into her body, Freya went through the Queen, ripping the shards of Arlo's soul right from her as she merged back with her brother as the Dioscuri. The Autumn Queen let out a blood-curdling scream as she felt the immense loss of energy. She gasped and clutched her heart, scrabbling to cling to whatever had just left her. Her chest heaved and her hands shook.

Zaria and Marigold instantly moved to catch the unconscious girl, forced out of the Queen's arms upon impact. They moved her to the corner where Marigold cradled her head in her arms while Zaria used Glamour to clean her up a little. She did her best to remove as much blood as possible, but the putrid iron smell still hung in the air.

The Autumn Queen was forced to her knees. Her face had lost its glow, and her porcelain skin was now tinged with gray. But the Dioscuri felt stronger now than before, and Arlo knew he could now match Freya's power which increased their strength as the Dioscuri. It was still strange to be conscious in his body with her, rather than allowing her to take over. But he would have to get used to it.

The Dioscuri, the helper of those who truly needed it.

Lord Bane had hung back once the Queen arrived, allowing her guards to do their work. Now he rushed forward to help his Queen, but Agent Harpy had grabbed Agent Eiríksdóttir's revolver from the ground and pointed it at his head.

"I *dare* you," Agent Harpy said. He raised his arms in surrender and stepped back from her, but his eyes kept moving to the side to make sure his Queen was okay. His eyes darted around the room as he began plotting his next move.

"Well don't just stand there!" the Autumn Queen snapped at her guard, who stood around, discombobulated, as they looked at one another, seemingly released from her allure.

The Dioscuri took a step toward her as she scrambled to her feet. She had lost some of her beauty with the depletion of energy. "You've lost," they said to her. "You will leave Terra and never come back here."

"The Imps," Lord Bane uttered quickly when he noticed a portal wouldn't open. "The Imps are trapping us here."

The Autumn Queen curled her thinned lips into a scowl. She clenched her hands into fists and screamed.

As if roused by a battle cry, the remaining members of the FeyForce leaped towards the Dioscuri. Imps poured through portals all around the Autumn Queen.

The Queen began ripping through the Imps that came after her, tearing them apart with her fingers and razor-sharp nails. In the chaos, Lord Bane lunged forward and knocked the revolver out of Agent Harpy's hand. She retaliated with a right hook that caught Bane on his jaw. He scrambled backward, assessing the carnage. With the Autumn Queen and her FeyForce on one side and the

Dioscuri and the Imps on the other, the battle seemed at a perfectly equal balance.

There was an internal battle between the Dioscuri as they faced what was left of the FeyForce. Arlo still hesitated before harming any of his former allies. Freya, on the other hand, had no such qualms.

*Not Sebastien*, he demanded, pulling Freya's hand back before she dealt him a fatal blow. Her hand missed, landing at the base of his neck instead, knocking him unconscious.

Arlo heard Freya grunt in annoyance. *'You know, being dead isn't the most terrible thing in the world. It's probably better than living with that thing as your Queen.'*

Arlo knew he wasn't in the position to argue. *I just don't want to kill my friends, okay? Even if they've betrayed me.*

Internally, he could almost feel Freya roll her eyes, but she worked with him after that.

In a rage, the Autumn Queen murdered many Imps, and Lord Bane fought to open a portal back to Fey. He was finally able to force a small opening, but just as he was about to call for retreat, an Imp popped through and pushed him back.

Zaria stood with her back to Marigold and the Book of Fate, fighting off any FeyForce or Queen's guard who dared come close. Marigold stayed hunched over the young girl, shielding her from the fighting and doing her best to wake her back up.

Lord Bane finally got the portal completely open. He practically dragged the Queen through it as he shouted to Kall-An to call for retreat. He and the Queen disappeared into Fae without another word. Commander Kall-An shouted for the FeyForce to fall back one by one through the portal until they all disappeared out of sight.

The portal vanished just as quickly as they fled.

The room was left reeking of blood and rotten flesh.

The bodies of many dead Imps lay in heaps on the ground.

Zaria stared at them with great remorse. The Imps had been her friends and allies, shielding her from Fae when she chose to become a traitor to her own people. She closed her eyes, unable to continue looking at them, and instead, directed her attention back onto the young girl still being cradled by her younger sister.

"We should have killed the Queen," the Dioscuri argued, the prominent voice was feminine. They stood in front of the spot where the portal had just closed.

"I took back my life from her. That is justice," they said back, Arlo's deeper tone louder this time.

Arlo and Freya continued arguing for another moment, temporarily splitting so that they could address each other directly. To the others in the room, Arlo simply appeared to yell at the air before Freya reunited with him again.

They turned their focus onto the Queen's guard who'd been left behind. Something had to be done about them. There were at least six of them in their presence, now left behind on Terra, cowering under the terrifying gaze of the Dioscuri. One by one, they slowly removed the masks the Queen had forced them to wear.

"You can stay here in Terra if you wish," they announced to the confused guards. "S.M.O.K.E. & M.I.R.R.O.R.S. can help with your integration into this society, but if you step out of line, you will answer to us. Or, you may return to Fae. The choice is yours."

The members of the guard all looked at one another. Slowly, each of them nodded in agreement to the terms. Arlo recognized many of them, some of whom he hadn't seen in a long time. He felt shame and wanted to look away, but Freya kept their focus on them for a moment longer before the pair looked at Agent Eiríksdóttir, who nodded in agreement.

"We'll be happy to assist."

The Dioscuri turned around. They looked down at the young girl, who was still unconscious.

"How is she doing?" they asked, their voice both separate and one all at the same time.

"She'll be okay," Marigold said softly, gently brushing strands of her brown hair out of her face.

"The force field weakened her significantly, and she lost a lot of blood. But she's a strong girl, and—" Zaria nodded in agreement with her younger sister. "She'll be okay."

## CHAPTER TWENTY

*20*

After a few hours, everyone had time to regroup after the fight. The fire lit beneath the brazen bull had been extinguished, luckily before any water sprinklers had gone off. Zaria had retrieved the marble from the bull, causing it to decrease in size again. She gave both pieces to Agent Harpy for data collection and storage.

The Queen's former guards were ushered to a secure holding cell until they could be properly processed. Arlo learned that the moment she'd realized they were in crisis, Agent Eiríksdóttir had sent the paper pushers of S.M.O.K.E. & M.I.R.R.O.R.S. to various safe houses where they could alert headquarters in Hawai'i and wait for further directions. Now, Agent Harpy sent out an alert to the agents who'd been dispersed in the surrounding states, telling them to be on high alert for unauthorized Fey activity.

The young girl had regained both consciousness and strength with a little nourishment that Marigold fetched for her. She was standing upright again, and color had been brought back to her cheeks.

Now, the group rested in Director Quartermaine's old office. Zaria placed her hands on the young girl's shoulders as her eyes wandered around the room to everyone. She supposed it was time for a proper introduction after what had just happened. Maybe even a little late for one.

She cleared her throat. "This is Echo, or," she hesitated, "At least, she's called Echo-01 for her documentation to be kept confidential. Secrecy was important, so we kept her existence on a need-to-know basis. Her name has been kept confidential for the safety and privacy of her and her family, who did not ask for this."

"That's impersonal," Arlo frowned and slowly approached the girl. It wasn't even really a name. It was a label. "Echo."

"But *necessary*."

"What is your name?" he asked. Even as young as she was, she was nearly as tall as he was. He tucked his chin down and tilted his head to the side. The girl known as Echo-01 hesitated. "You really gave us a scare back there."

"You told me not to tell the Queen my name."

Arlo smiled. "And that probably saved your life." She stood silently for another moment. "Do you want to be called Echo?" he asked. She shook her head. "What name do you prefer?"

"Friday," she said softly.

He smiled. Friday. He wondered if that meant she was born on a Friday. Though how funny it would be if she wasn't. A Friday who wasn't born on a Friday.

"How old are you, Friday?" he asked. His voice was soft and offered comfort.

The moment she told him her name, Friday trusted him immediately, and she had every reason to. Even so, she still looked up at Zaria for approval, just in case. Zaria nodded encouragingly. Friday's eyes then fixated back onto Arlo.

"Eleven," she said, still speaking in a tone just above a barely audible whisper. Friday was a very different girl than whatever seemed to take over her body when the Book of Fate came forth. It was an interesting sight, but one he could go without seeing again for a while. The three eyes were jarring, and the smell of blood still circled his nose. Her dress was stained red.

"I remember being eleven," Arlo said. Friday's eyes shifted to the left. Arlo narrowed his gaze before looking at Freya. "You can see her?" he asked.

Friday nodded. "I remember her when I first met Uncle Finn. She's pretty." Freya smiled for a moment, only for it to disappear at the remembrance of what happened to

Director Quartermaine. Friday began digging into the pocket of her gown and fished out a folded piece of paper. "I have another drawing for him."

Zaria frowned. "Oh, Friday, he's—"

"Don't worry, I know. You don't have to say it." Friday unfolded the artwork in her hands and looked down at it. Zaria and Arlo exchanged glances with one another. Of course she knew. Why wouldn't she know? She was the Book of Fate. "There were things he wanted to know, but I couldn't tell him." Friday frowned and folded the piece of paper back up before handing it to Zaria. "I guess I should have paid better attention to his timeline."

Zaria stared at the piece of paper being handed to her, but she didn't move to grab it right away. She was hesitant and kept looking between the piece of paper, Friday, and Marigold, before her eyes wandered over to Arlo, who raised his eyebrows at her. Slowly, she accepted it. "Shouldn't you be giving this to Arlo and Freya?" she asked.

"Why?" Friday asked. "He isn't staying here." Zaria raised her own eyebrows and glanced at Arlo, who quickly averted his gaze. Friday's eyes wandered between the two of them before settling on Arlo's hands. "I'm sorry you do not have a soul mate," Friday said quietly, still observing Arlo's hands.

Arlo frowned, also looking at his hands.

"What do you mean?" he asked, turning his hands over. He forced himself not to look at Marigold, but he felt a density in his chest that hadn't been there a moment before.

Friday stared silently, almost sadly.

"There's an East Asian belief of the Red Thread of Fate. It's thought to be a single invisible string around the finger linking those destined to meet as one another's true love," Zaria eventually answered for her. "She likes to look for them. She's always looking at hands."

"It's always sad when the string comes undone for one person but not the other." Friday looked at her hands. She raised them and wiggled her fingers. "Sometimes if you're lucky, the lunar matchmaking god will tie another around your finger."

"You're too young to be worried about love," Zaria said, smiling gently. She hadn't yet looked at the drawing Friday had handed her.

"Oh—I'm not worried. I'm not interested in finding love. That's disgusting. I don't even want to be here." She sat back on the couch in the corner and looked up at the ceiling.

There was a small pain in Arlo's gut when he realized she didn't mean in *this room*. She meant in *this world*. In this life. He could feel her forlorn energy even from across the room. They were connected to one another; he was sure of it.

Friday looked over at Arlo, as if aware of his sudden realization.

He stiffened and looked down. He felt as though the simple discovery had somehow been an invasion of her privacy. He wondered if Freya could feel it too.

"Do you know much about human sacrifices?" Friday asked.

Arlo exchanged glances with Zaria, who shrugged. He then looked at Freya, who avoided catching his gaze. Freya was clearly more than aware of how disturbing Friday could sometimes be. This remark wasn't the first. While a little dark for an eleven-year-old, Friday was no ordinary eleven-year-old.

"Not really," said Arlo, unsure of what to say. He was unsure of what else would follow. *What could follow a question of human sacrifice?*

"I looked into it a little after my grandpa died. I missed him, and I thought—well—obviously I wanted to bring him back." Friday looked at Freya curiously. "But I suppose the dead come back on their own. Just not always in the way we expect."

"I don't mean to interrupt," Zaria said, looking at the now unfolded paper in her hands, "but what is this,

Friday? What am I looking at?" she asked as she looked up at the eleven-year-old.

Friday glanced down at the paper, and just as she looked up, her third eye reappeared on her forehead. Only this time, the eye wasn't just an eye symbol. It was a true third eye, with lashes, an iris, and a pupil. It startled Agent Eiríksdóttir, who instantly touched her own forehead and looked away.

"The Infernal Artifacts," Friday said. Her three eyes blinked in unison before the third one disappeared again, submerging itself back into her skin like it was never there in the first place. Agent Eiríksdóttir had found the courage to look at her again, only to realize the eye was gone. She shook her head and blinked several times, wondering if she'd imagined it.

Arlo looked at the drawing. It depicted two young women and a young man. The woman in the middle had three eyes and four arms with strings tangled on her fingers—Arlo assumed that portion was a self-portrait as Friday already looked strikingly similar to the figure even as a child. The other woman looked as though she were decaying, and the man's skin was a golden color. Arlo frowned.

"So there's three?"

"That will meet at this point in time, yes."

"That's vague."

Friday tilted her head and lifted her shoulders. "The years to come will be interesting."

"To say the least," Agent Eiríksdóttir added.

"What happens to you?" Arlo asked, his eyes looking down at the drawing, particularly of Friday's depiction of herself. "You look—"

"I try not to look at my own Fate," Friday answered quickly. "I don't want to know what becomes of me—or doesn't. Besides, there's a lot of other people to serve as a distraction. But this came to me in a nightmare. I had no control over that."

"Do you have nightmares a lot?"

Friday hesitated, then nodded.

"When does this happen?"

"About two decades from now, give or take a year or two. I don't know the exact time."

Arlo inhaled sharply through his nose and looked over at Freya. She was surprisingly quiet throughout the whole thing. Friday looked at her too.

"He would have loved to have seen this," Freya mumbled softly, clear she was speaking about Director Quartermaine.

Arlo studied his sister's face for a moment. Her eyes stared out the window and her words came slowly, as if each syllable had to wade through an ocean of grief in order to be heard. In the absence of the adrenaline of battle, her face had relaxed to reveal an emotion deeper than sadness. Freya had known Finn for a long time—during a very lonely time. Not only had he been her oldest friend, he had been her only friend on Terra.

Arlo's face softened as his own sadness settled over him. He thought of Salvatore first. His closest friend who had been forced to kill himself right in front of their eyes. Even with the endless list of how Fae had betrayed him, the transgressions they were responsible for, even after all they had done to Arlo, Salvatore had been a dear friend. Arlo wondered if Salvatore had his doubts about everything that was happening. *He must have*, he thought.

"His heart and his mind conflicted," Friday said as if she knew what Arlo was struggling with internally. "He didn't know what to listen to."

"What about Acacia?" Marigold asked. Arlo jumped slightly. For a moment, he'd forgotten she was even there. He hung his head, avoiding eye contact. "Is she going to be okay?"

Friday frowned, and then her expression smoothed. She opened her mouth to speak and then closed it again. Friday closed her eyes and inhaled deeply. The third eye emerged on her forehead again.

"You really had to ask," Agent Eiríksdóttir muttered, eyes glued in horror once again at Friday's forehead. She massaged the goosebumps forming on her arms. "It reminds me of the book from Hocus Pocus." Eiríksdóttir shuttered.

Agent Harpy shot her a glare.

All three of Friday's eyes were open then, and she muttered something under her breath that, while it was clear she had said something, no one could make out the words. Fresh blood began to soak into her gown again. Freya grabbed Arlo's arm, her hand sinking into his as she practically latched onto his skeleton.

"Stop!" the voice of the Dioscuri came out of Arlo's mouth, his eyes turning white as his pupils split.

Friday blinked several times, nearly losing her balance as she tipped sideways off the couch. Agent Harpy was quick to catch her. Friday's third eye disappeared into her forehead again as she fluttered her eyes.

The Dioscuri glared at Marigold before approaching Friday. They touched the side of her cheek. They were a unique blend of both Arlo and Freya. Arlo was the solid form, but you could see Freya's blueish ghostly form outlined over his. It was like watching a 3-D movie without the red and blue glasses. Freya looked almost like an echo, but their white eyes were aligned.

"Are you okay?" Their voice was strange too, two voices speaking in unison.

Friday nodded. She looked up at Agent Harpy as she stood up. "Thank you," she said softly before looking at

Marigold. "She'll be okay, but you won't see her for a while. Both of you won't." Friday glanced over at Zaria. "But you won't like it when you do see her again."

Zaria stiffened a little, slightly bothered by what Friday had decided to add. She didn't like the vagueness in her response and would have preferred not to know at all.

"I'm sorry," Marigold said quietly. "I wouldn't have asked if I—" she looked down at the fresh blood soaking the front of Friday's dress. "I just—my sister—" She stepped back, feeling deeply out of place in the room.

Friday only shook her head and waved her apology away.

"This?" Friday asked, pulling on her bloodied gown. "I'm used to this."

"Come," Agent Harpy said, still holding Friday steady. "I think you should sit down. I don't want you to hurt yourself any further." She helped Friday back onto the couch before looking over at the Dioscuri. "Are you both—present?"

The Dioscuri turned their heads one way, then the other. Freya seemed to move just a fraction of a second slower than Arlo.

"Yes," they said together. Freya closed her set of eyes and pulled herself away from Arlo.

Arlo quickly rubbed at his temples. "That actually really fucking hurt, Freya," he mumbled. "What the hell was that?"

"I'm sorry," she said, appearing beside him. "But look at her. I couldn't help it."

Arlo looked over at Friday. She was saying something to Agent Harpy, but he couldn't hear her. He figured he shouldn't be eavesdropping on their conversation anyway. At least she was okay now.

"This is what you did in the bull, right? I thought you could only force me to share the body when I was unconscious."

She nodded. "I can only *fully* take over your body when you're unconscious. But I didn't do that. I just… both of us were occupying it consciously at the same time. I don't technically need your permission or anything. It's just easier when you're on the same page."

"Please don't do it again," he said, still rubbing his temple. "I don't know if I can take it a third time in the same day."

She tilted her head sympathetically. "I'm sorry."

Arlo moved his elbow to nudge her arm in a joking manner to hint that he was only kidding with her and not actually serious but was a little surprised that instead of his elbow going right through her like he had anticipated, he'd actually nudged her. He furrowed his brows slightly as the both of them looked down at their arms.

"You felt that?"

Freya nodded.

Friday watched the two of them stare at each other in confusion. A small smile peeked at the corner of her mouth before she directed her attention back onto Marigold to tell her to stop apologizing for the millionth time. She looked down at Marigold's hands. The string tied around her finger was black.

Black strings were never good.

"You do know she's depressed, right?" Arlo asked, turning to Zaria.

"Sure, among a series of other things." Zaria shrugged, seemingly unbothered by Arlo's observation. "But wouldn't you be? Depressed, I mean. Look what she has to deal with. She's just a kid."

Arlo sighed. "She's a unique girl, that's for sure. Where are her parents?"

"Nearby. They wanted to get help for her, which is why she's here. Which is how we even found her in the first place. Her case was unique, and she was sent to us from the facility in Hawai'i."

"What's wrong with her? I mean—the blood just keeps coming."

"I guess you could call it a medical anomaly, but it's not very scientific." Zaria shrugged. "I mean, she's the Book of Fate. This is something we've never dealt with before."

"Don't forget about her mom—" Agent Eiríksdóttir chimed in.

"There's that too," Zaria said, just before pursuing her lips together. She chewed on the inside of her cheek. She had almost forgotten Agent Eiríksdóttir had seen Friday's file. She had been holding it when the two of them first met.

"What about her mom?" Arlo asked curiously.

Zaria looked pained by his question and didn't answer it. "It doesn't matter anymore. It's been made clear she can't stay this way."

"What are you talking about?"

"We have to bind her abilities. She needs to be concealed. From *everyone*. The Fey know all about her existence now, as she is. More will only come for her. More beings, more creatures." Her gaze met Friday's. "I'm sorry."

"It's okay," Friday answered quietly from where she was sitting and fumbled with her gown. "I knew this was going to happen."

"Of course you did," Zaria said softly with a smile. "At least one thing's for certain, no one will ever be able to startle you, huh? You're always going to see them coming." She winked at her. Despite saying this, Zaria wasn't sure the extent of what the Glamour would really do. Her intention was to merely reassure Friday—and she was positive Friday more than likely knew that.

Friday smiled before giggling a little. She took a deep breath and looked at her hands. "I'm ready for my life without…" her eyes fell to her bloodied gown and she moved her fingers as if they were still tangled in glowing strings.

Arlo smiled too, but it soon faded. He could only hope this meant she would have some semblance of a normal life. It was the first time he had seen her face light up. The first time he had heard her laugh. It was like music to his ears. His eyes began to water a little. He felt horrible. How could Destiny be so cruel to this child? Freya touched Arlo's arm, and he closed his eyes.

"Do you want to leave the room?" she asked quietly. "This might trigger bad memories for you, watching Zaria do to her what she did to you all those years ago."

Arlo inhaled deeply and directed his attention to Friday.

"Would you like us to stay?" he asked sincerely, tilting his head toward Freya.

Friday looked at the two of them, her eyes wandering back and forth between the twins. She nodded and uttered a very quiet *please.*

Arlo looked over at Freya, and she nodded in agreement, her hand slipping into his.

“Then we’ll stay,” they said together.

# CHAPTER TWENTY-ONE

*21*

Arlo stood in the break room of S.M.O.K.E. & M.I.R.R.O.R.S with Freya. He clutched a warm mug of hot coffee in his hands as he looked over at his sister who was going over the events that had taken place in her mind. He had allowed Freya to take over his body long enough to change her clothes and get out of the ballerina outfit she had been stuck in since she died. Now, her hair was bound in a loose ponytail, and she wore a white button-up beneath a forest green cable knit sweater vest and jeans.

"I don't know why you'd choose to wear *jeans*," Arlo commented once he had regained consciousness. Luckily, anything she did in his body also left when she left. "They're uncomfortable to lounge around in, and pretty much anything is more comfortable. Jeans don't even exist in Fae." Arlo was definitely the dressier of the two, wearing black slacks, a belt, a black button-up, and a burgundy vest.

"You forget I don't feel stuff like that once I'm intangible," she replied matter-of-factly, shrugging. "And no one's going to see me. I could wear pajamas if I wanted to."

He tilted his head in consideration. She had a point.

"What's that?" she asked, acknowledging a cell phone on the counter.

Arlo followed the direction of her eyes and picked it up. "I found it when I first got to Terra. I was intending to keep it as a souvenir when I went back to Fae, but it turns out Destiny had other plans, I suppose." He turned it over in his hands. "It was severely damaged, and I was just messing around with it, and I realized—well, I sort of accidentally fixed it." He held it out to her to examine. "I've never healed something that wasn't alive before. But apparently I can." He turned it over in his hands again before tucking it into his pocket.

Even though he'd just revealed a new discovery of his power, Freya looked distracted. She fidgeted with her sweater, pulling the sleeves over her hands and tapping the edge of the table with her finger.

"What are you thinking about?" he asked, pulling the cup to his mouth as he leaned against the counter. Freya only shrugged.

"So much has happened, and Finn's—I mean Director Quartermaine—" her voice faded.

"You loved him, didn't you?" Arlo asked, cutting her off gently.

Freya's mouth opened, and she looked at Arlo in surprise. But eventually, she lowered her gaze. "I don't know how to answer that."

"You don't have to."

He walked over and took a seat across from her.

"I'm just glad he found me," Freya said quietly. "I needed a friend."

"I think he did too." Arlo sat back in the chair and placed the mug on the table. "He seemed like a good man, just a little rough around the edges—maybe a little terrifying with black eyes and stuff. But a good man nonetheless."

Freya smiled but didn't look up to meet his gaze.

"I wonder if he's with his brother."

"His brother who's like us?" Arlo asked.

Freya nodded. "The Corpse Walker. He helped win the Pacific War during the forties."

"How old was Director Quartermaine during the war?" Arlo frowned as he did the math in his head. It was currently 2002. "No way he was old enough to actually—"

Freya shook her head. "No, he wasn't drafted or anything. He was younger than Friday."

"The Infernals don't mess around, huh? Dragging kids into this shit." Arlo etched his thumb against the edge of his mug.

"I don't think they really dictate it. They just… know what's coming. We all have a part."

"What happened to the Corpse Walker?"

Freya shrugged. "Finn said he disappeared. He said he knew the moment his brother was gone. There were no traces of him or the demon he fought on Guam. They were both just *gone.* He said Mrs. Sharp and the R.A.V.E.N. organization looked tirelessly for him, but they never found his body."

Arlo pondered for a moment.

"Do you—"

He and Freya looked up in surprise as someone knocked gently. Marigold stood in the slightly open door, her knuckles raised to knock against the doorframe.

"Sorry, am I interrupting something?" she asked, though to her, Arlo appeared to be alone in the break room.

His gaze dropped to Freya. A small smirk peeked at the corner of her lips as she rose from her seat and disappeared through the wall behind her.

"Not at all," he said and stood up. "Care to join me? I'd skip the coffee, though, it's awful."

Marigold laughed. He pulled out her chair and took a seat after she had made herself comfortable. The break room wasn't much. The table was stained. The floor boasted several broken tiles. One of the cabinet doors was hanging loosely from one hinge, and the refrigerator hummed noisily.

"It's a bit of a downgrade for a second date unfortunately," he commented.

Marigold kept her smile and shook her head. "Definitely no White Crest."

"That feels like a lifetime ago."

In a way, it was.

A moment of silence passed between them. Marigold looked at her hands, and Arlo found himself considering a stained tile near his foot. It wasn't that he didn't want to look at her—he did. But now that they were alone, he found that he felt almost shy—a very new feeling for him. In her mind, he was a totally different species now. So much had happened, and he felt wrong-footed, unsure how to broach the topic.

"I didn't know," she said quietly, breaking the stillness. "I didn't know that you weren't—"

Arlo shook his head as he sighed in relief. "I didn't think you did. I doubt anyone outside the Queen and the FeyForce knew what I really was. I'm not sure I even know what I *really* am at this point."

"It's horrible, what they did to you."

"I got to meet some pretty amazing people though," Arlo said. He reached for Marigold's hand, and she withdrew it before he managed to touch it. He withdrew his hand back to his side of the table awkwardly, but he didn't put it back in his lap. He tilted his head, searching her eyes. "What's wrong? I thought we—"

Marigold smiled sadly, apologetically. "Arlo, I'm not in the right place right now," she said and looked down at his fingers that were still outstretched to her. "And I don't think you are either."

Slowly his fingers curled in toward his palm, and he clasped his hands in his lap.

He felt as though an anchor had just been dropped in his gut, and he forced himself to inhale. Exhale. Smile.

Deep down, he knew she was right.

Within the past few days, his identity had changed fundamentally. He was human. He had a ghost sister. He was unsure of his own mortality. He'd unlocked the whole history of his life—a life that included a not-insignificant romance with an Elven Princess, a romance that had caused the Book of Fate to be stolen in the first place.

He knew there was still a lot he had to process regarding Halina.

He knew it was unfair to Marigold, and it was unfair to the memory of Halina for him to try to pretend like she didn't exist.

Yet part of him had hoped they could try.

In a life that felt uprooted, Marigold's presence seemed to tether him to something outside of the world's crises.

"How are you doing, though?" Marigold asked. "I wanted to make sure you were okay."

And there it was. Her kindness that persisted through every obstacle. Arlo's chest felt tight, but he did his best to brush away the feeling. Even so, he felt her tenderness as her eyes wandered over him, attempting to look for any possible injuries. Arlo, of course, didn't have any aside from the mutilation of his ears by the Fey, which no longer bothered him. He could heal himself.

"Though you seem to be in pristine condition," she noted.

"Only on the outside," he admitted quietly. Arlo cleared his throat. He wanted to stay sitting in the break room with Marigold, but he knew it was time to move on. He stood, and she followed his lead. "What will you do now?"

"I'm going to stay here in Terra," Marigold said as she looked up at him. "I can't return to Fae—not after that. I don't know what's going to happen with the Autumn

Court and the Queen… I decided I'd stay and help Zaria if I can."

"I'm sorry," he said. "I know this isn't what you wanted from life."

"Not everyone gets what they want," she said softly. "I suppose it was time to wake up from my little fantasy—as Acacia would call it." She took a hesitant step towards him. "I can't imagine this is what you wanted out of life either."

He chuckled and raised his brows. "Certainly not what I expected." Arlo took a step closer to her. He reached for her hand, and his thumb grazed over the smoothness of her soft skin.

"You know I could have loved you," he whispered.

Marigold watched as he gently kissed the back of her fingers. A smile tugged at the corners of her lips.

"I know," she answered, matching his volume. While to many, Marigold was just a silly little girl, she wasn't stupid.

Arlo rubbed at her hand a moment longer.

"Are you worried about Acacia?" he asked, his gaze lifting to meet hers, but she continued to watch his thumb move over her fingers.

"I'm worried about anyone who gets in her way."

"Me too."

Arlo looked up and saw Zaria standing in the doorway. She locked eyes with him for a moment before dropping her gaze to meet Marigold's when she turned around. Arlo was intensely aware of Marigold's warm hand still resting in his palm.

"Are you sure about staying in Terra?" Zaria asked. "It's nothing like Fae."

Marigold didn't hesitate to nod.

"Yeah, it's a lot uglier and dirtier—" He was met with glares from both Aster sisters. "What?" he exclaimed with a laugh. "You can't tell me that's not true. It's disgusting here. Look around."

Zaria rolled her eyes and nodded toward the hall. "Come on. The new director would like to have a word with you."

"Am I in trouble?" Arlo asked as he cocked a brow, reluctantly letting go of Marigold's hand. Marigold quickly crossed her arms over her chest.

"Wouldn't surprise me if you were," Marigold chipped in, grinning up at Arlo.

He nudged her playfully.

"Is your sister nearby?" Zaria asked.

Arlo's eyes wandered around. "I'll find her."

"We'll catch up with you in a minute then," Zaria said, motioning for Marigold to join her.

Marigold followed Zaria out of the break room, and Arlo turned to the sink to wash his coffee mug. He was surprised at how much it hurt to say goodbye to a life he hadn't even wanted a week ago.

He took a few deep breaths before considering where Freya might be. He tried saying her name a few times, just in case she was hiding in the wall. When nothing happened, he paused, considering. Arlo dried the mug and returned it to the rack before leaving.

He stepped into the elevator and clicked the button marked 8. Even as the elevator rose, Arlo's heart sank. He knew where Freya would be.

As soon as the elevator doors opened, there was Freya, on the ground, kneeling beside a faint copper stain on the industrial office carpet.

"They're efficient," she said quietly, running her fingers over the stain. Arlo could still visualize the Director's body on the ground. He could still clearly picture himself kneeling beside him, arms and hands covered in blood as he tried, and failed, to save his life. "It's not even damp anymore."

Arlo knelt beside Freya. He studied her face as she continued to gaze solemnly at the floor.

If ghosts could cry, he was sure she would be. His hand reached out for her, and she pulled away.

"Freya," he said, reaching for her again. This time she let him put his hand on hers. He wrapped his arms around his sister, holding her tightly.

She finally forced herself to look at him.

Arlo clenched his jaw.

As it turned out, ghosts could cry.

# CHAPTER TWENTY-TWO

*22*

They were expected to meet right away in the Director's office of S.M.OK.E. & M.I.R.R.O.R.S., but Arlo gave his sister a moment to make sure she was ready before they approached the door. He looked over at Freya who had stopped in the hall abruptly.

"Are you going to be alright?" he asked.

Freya didn't speak. Not immediately, at least. Her eyes were focused ahead at the door. While a new name hadn't yet been added, Finn Quartermaine's nameplate was already removed from beneath the 'Director' title.

"Efficient," she muttered softly to herself.

There was nothing he could do or say that would make any of this better. Director Quartermaine had technically spent more time with Freya than Arlo had. For all he knew, Finn knew her better than he did. Arlo was her brother, but Freya lost her only friend.

He reached his hand out toward her. She looked down at his fingers and sighed. She didn't reach for him straight away, but Freya knew better than to think she could linger in the hallway forever. Touching the tips of his with hers, she merged into him and the Dioscuri entered the room. Arlo could feel Freya's pain in his chest as they looked around the office. Much of Director Quartermaine's personal belongings had already been cleared out. What was left mostly sat in a few brown cardboard boxes by the window, a handful of personal items peeking over the edge. The furniture had also been rearranged. The desk was pulled away from the wall near the window and sat to face the door with two chairs in front of it. The couch was near the window now, and the walls were bare, absent from Director Quartermaine's achievements.

Agent Eiríksdóttir stood leaning against the front of the desk. The Dioscuri turned toward the person standing behind it and met eyes with Harpy. She still had the deep scar going down her face that Arlo hadn't been able to fully heal. Her hair was bound back in a high ponytail and she was dressed in a black suit with her gun holster positioned on the right side of her hip. Her right hand held her left wrist in front of her body, and she tilted her head as she observed what was standing in front of her.

"Arlo, Freya."

"Director?" The Dioscuri said in unison.

"That's so weird," Director Harpy said as she raised her eyebrows.

"That's so cool," Agent Eiríksdóttir had uttered at the exact same moment.

The two of them exchanged glances with one another.

"Director Quartermaine left some big shoes for me to fill," Director Harpy said. "I hope I can do this organization justice. He was here from the very beginning, and he was brilliant."

Freya stared at her with a grave expression etched on her face. He had been there from the beginning. He had started the facility in Chicago.

"He was brilliant," the femininity in the Dioscuri's voice was more prominent as Freya nodded. "This was his… everything. This meant everything to him. But you'll do great, Director Harpy. I believe—we believe in you. If someone were going to take his place, he'd be glad it was you."

"Thank you," Director Harpy said with a very subtle smile. She swallowed and blinked a few times at her suddenly glassy eyes as she motioned the Dioscuri to have a seat. She also took a seat in the swivel chair. Her fingers massaged the nub of her left arm. "So, Friday said you were leaving, if I'm not mistaken?"

The Dioscuri nodded. Freya's facial silhouette looked one way while Arlo answered the question: "I can time travel, but I can't interact with or change the past—Freya, on the other hand, can travel to the Underworld. Maybe together we can find out more about what's going on, and what all this means—I mean the Book of Fate is a *person*. A living, breathing *human* girl."

Director Harpy's eyes widened as she looked away, tilting her head slightly. She cleared her throat, "Well…"

The Dioscuri cocked a brow as Arlo continued to speak for them, "Well, what?"

"I don't think she's completely human, exactly." Director Harpy sat back in her chair.

"What do you mean?"

"She's part Yokai," she finally admitted. "The demonic gene runs through her veins. I saw it in her file but likely would've missed it if Agent Eiríksdóttir hadn't highlighted it as a potential concern. Director Quartermaine detected it in 1992 when she was first hospitalized as a baby. That was actually what first put her on S.M.O.K.E. & M.I.R.R.O.R.S.' radar."

Arlo furrowed his brows in confusion. "Yokai?" he and Freya asked together. He blinked a couple of times. Her echo was going to take some getting used to. "What's a Yokai?"

"It's a… well, like a demon," said Agent Eiríksdóttir. She twisted to look at the files scattered on the desk and picked out one of the drawings of a monster. "They're what came through the portal in Guam during World War II," she said as she handed it to the Dioscuri. "We, our organization, figured at least some had escaped the island."

The picture depicted a fierce troll-like creature baring teeth and fangs. It sported horns and a black mane which stood out against its red skin.

"This is what she is?" Arlo asked as they handed the picture back to Eiríksdóttir.

"We don't know what she is exactly, but this is an Oni." She returned the photo to the file. "Whatever she is could look like this, or worse."

"But how aware of it she is, we're not sure," Director Harpy continued. "And she hasn't said anything about it herself or shown any symptoms… It might just be in her ancestry. It may be nothing to worry about, but we'd rather be safe."

"So she's a demon *and* the Book of Fate?" Freya's voice was prominent.

"That's—not concerning at all," Arlo's voice added.

"I'm sure Destiny has his reasons."

"Where is she, anyway?" the Dioscuri asked together.

"Safe," said Zaria as she entered the room with Marigold as the Dioscuri twisted their body from where they sat to look back at the door. "We just came from visiting her."

"Can we see her?"

"It's probably not the best idea, truly," Zaria said, her expression indicating her remorse for the situation. "I would have liked for you to be able to say your goodbyes, but I don't want your presence to potentially trigger anything with the energy of the Book of Fate. I struggled to contain it as it is. I feel like you guys are some kind of… key or magnet of some sort. I just can't risk it. We can't risk it. Since your abilities came *from* the book. It's just too risky." The Dioscuri considered her words for a moment before nodding in agreement. "But know that she's doing well," Zaria added with a nod. "And the bleeding has stopped. Finally."

The Dioscuri smiled. They then fished the cell phone out of Arlo's pocket.

It was a Nokia 3390.

"Don't lose it," they said as they handed the phone to Director Harpy. Arlo's voice was the stronger of the two as they spoke. "I used my abilities to fix it so a piece of me is basically in there, and I'm going to want it back eventually."

Agent Eiríksdóttir tilted her head in observation. She looked down at the phone in Harpy's hand, a large smile plastered on her face as she looked up at the Dioscuri.

Director Harpy furrowed her brows as she took the phone. "It's kind of weird how you just get put back together like some kind of Frankenstein." She remembered watching him steal energy from Acacia during the fight with the Fey, and something strange happened between the Dioscuri and the Autumn Queen that appeared to make them stronger while weakening her at the same time.

"Frankenstein was the doctor actually," Agent Eiríksdóttir corrected. She was still smiling brightly as her eyes darted back and forth between the phone and the Dioscuri.

Director Harpy glared at her. "Will you *stop* that?"

"Sorry," she uttered while Zaria and Marigold held in their chuckles.

"How does it work?" Director Harpy asked. "If I call, will you answer?"

"Sort of. Maybe. Didn't exactly have a moment to really test it out. Haven't been able to get far enough. It should work more like a transmitter though. Or well, I hope. It'll send a signal to us that you need us, and we'll come back. Be nice to it, though."

Director Harpy frowned and looked down at the phone in her hand.

"Be nice to it?" she asked. "It's a phone, Arlo."

"It's part of me," he said. It was then Director Harpy noticed the digital smiley face that appeared on the screen. "Just don't break him."

"Great," Director Harpy sat back in her chair again as she rolled her eyes dramatically, placing the phone down on the desk. "I have my own little Pocket Arlo."

"You're welcome," they said as they got up from where they sat.

"You're sure you can't stay?" Director Harpy asked. "We could really use your help."

"We'll be just a phone call away," the Dioscuri reassured, tilting their head as they acknowledged the phone. "But we have to find out what's going on with these Infernal Artifacts becoming human. It's affecting a lot of realms. This is bigger than just Terra or Fae." The Dioscuri looked back at the Aster sisters. Marigold averted her gaze until they directed their attention back onto Harpy. "I'd rather we be ready than not know what to expect."

"Be safe," Director Harpy said.

"Yes, ma'am."

Director Harpy rose from her seat too. Shaking hands with the Dioscuri was a strange experience. The Dioscuri turned to leave, nodding to Zaria and Marigold.

"What about the funeral?" Marigold quickly asked as they reached for the door.

Their hand paused over the handle. Arlo kept quiet while Freya pondered what to say. He felt it wasn't his question to answer. Their white split eyes darted around the room before returning to the doorknob where their hand continued to hover.

"We'll be there," she answered quietly. "But for now, we need to prepare for our journey." They turned around and gave one last look to each of the members standing in the room, from Director Harpy, to Agent Eiríksdóttir, then to the Fey women, Zaria and Marigold.

The Dioscuri nodded.

"We'll be seeing you," they said together and left the office quickly, allowing the door to click shut behind them.

Director Harpy looked down at the phone again. It was no longer just a smiley face on the screen, but a small digital Arlo had appeared. Agent Eiríksdóttir peered over at it.

"How cute!" she said with a grin. "He's like a little tamagotchi." Eiríksdóttir chuckled and clapped her hands together. Her grin was still as broad as it could be. "I wonder if you have to exercise him and feed him and stuff."

"What's a tamagotchi?" Marigold asked as she looked up at Zaria who shrugged.

Director Harpy rolled her eyes and slipped the phone into her pocket.

"I will buy you one," Agent Eiríksdóttir told Marigold as she got up from her lean against the front of the desk. "I think you'll love it. It's like a digital pet."

"Please don't," said Zaria. "Marigold could barely keep plants alive."

"Hey!" Marigold said as she elbowed her sister.

# CHAPTER TWENTY-THREE

*23*

Director Harpy sat at her new desk, staring at the different left arm and hand prosthetic prototypes S.M.O.K.E. & M.I.R.R.O.R.S. sent to serve as her replacement. The one that looked the most like a hand was also the most useless, purely cosmetic, but the one that could perform the most tasks made her feel like a cyborg.

When she sat back in her chair, her gaze wandered over to a photo of her standing with Director Quartermaine after she had just joined the team. Director Harpy clenched her jaw. She had never been a vain woman, but she had never felt uglier than she did in that moment. The large scar on her face nearly blinded her in one eye and left her feeling disfigured. She glanced in the mirror hanging on the wall and touched the scar that ran deep in her face. While she wasn't blind in that eye, it was still clouded, and it affected her vision more than she wanted to admit. She made a mental note to request an assessment for corrective eyewear. But even as she did so, her heart sank slightly.

She'd always prided herself on her physical and mental abilities. Now, her physical abilities felt decimated by her recent torment by Fey, and the mental demands of being the new Director challenged her more than she wanted to admit.

Director Harpy's eyes fell onto the photo of Director Quartmaine she'd kept. He was younger in the photo, and he stood at the Pearl Harbor Memorial with Dorothea Sharp and Ingram-Zander Stolly. He had been so young when he came to Chicago and dedicated his life to this work. She was still uncertain she would manage to pull it off without his guidance. More than once already, she'd picked up her phone to text him a question only to remember that she'd never be able to seek his mentorship again. Her eyes shifted over to Mrs. Sharp in the photo. Harpy then looked at the several different prosthetic options before looking back at the photo. Harpy narrowed her eyes and glanced at the old black rotary phone.

She sat up suddenly and fished her own cell phone from her pocket. She opened the top desk drawer and pulled out Director Quartermaine's address book as she flipped for Mrs. Sharp's phone number and quickly punched it into her phone.

It started ringing.

Unfortunately, there was no answer, and she was directed to an unnamed voicemail.

Director Harpy exhaled deeply as the automated voice repeated the phone number back to her. "Good morning, Mrs. Sharp. My name is Prudence Harpy, and I am the new director of the Chicago branch of S.M.O.K.E. & M.I.R.R.O.R.S. I understand you engineered the existence of the Corpse Walker's spine whip, *Marfóir*. I was wondering if I could ask a favor. Please get back to me when you have a minute—and I'm sorry for your loss," she added, as she glanced at the photo of the three of them, narrowing on Finn. "Director Quartermaine was a good man."

She ended the phone call on her Motorola and dropped the phone on her desk in front of the prosthetics.

A knock sounded at the door just before it opened.

"I don't mean to interrupt, but I have news regarding Echo-01—I mean *Friday*," Agent Eiríksdóttir said as she entered the office holding a manilla folder. Her usual cloud of black hair was now braided and tied back. "Her parents are here. They would like her to be released to them. She was originally scheduled to return to our facility in Hawai'i before returning home. Is that a good idea? That we release her now, I mean. I'm not sure what to tell them, but we have to tell them something."

Director Harpy sighed, wishing more than ever that she could talk to Director Quartermaine. Just one last time. She picked up her phone and stood up as she put it back into her pocket.

"Well, we can't hold her here," she started as she began putting things back into the drawers of her desk. "There's nothing more we can do for her at this point. Zaria eased her pain and mostly blocked the Book from harming her, so hopefully she'll live a relatively normal life for now." She turned to give Agent Eiríksdóttir her full attention as she leaned against the edge of her desk and crossed her arms. "But I mean, she is still the *Book.* It's as much a part of her as her skeleton is. It could probably re-emerge on its own if it really wanted to. We'll just have to keep a close watch from a distance, but that will be easier with the consent of her family. Do we know if her mother is aware of her Yokai heritage? Or if their family is going to be a problem?"

Agent Eiríksdóttir shrugged and hugged the folder close to her body. "I'm sure I could look into it. I don't think it's something I can openly ask. Her mother's maiden name should be in Friday's file, right?"

Director Harpy nodded.

"What should we tell her parents in the meantime?" Agent Eiríksdóttir asked as Director Harpy reached for her jacket. "Should we tell them what happened? With the Fey?"

Director Harpy thought back on the terrifying sight of Friday when she entered her hospital room as she shrugged on her jacket. "I don't really think we should… tell them that. We shouldn't worry them unnecessarily."

"Unnecessarily? You don't think we should warn them? So that they can protect—" Agent Eiríksdóttir bit her tongue as she tilted her head at the realization. How exactly were Friday's parents supposed to protect her anyway?

"Have Zaria handle it. She'd be the best in giving them direction with Friday."

"Yes, ma'am." Agent Eiríksdóttir grinned at Harpy before leaving the room to find Zaria.

***

In Hawai'i, Dorothea Sharp walked over toward the beeping phone that alerted her of a new voicemail waiting in her messages. People rarely called that line anymore unless it was important. Very important. Very classified.

She looked down at the number, though she didn't recognize it.

Out of curiosity, she played the message.

Mrs. Sharp had to take a seat as the message played back. She had been so disconnected from S.M.O.K.E. & M.I.R.R.O.R.S. since becoming a grandmother, she hadn't even heard of Finley's death. Her heart sank. She could hardly think of Director Harpy's request. Dropping her phone, it clattered to the ground as she buried her face in her hands.

She remembered cradling the young boy when they rescued him from Guam. Holding his hand while he lay unconscious in the hospital. It was caring for him in those brief moments that gave her the confidence to become a mother in the first place, and now he was dead.

And she had been dodging all of his phone calls.

The guilt felt like a searing hole in her chest.

Mrs. Sharp gasped for a few short breaths before she succumbed to the grief, crying out in pain as she hunched over, sobbing into her hands.

"What's wrong, Gramma?" a small voice asked.

Mrs. Sharp looked up to see her granddaughter pick up the cell phone she had dropped. She looked up at the older Sharp woman with her large eyes, bushy little brows, and frizzy brown hair framing her chubby heart-shaped face. Mrs. Sharp quickly wiped her cheeks and mentally told herself to pull herself together. She could not cry in front of her granddaughter.

"Grandma lost a friend," she said softly, opening her arms to her young granddaughter who immediately crawled into her lap.

Mrs. Sharp took the phone from Teddy's small hands and put it down on the table. She inhaled deeply. "Grandma has to go to work," she said then, glancing at the phone on the table as she thought of Director Harpy's request. She could only wonder for the time being why exactly she was asking about the Corpse Walker's spine whip. "Would you like to come with me to Pennsylvania?"

Her granddaughter's face lit up and she nodded immediately.

# CHAPTER TWENTY-FOUR

*24*

Finley Quartermaine's funeral was held in his hometown of York, Pennsylvania at the same venue his brother's had been nearly sixty years prior. Mrs. Sharp was overcome with deja vu. While she had been to Pennsylvania, she hadn't specifically stepped foot in York since. The small town hadn't changed much in the last sixty years, and Mrs. Sharp wouldn't be surprised if the podium was the same one Finley had stood at for his brother's funeral, his knuckles white as he'd clutched the sides, steadying himself as he delivered the eulogy for his own brother. It seemed like so long ago, and yet it was such a prominent memory in her mind. He had been nearly ten years old by the time World War II ended. Mrs. Sharp could see him standing up there with his parents on either side as his brother's casket had been carried down the aisle. In the absence of a body, the casket had been empty, but the director of R.A.V.E.N. at the time had felt that it was an important symbol.

She closed her eyes and tightened her grip on her granddaughter's little hand.

"Can you feel anything?" she asked her granddaughter.

The young girl looked up at Mrs. Sharp. She paused for a moment and closed her eyes. Tightening them shut, she then shook her head almost immediately after. She looked up at her grandma again and shook her head once more. However, Teddy's attention was soon drawn elsewhere. She stopped suddenly and quickly turned her head.

Mrs. Sharp frowned as her granddaughter squeezed her hand. Mrs. Sharp looked around, scanning the crowd and their surroundings to see what Teddy was looking at. Her eyes then widened once she had found it. A chill ran down her spine as goosebumps covered every inch of her skin.

There in the background, off in the distance, stood Death.

She clenched her jaw and turned away, pulling her granddaughter with her. That was not what she had in mind. Mrs. Sharp had a briefcase in her other hand and scanned the crowd further, diverting her attention away from the Infernal. The majority of people in attendance were agents who worked for S.M.O.K.E. & M.I.R.R.O.R.S.

from various facilities throughout the country, but she was intent on finding one person in particular, and she made a beeline for her the moment she found her, still troubled from the Death spotting. Something pricked at her neck that made her uneasy, but she didn't dare turn around.

"I didn't mean to do this here," Mrs. Sharp started as she approached two women, "but I knew I would find you here, Director Harpy." She then held up the briefcase in her bandaged hand and offered it to her. "I have what you requested."

Director Harpy furrowed her brows as she frowned slightly. She looked down at the briefcase Mrs. Sharp held out to her before glancing at Agent Eiríksdóttir. She returned her gaze to Mrs. Sharp as she swept the end of her ponytail over her shoulder. "But I didn't even get to elaborate—or tell you what I needed—you never called me back to discuss anything—"

Mrs. Sharp tilted her head, smiling slightly. "I have my resources, Director." Her gaze dropped for a moment to the prosthetic left arm Director Harpy wore. "I heard about your injuries. I figured you desired a prosthetic you'd be able to properly use in your—*unique*—line of work. Was I wrong in my assumption?" Mrs. Sharp asked, her gaze returning to meet Director Harpy's. Mrs. Sharp tilted her head, carefully examining the scar on her face.

"Not at all," answered Director Harpy. "Spot on, actually."

"Then please accept this—consider it a gift, for your promotion." She offered the briefcase to Director Harpy once more, who finally accepted it with her right hand. "Thank you for calling me," Mrs. Sharp added, glancing at the picture of the elder Finn Quartermaine sitting on the table they stood beside. "I had no idea."

Director Harpy was good at hiding the pained expression that threatened to surface on her face. "I'm sorry you had to find out that way."

Mrs. Sharp shook her head. She tucked a few loose strands of gray hair behind her ear as Teddy swung her other arm back and forth in her hand. "I'd rather have heard the news from someone who knew him personally than from an informal letter in the mail or the newspaper obituaries."

Director Harpy nodded.

"I understand."

"It was nice to meet you, Director Harpy." Mrs. Sharp then turned toward the other woman.

"Agent Ruthie Eiríksdóttir," Eiríksdóttir said immediately with a broad and bright smile plastered across her face. "It's an honor."

"Pleasure to meet you, Agent." Mrs. Sharp tilted her head before turning away from the two of them. As she did so, she briefly made eye contact with the Dioscuri. She felt her heart stop for a moment as the strange being looked down at her granddaughter. Dorothea Sharp tightened her grip on her granddaughter's hand, as if she were afraid she might lose her.

"You were a gift, Theodora Sharp," she said in a low whisper, unsure if Teddy could even hear her as they walked into the sea of people. "Never let anyone make you forget that."

The Dioscuri watched from afar as the two Sharps merged back into the crowd. Their eyes followed her granddaughter through the cracks in the walls of people.

*'What do you think?'* Freya asked Arlo as they continued to observe her and her granddaughter from afar. Mrs. Sharp seemed like she had her fair share of secrets.

*I'm not sure*, he thought back, their eyes a glowing white. They tilted their head, Freya's face blurred slightly. *She's up to something, though. She knows something.*

*'And her granddaughter… something's not right.'*

It wasn't that they thought Mrs. Sharp's showing up to the funeral with a briefcase was strange. Rather, the Dioscuri could sense an unnatural energy from the granddaughter. And Dorothea Sharp was clearly intensely protective of the young girl. She had dark hair and skin that seemed slightly more pale than usual—perhaps a genetic anomaly. *Perhaps.*

The Dioscuri remained in the background. When Arlo asked if Freya wanted to move closer to pay her respects, she'd hung back.

*'I'm just—I'm not ready to even see his picture.'*

Arlo had nodded, and they'd hung back. It was easier this way anyway. They didn't want to draw undue attention to themself from the surrounding agents or by any Fey or beings who may mean them harm. Fortunately, if anyone was there who wished them harm, they remained hidden.

The last thing Freya wanted was to cause a scene at Finn's funeral.

Suddenly, someone bumped into them, causing the distracted Freya to slip right out of Arlo's body. Arlo turned around to face an elderly, frail man.

Arlo gasped.

The man's mouth had been sewn shut.

Arlo quickly took a stumbled step backward. The man's sunken eyes were completely black, and he looked from Arlo to Freya.

Arlo blinked, and the man was gone.

"What the hell was that?" he asked under his breath, looking around.

"*Death*," she said softly. His skin crawled. "We need to go."

Freya quickly merged back in with her brother. The Dioscuri backed away from the rest of the crowd and vanished.

***

While many of the agents enjoyed the offered refreshments after the funeral service, Agent Eiríksdóttir stood to the side with Director Harpy, holding Dorothea Sharp's briefcase open for her. Inside was a beautifully crafted left hand, wrist, and part of the forearm. It looked real enough, its fleshy color perfectly matching Harpy's warm ivory skin. Director Harpy held her right hand beside it; it was the perfect mirror image.

"I wonder what it's capable of," she muttered softly as she took off the prosthetic she currently wore and put on the other. It came with a cuff to secure it to her elbow. She fixed it onto her arm and flinched. A searing pain shot up what was left of her actual arm, up to her shoulder, and directly to her neck.

Flashes of Acacia and Salvatore invaded her mind. Flashes of Acacia grabbing Harpy's wrist forcefully and slicing her arm clean off. She remembered the blood spraying her just before Acacia slashed her face and damaged her eye.

Director Harpy shook her head and took a step back.

"Are you okay, Director?" Agent Eiríksdóttir shifted the case in her arms and reached out to steady Director Harpy.

The Fey had used Glamour on her to get her to lead them to their weapons vault and Acacia walked away with one of the worst ones they contained. She frowned slightly as her head pounded.

"Director?"

She could distantly hear Eiríksdóttir's voice fading in and out. Harpy did her best to focus on it and bring herself back to the present. She blinked several times as she reached out to grab Agent Eiríksdóttir's arm.

"Are you okay?" Agent Eiríksdóttir asked.

Finally, Director Harpy nodded, looking down at the prosthetic. She then wondered what exactly Mrs. Sharp had given her. After all, Harpy had brought up the famed spine whip of the Corpse Walker. She had her doubts this was any normal prosthetic and not enhanced in any way.

While it took a moment to adjust, it was as though the prosthetic connected to the phantom hand Director Harpy felt. She wiggled the fingers of the animatronic. It was a strange sensation. It was like having her hand back. She looked through the briefcase and found a note that highlighted features of the hand, but there was no mention of how exactly it was forged. Still, the corner of Director Harpy's mouth lifted a little before she closed the briefcase that now contained her old prosthetic.

Her eyes wandered back toward the Sharps as she tried to refocus on the present. "I wonder if that's her," she said finally, taking the briefcase from Eiríksdóttir.

"Who?" Eiríksdóttir asked as she looked around.

Director Harpy fished a piece of paper out of her pocket with two fingers and unfolded it as she handed it to Agent Eiríksdóttir. "The other girl from—Echo's—drawing."

"Dot Sharp's granddaughter?" Agent Eiríksdóttir frowned. "No way."

"When I was cleaning out Director Quartermaine's desk, I found a few interesting things. I think we should keep her on our radar."

"She's just a kid, Harpy," Agent Eiríksdóttir said as she handed the drawing back to her.

"Kids age. They turn into adults. Those adults don't always become good people." Director Harpy's eyes shifted from the little girl to Mrs. Sharp as she folded the paper back up. She narrowed her eyes as she frowned slightly against the sun. Agent Harpy lifted her hand to shield her face with the paper. "And she seems like she's hiding something, doesn't she? Is she always like that?"

"Dorothea Sharp helped the United States win World War II," said Agent Eiríksdóttir, defending the elder Sharp. "She's a good person. She made you your prosthetic—which you barely had to ask for. She does what's best for the country—and she worked on the Manhattan Project."

Director Harpy didn't take her eyes off the elegant older woman. "And a lot of people died for that win," she retorted. "She also worked with Hayden Dáithí, the *Corpse Walker*."

"Who was a war *hero*," Agent Eiríksdóttir said, stressing the ending of her sentence. "I think you're overthinking this. Seriously, the Corpse Walker did a lot of good for the world."

"He was also affected by an artifact. I mean you really think she wouldn't know anything? How would hearing from me be the first time she heard of Director Quartermaine's passing unless she was extremely distracted." Agent Harpy continued to observe Mrs. Sharp and her granddaughter for a moment longer before finally tucking the drawing back into her pocket. "I mean, I'm not going to do anything right now," she said. She shielded her face and away from the sun. "Besides, we have bigger problems to worry about."

"Like what?" Agent Eiríksdóttir asked while Director Harpy's eyes settled on one of the pictures of Finn on display. Director Harpy's gaze slowly lifted to meet Agent Eiríksdóttir's.

"Like where the hell is Director Quartermaine's body?"

# *epilogue*

The Dioscuri stood at Ka'ena Point, which was the westernmost tip of land on the island of O'ahu. The moon was shining brightly overhead, and the stars twinkled vibrantly in the dark sky, unobstructed by the light pollution of the faraway cities. It was beautiful out there in the cool night, but Arlo was focused on one thing: the depths below.

*Are we sure about this?* Arlo asked, observing the dark blue waters crashing up against the very low rock. He inhaled deeply and turned his head one way, while Freya's echo kept looking down at the bottom. *Can't we go down there and just wade into the water?*

*'It is the* leaping *place of souls,'* Freya responded, holding particular emphasis on leaping. *'It's one of the most direct paths. You're the one who made the decision we were going, remember? We have to leap.'*

Arlo drew another deep breath.

"I feel like I'm about to leap to my death," he muttered aloud. "I mean, I am still technically alive. Even if I am over a hundred years old. This is not something a hundred-year-old man should be doing, actually."

"Go to sleep then," she said nonchalantly. "I'll jump. What you aren't aware of won't hurt you, right?" He could feel her smirk tugging at the corners of his lips. Her words weren't making him feel any better. Not in the slightest.

"How am I supposed to go to sleep knowing what you're going to do?" he asked, looking down at the water again before looking out at the vast ocean.

"We have to find out what's happening, Arlo," Freya insisted. "I don't think we'll find answers here. We've already come across two Infernal Artifacts." Two Infernal Artifacts had surfaced in the last one hundred years. The one Halina had brought to the Iroquois Theater and the one Director Quartermaine had come into contact with in the forties as a child. She had her worries about what the future might hold, and what else would surface. "Friday said the years to come would be interesting. She didn't exactly say they would be good."

"She didn't exactly say they'd be bad either," Arlo countered. "Are you sure this won't hurt?" He took a step closer to the edge and looked down again; a few rocks skittered down the side. Goosebumps covered his body as the hairs on his neck rose. He wasn't sure if that was from the cool winds nipping at them, or from fear.

"No," Freya said bluntly. "I'm not."

"Wow. You're *really* good at pep talks, you know that?" he said sarcastically.

"I'm just being realistic and there's no use in sugar-coating this." Freya pursed her lips together and tilted her head to the side slightly as she observed the immense ocean before looking down at the waves crashing against the island of O'ahu. "Would it make you feel better if I assured you that you would at least survive?"

He could have rolled his eyes at her remark.

"Given where we're going, not really. I'm sure we'll make it there one way or another." Arlo chuckled a little at his joke, and Freya smiled. They were going to the Underworld. His survival wasn't exactly crucial.

*'Are you ready?'*

He wanted to say *no*. But all that had happened over the last few weeks were things he had not been ready for. The power of being Dioscuri did not make him feel protected or invincible. Finn Quartermaine had still died, and who knew what had really happened to Finn's brother after the Pacific War? Everything felt unknown—potentially dangerous.

*'Arlo?'*

He inhaled deeply and closed his eyes before taking a leap of faith. It was now or never, and he wanted to be awake.

It was not just Freya or Arlo, just as it was never only Castor or Pollux. Arlo felt honored by the nickname, and he wanted to do it justice.

They held out their arms as the crashing waves rushed towards them. Their eyes opened, and the world split open in a flood of white light.

*The Dioscuri has come to power.*

*THE DIOSCURI WILL RETURN*

If you enjoyed this novel,
please consider leaving a review.

Thank you.

# *Q&A with*
# *THE AUTHOR*

## *What are the Infernal Artifacts?*

The Infernal Artifacts are artifacts that belong to the Infernals and believed to be the strongest artifacts in existence. Infernals are the first beings, and children of the Creator. In my universe, the Creator and his children existed before all else, including prior to the existence of Gods and Goddesses.

## *What inspired Dioscuri?*

When it comes to my ideas, there's never really one thing that inspires them. They come to me fully formed and I just have to do the research to make sure I can make it make sense and flow together.

I started this project building the Underworld and didn't really think of the plot. There are different 'countries' in the Underworld similar to the way we have different countries in our world, or the land of the living. I wanted the Underworld to almost mirror our world, influenced by different cultural beliefs, and that helped develop the idea for the Infernals, and so on. The Underworld will be explored as the collection progresses. There's something about death that has always fascinated me. The way it lingers and how people never fully leave us, whether it be in memory. the impact they have, or by what they leave behind.

As mentioned in the book, 'Dioscuri' is more of a title rather than specific to Castor and Pollux. It is a being in its own right. I love legends and I love mythology. I think there's a lot to learn from them and things like that definitely inspire me greatly. I guess a lot of things inspired this book. A lot of things inspired the collection itself. I can't wait to continue with this project and watch it grow.

*How many books will be in the Infernal Artifacts Collection?*

I don't know. I could give an estimate, but I don't want to give a definite answer and change my mind later on—but there will be a lot. I have it all planned out and I know how it ends, I just don't know how many books it will take for me to tell it in its entirety. Generally, there are several different book series that all connect for an overarching plot. So the next book that will be released won't be a Dioscuri sequel, but the first book of the next series. As you may have noticed in the beginning of this book, it listed this as the first in its own series but the second in the collection.

The collection will encompass the entire project from start to finish. The entire overarching plot will be throughout all of the books. It will have as many books as I feel it takes to complete the story. There are so many stories to tell in addition to the main one and while there will be many books, I do encourage reading them all, even out of order if this happens to be your first. I encourage going back to reading Corpse Walker. There's a lot of little hidden gems.

*Is there a specific reading order to keep in mind when going into these books?*

Truthfully, you can read it in timeline order (the order they are being released) or by series. But even if Dioscuri happens to be your introduction into The Infernal Artifacts Universe, you can still go back and read Corpse Walker if you want a better understanding. As long as you start with the first book of any series within The Infernal Artifacts Collection, you should have no problem going back to read the others.

So there's a timeline order and there's a reading order once each series is established, but starting out, any mini series can be your first.

My goal is that these books are written in a way that gives enough information to those who are only just starting out without confusing them, while also not repeating myself and providing new information to those who have read everything thus far and are keeping up with the collection.

*Will we learn more about the Dioscuri's travel down to the Underworld?*

Absolutely. Just not right away. I promise it'll make more sense as more novels are out and the overarching story comes together. The way I am releasing the books makes the most sense from a storyteller's point of view, but there will be a Dioscuri sequel that touches base with what they're doing down there.

*There are a lot of books out right now about fairies. Did that inspire you to write about a Fae realm?*

Definitely not. I wish I could insert emojis because I would insert the one with an awkward smile and a little drop of sweat right here.

I needed a lot of outsource help from people who were interested in the Fae and loved those types of books. I've never written about Fae or their realm, and knowing there are a lot of books about fairies currently out was actually very intimidating and that wasn't exactly something I wanted to compete with. Though for some reason, I couldn't bring myself to use another type of being. They just had to be Fey. It had to be the Autumn Queen. I argued with myself a lot over this. That I could change it to anything I wanted to. Why was I writing about something that was already so popular?

Unfortunately for me, my ideas are as stubborn as I am and I couldn't bring myself to change it.

*Will we see more about the Elves?*

Of course but this wasn't their story.

With the Elves, I wanted to provide enough information for them to play their part in this and with Arlo, since what the Elven King did was very important, as what the Elven Princess did. I couldn't leave those moments out, but that certainly isn't the last you'll see of them.

*What about Halina and her mother?*

Absolutely. There's a lot there that needs to be explored with Halina, her family, and the Elves entirely, but again, Dioscuri wasn't their story. There will be more about them in the future. This certainly isn't the last you've seen of them, especially Halina.

*Why didn't the Elven King try harder to protect Halina? Why didn't he try harder to not kill her?*

The Elven King is a very interesting character to me and he understands something about the Book of Fate that many do not. It cannot be changed. Even if he did not cause the theater fire, something else would have. She was always going to die at that point in time. From a fire.

The Elven King had already experienced what it was like to try to change Fate. He even admits to it regarding his father. He knew there was no way around it, even with falling in love with his wife and them having their three children. It was all part of Fate's design for him and the inevitable would happen: he would be responsible for Halina's death. The Elves are also old beings in their own little pocket of the universe. He knows better than to interfere with beings older than he is. His blackened fingers are a mark of his cursed knowledge.

Keep in mind though, the Elven King's knowledge only extended until 1991 when the Book changed forms. So he didn't know what would become of Arlo until he saw it and he doesn't know what the future holds from there.

*Will Arlo and Halina ever see each other again? Is there a chance he may see her portrait? Something?*

Maybe...or maybe not. This one I won't answer for many reasons. You'll just have to keep up with the future books and find out for yourself!

*What will happen to Friday?*

Unfortunately, a lot will happen to Friday between where we leave her in Dioscuri and when she makes another appearance. I will not elaborate, haha.

*So we've learned primarily about Death and Destiny but what about the third one mentioned: Dream? Will we get more information on him soon?*

Yes. More information will be revealed about him and his artifact soon. Unfortunately I feel like it is currently too early for me to give out too much information on him at this time.

*Just in case I don't like the next book in the collection, will I be able to finish the Dioscuri series and still understand his story?*

Yes. I am writing the novels in a way that you will either be able to enjoy them as a collection or as individual series. You will not have to read all of them to enjoy the stories.

This project is intimidating for me as a writer, so I'm sure from a reader's perspective, it can be a lot to take on.

*Are you considering expanding on this universe?*

Actually, yes. I mean, my plan for this universe is already fairly extensive, but I often think about writing sidequels and short stories to go along with them. However, I currently have a lot on my plate. It's definitely something I am highly considering though. Not sure if it would be something I would publish or have it exclusively available somewhere.

*Are you currently working on any other projects?*

Somewhat. I have revisited an old series I originally published back in 2016. The first was republished in February 2023 and its sequel will be released soon.

I have a few smaller side projects I've started, but these two will take up the majority of my time and focus until I'm a bit further along.

## *About the Author*

Ralynn Kimie was born and raised in Honolulu, Hawai'i. She would spend her days eating sushi all day every day with her miniature dachshunds if time (and her wallet) would allow it. She maintains awful relationships with both coffee and sleep, and forgot what it's like to have a social life as she constantly buries herself in her hobbies. Never satisfied with the limitations of her own humanity, she has found a way to exist in worlds she'll never truly get to live in and gets to share them with others through her writing.

For more information, check out her website below:

*www.ralynnkimie.com*

# *ACKNOWLEDGEMENTS*

Thank you to everyone who worked on this novel and helped make it what it is today.

Thank you always to Rachel Fernando, Heather Hanson, and Kristen Vasquez, who have been with me from the very beginning of my writing journey for nearly two decades now. Your unwavering and unlimited support has been the spine of every project I've completed.

Special thanks to my fantastic friends, Stephanie Agarpao, Kristy Carroll, Ka'ipo Castillo, Daina Elvenia, Chelsea Gillihan, Joshua Hammer, Sgt. Jack Huber of the Marine Corps, Chez Maae, Sgt. Lucas Morgan of the Marine Corps (and his wonderful family), Sunshine Pregana, and Steven Yokota. Without your daily encouragement through all of my doubts in myself and in my work, I would not have finished this.

Thank you to my family, always, for being especially forgiving when I miss get-togethers due to writing conflicts.

I also wanted to take a moment to especially thank those who helped me get through losing my dog Twix, in February earlier this year. She had been part of my life for so long and her death shattered me. I was in the middle of working on Dioscuri when she passed and it sort of felt like time stopped. I was struggling a lot mentally and there were several moments where I wanted to quit writing and commit to something else entirely. Twix was sixteen years old when she died and I basically lost a member of my family.

Twix was a rescue from the Waimanalo Puppy Mill. She was one of the mothers used for breeding and very malnourished. Special thank you to my cousin, Sherri Barrett, who fostered her and blessed my life with her. Twix was fearless and strong and stubborn and I miss her every single day.

Lastly, I beg forgiveness from all those whom I have failed to mention. Please know that I appreciate you and your support with the entirety of my heart.

Made in the USA
Columbia, SC
26 April 2023

15809135R00257